LEGEND OF THE LAST SWORD IN THE WEST

LAST SWORD IN THE WEST
BOOK 7

RYAN KIRK

WATERSTONE
MEDIA

For Loretta

1

Elzeth shouted for help.

His call was nothing like the silent conversations he and Tomas held daily. This was more primal, raw, and beyond human hearing. Tomas heard only the whisper of the afternoon breeze through overgrown prairie grasses. Intermittent thunder rolled across the plains like surf breaking over a distant shore.

When Elzeth shouted again, Tomas felt the call in his bones. His eyes darted across the sea of grass, searching for any sign of movement. Sagani took all shapes and sizes, and he feared one passing by undetected.

"Anything?" he asked.

"Not yet," Elzeth answered.

Their plan, if it even deserved the name, was born of desperation. Angela hovered on the brink of death. Her wounded body pushed her soul toward the gate, even as her soul clung to the world. She'd been unconscious since Tomas had found her, but there was no ease in her expressions. She fought the hopeless battle against the pull of the gate alone.

But hopefully not for long. Elzeth called to his brethren again. Tomas's bones resonated with the call, like a church bell struck too hard by an overeager acolyte.

Tomas couldn't separate his feelings from Elzeth's. The veil between sagani and host had grown so thin that emotions danced freely between them. When their emotions aligned, as they did now, Tomas's grief felt doubled. Elzeth, naturally, hadn't shared Tomas's stronger feelings for Angela, but he had liked her. They both wanted her to live.

One call followed another, draining the last of Tomas's meager strength.

He feared their efforts were for naught. Sagani had once roamed the frontier freely, but they grew increasingly absent. Travelers, hunters, and innkeepers told different variations of the same tale. Sagani were disappearing, and no one knew why.

They were hard to hunt and impossible to eat, so it wasn't likely that settlers caused the disappearance. Everyone agreed on that, but little else. Tomas had listened to plenty of guesses over the months, some more outlandish than others. Sagani were migrating west in massive numbers, fleeing the incoming tide of humanity. The church hunted them down. They were dying off because of disease or lack of prey. Everyone had their own theory, but Tomas found them all lacking. Elzeth held them in contempt.

Right now, though, he didn't give a damn about the reasons. He just needed one sagani to be nearby. He needed one sagani to answer Elzeth's plea.

High above, something let out a piercing cry. Tomas covered his eyes and looked up. A lone hawk soared in the winds ahead of the storm, staring down at them like they were prey.

"Is that—"

It didn't give Tomas time to finish the question. The hawk folded its wings and dove toward them. Its eyes blazed gold. At the last moment, it spread its wings wide and slowed its descent. It landed a few feet away.

"Can you talk to it?" Tomas asked.

"Not like we talk. Hold on."

Elzeth vibrated within Tomas's core. The feeling was like the call Elzeth had put out earlier but more subtle. The hawk made no move.

"Put Angela down and back away," Elzeth said.

Tomas shook his head. "I'm not leaving her side. Not again."

The hawk fluttered its wings and jumped a small step back. It looked to the sky as though plotting a path between the approaching clouds.

Elzeth said nothing. His last suggestion hung like a heavy stone between them.

"Fine," Tomas said.

He shifted Angela and laid her down gently. He clenched his fists before he did something foolish and sentimental, like brush the hair from her face. Her brow was furrowed as though she were focused on a difficult problem. Her skin was pale, and sweat beaded on her forehead.

Tomas backed away on his knees. Each shuffle was harder than the last, not because of injury or weakness, but because he couldn't bear to part with Angela in what might be her last moments. Five paces away, he stopped, unable to retreat any farther. He watched and waited, fighting the urge to scramble forward and scoop Angela up in his arms again.

The damned bird was in no hurry. It stared at Angela with those golden eyes, blazing with an inner light no other animal possessed. It grew, nearly doubling in size before

Tomas's eyes. Then it finally hopped forward and landed on top of Angela.

The sight of its claws digging gently into her wounded stomach almost broke Tomas's resolve to remain away. He held his breath and imagined heavy chains fixing him in place. He couldn't help Angela, but one wrong move might shatter her last chance at life. Tomas clenched his fists tighter and pressed them into his thighs. He tried closing his eyes, but not knowing was worse, so he abandoned the attempt.

Angela's eyes opened for the first time since he'd found her, and it took every bit of his control not to rush forward. The hawk's golden eyes reflected in her own gaze. They stared at one another, and Tomas had some sense of what passed between them. He and Elzeth had shared a similar moment a lifetime ago.

The relationship between sagani and host was mutual. The sagani offered its gifts, and the host weighed the benefit of those gifts against the known costs. If Angela accepted, she would live, stronger and faster than before. But the blessing carried its own curse. If she accepted, she would someday go mad with the sagani's power.

Tomas didn't know what Angela would choose.

When he'd first met her, she'd been ambivalent about the relationship. She didn't hate hosts, nor did she consider the sagani evil. But she'd also been content with her lot in life and was prepared to live out her natural lifespan. Becoming a host offered her nothing of value.

For most, the threat of imminent death would be enough to change their mind, but Tomas wasn't so sure that way of thinking applied to Angela. She had a warrior's heart, and she'd made her peace with death long ago. Perhaps she'd let her days end here, content with what she'd accomplished.

He wanted her to choose life, but his motives were selfish. He wanted her presence in whatever days remained to him. But he couldn't force her to stay. All he and Elzeth could do was give her the choice.

Marshal and sagani continued to stare at one another, the offer still on the table but fading fast. She didn't have long to choose. Her skin was as white as freshly washed linen, and the pool of blood beneath her had grown noticeably wider. If Tomas lived long enough, he'd ensure Rachel suffered for her lies.

Angela tore her gaze away from the sagani and looked at Tomas. He couldn't guess at her thoughts, and he feared how any gesture would be interpreted, so he remained perfectly still.

Angela's breath shuddered, and she closed her eyes again as the last of her strength faded. The hawk remained unperturbed by the developments, its gaze never wandering from the wounded marshal. The rise and fall of Angela's chest slowed, and Tomas feared she had chosen death. He bowed his head. At least he'd given her the choice and allowed her to choose the time of her departure. It was more than most received.

The hawk spread its wings wide and flapped. To Tomas's sagani-aided vision, its aura brightened until it embraced Angela. Hundreds of tiny threads extended from the hawk, shooting like arrows into the fallen marshal and weaving into her body. Each looked as insubstantial as a spider's web, but Tomas guessed no sword was sharp enough to cut them.

A flash, bright as the lightning that had chased them out of Porum, blinded Tomas. He closed his eyes and flinched away, but there was no sound, heat, or wind. He blinked the afterimage away. By the time his vision cleared, the hawk was gone. Tomas felt it, though.

Tomas scrambled forward. He pulled Angela back onto his lap and held her close. Her breathing steadied, and color returned to her cheeks. He cradled her head in his right arm. With his left hand, he reached down and pulled open the tear in her shirt. The cut on her abdomen had closed, and the scar faded fast. Her skin wasn't burning, but Tomas didn't question why. Though he'd seen the birth of a host twice in his life and experienced it once, he didn't understand it. No one did.

A few minutes later, Angela's eyes fluttered open. They flashed gold before settling into the light brown he was familiar with. "You're alive," she said.

"I could say the same about you."

"I thought Ghosthands had killed you. When he entered the car, and you didn't return, I thought you'd lost."

Tomas's hopeless chase of the train had given him plenty of time to reflect on Ghosthands's motivations. The assassin had chosen not to kill him. "Oh, I lost, but I think he wants me to suffer. He knows how close I am to madness and believes it's the greater punishment. I wish I could say he was wrong."

Tomas became self-conscious. Angela's life had changed more than his today, and here he was, talking about himself. "How are you feeling?"

She considered the question for so long that Tomas worried she was in shock. "Odd."

"You're a host now. It's going to take a while to get used to it."

"You'll guide me, though, won't you?"

Tomas suddenly realized how close she was. Though most of her health had returned, she'd made no effort to extricate herself. Tomas felt her strong heart beating in time with his own.

He'd nearly given himself up as lost for good. If Angela had chosen to die, Tomas would have soon followed her to the gate.

He swallowed the lump that formed in his throat and made it difficult to breathe. She had a second chance. Her years ahead, though numbered, could be some of her best. The sagani burning within her would enhance her considerable skills, so many paths were open to her.

Tomas's near future wasn't so enticing. Madness nipped at his heels, and he couldn't escape its dogged pursuit for much longer.

He made himself a promise.

He wouldn't surrender. Not until the last possible moment. Until then, he'd support Angela with every bit of strength remaining to him.

He looked into her eyes to answer the question.

"For as long as I can," he said.

2

By the time Angela felt well enough to stand, the remnants of the storm grew close. Tomas brushed the dirt and grass off his pants and watched the clouds gather to the west. The horizon darkened, but the lightning and its accompanying thunder weren't as fierce as in Porum. After chasing them miles across the prairie, the storm had lost much of its energy.

Tomas sympathized. Some of his strength had returned while resting beside Angela, but his body was broken and sore. Fresh bruises mottled his arms, legs, and back. Light efforts made him breathe hard.

Angela had just returned from the brink of death, but thanks to her newfound sagani, was healthier than him. He tried not to be jealous and almost succeeded.

"So, what next?" Angela asked.

Tomas gestured toward the tracks. "Not much point in returning to Porum, and I suspect we're closer to Dodge, anyway. Might as well follow them and learn what happened."

Angela agreed, and they set off down the tracks, the

storm chasing them with its dying breaths. Their shadows grew long in front of them as the sun fell toward the western horizon.

"You called for the sagani, didn't you? You and Elzeth," Angela said.

"It was the only chance you had. I wasn't sure if you would accept it or not, but I wanted you to have the choice."

"Thank you."

Tomas had a long list of questions. It was rare to spend time with another host, and most were reticent to speak about their experiences. How did she guess her sagani had been called? Did she speak to the hawk like he did to Elzeth, or had she intuited it?

Narkissa had implied Tomas's relationship with Elzeth was unusual. Angela might provide a way of finding out for sure.

Before he could ask the first of many questions, she said, "Would you mind walking ahead for a bit? I won't be far behind, but there's a lot to think about."

She smiled to shield him from the hurt of her words, but it was only partially successful. He understood her need for time and space well enough. After nearly dying, it was a small ask. It still sounded like she wanted space from him.

"Of course," he said.

"Thanks."

Her steps slowed, and Tomas inched ahead. He walked near the edge of her shadow for a while, then left that behind, too. He glanced back occasionally to make sure she hadn't stopped completely. She let herself fall about a hundred paces back, then matched his pace.

He tried to think about something besides Angela, but it was hard with her so close.

The sun fell below the horizon, bookmarking the end of

a terrible day. Angela was alive, and that was something, but Ghosthands had escaped with Rachel, who'd been a believer all along. The day's battle had left a trail of bodies that would stretch from Porum to Dodge. Their loss would echo across the plains louder than any cannon.

And those were only the immediate effects. Rachel knew something about the nexuses, something so extraordinary the church had sent their most feared assassin to retrieve her. Gavan and the army had suspected she was important, but they'd underestimated how important. That the church wanted her so desperately bode poorly for the future. The church had perverted the power of the nexus in Kimson to destroy half an army. He feared the weapons Rachel's knowledge might lead to.

Though he was aware of the magnitude of today's loss, his thoughts never drifted far from Angela. The world could burn, so long as she was well. The physical transition to becoming a host took time to adapt to, but it was straightforward enough. Angela had considerable martial training, so the transition would be easier for her than for some.

The harder transition was in the mind. A new host had to get used to another presence, a constant companion. All humans needed time alone, but even though Angela was walking by herself in the middle of nowhere, she would never be truly alone again. Many feared hosts and those influenced by the church's philosophy hated them. Society's prejudice was a heavy burden, and that was if one never thought about the madness that haunted their every step.

There was so much he wanted to say. But she wanted to work through the problems on her own. He could do nothing but walk ahead and be ready to help if she asked.

(###)

They walked alone but together the whole night. Tomas's calves and thighs screamed obscenities, but he didn't dare use Elzeth to ease his burden. He feared the slightest use of the sagani would tip him over the precipice of madness. Angela kept the distance between them the entire night.

His stomach rumbled, and his mouth was dry, but they had no food or water. Ghosthands hadn't been kind enough to throw their supplies off the train after them. Angela didn't even have a sword. The only way to save themselves was to keep walking. Tolkin and Shen both rose and fell and when the sun rose in the east, it revealed the town of Dodge ahead of them.

Angela caught up to Tomas, and they walked side by side. Her presence reassured him. He'd worried she had changed her mind and that she now wanted nothing to do with him.

Her first words put that fear to rest. "Thank you for the time. I didn't mean to worry you, but I needed to get my feet under me."

"Did you come to any conclusions?"

"Yes. I'm glad that you let me choose, and I'm grateful to still be alive."

Her words loosened the knot that had been tightening in his chest all night. "I'm glad to hear it," he said.

They approached Dodge together. It wasn't much of a town. It looked more like a wart on the endless prairie than any place worth stopping. The town wasn't more than a dozen buildings built around the railroad. Tomas imagined it served as a place for farmers and ranchers to load their grain and cattle onto trains heading east, but it hadn't grown into anything larger.

"Any marshals here?" Tomas asked.

"Not that I know of."

Tomas had feared as much.

No one greeted them when they came into town, and for lack of a better destination, they made their way to the one-room building that served as the train station. They knocked, and a heavyset man answered the door. He had bags under his eyes. He took one look at the two of them, his eyes lingering for a moment on Angela's badge.

"You two here about the train?" he asked.

"We were on it," Tomas said.

The man sighed, then stepped to the side. "Might as well come in, then. I'll get some tea started."

Tomas and Angela entered. The small building felt even tinier inside. It served as both station and house. A sturdy bed rested against the south wall, close to a small wood-fired stove and an equally small table with only one chair. A dividing wall ran across most of the space, separating the living area from the work area. Tomas poked his head around and saw the ticket window, train schedules, and a desk with a large ledger. Both sides of the building were kept orderly.

Tomas and Angela introduced themselves. Their host's name was Cline, and he'd been running the station in Dodge since the day it was built.

"And I've never seen anything like the train that came through yesterday. The first two cars were soaked in blood. They had shot out windows, which was probably for the best because the corpses were raising a stink. Don't think I've ever seen so many bodies in one place," Cline said.

"What happened when it arrived?" Angela asked.

"Train pulled in right on time, just like we expected. I had everything squared away here, but then I heard a bunch of shouting. As I went to investigate, a man and a woman stepped out of the first passenger car. They were both covered in blood, and I thought they were hurt. But the man gave me a stare that made my blood run cold, and I backed away."

Cline swallowed hard. "I checked on the first train car and saw the slaughter. I'm ashamed to say I lost my lunch. No one had seen the conductor, so I talked to the engineer up front. He knew little, but it was enough to put together a rough idea of what had happened."

"What did you do?" Tomas asked.

Cline stared down at his feet. "Truth be told, I didn't know what to do. It's just me here, and I couldn't handle that many bodies. I had a few passengers who were supposed to disembark here, but when they saw the man and woman get off, they decided they wanted to stay on the train. The passengers getting on climbed on in a hurry, and the train was off a few minutes later. The faster it left my station, the happier I was."

Angela rubbed the bridge of her nose. "Do you have any idea how many laws you broke?"

Cline shrugged. "What was I supposed to do? We've got no marshal here, and I don't know where those bodies belong. Most were army, by the look of it. There's a base at the next stop, so they'll have someone who can treat them well."

"What about the two who stepped off the train? What happened to them?" Tomas asked.

"They stole some horses and rode north," Cline reported.

"No one tried to stop them?"

"Again, we don't have any marshals here. Dodge is a quiet town. Word about the train spread fast, and most people saw no sense in picking a fight."

Tomas supposed he couldn't blame the townspeople, but it smarted that Ghosthands had been able to simply step off the train and ride away.

Cline poured them tea, and they asked a few more questions, but it was clear there wasn't much for them to do here. Tomas thanked Cline for the information, then asked if there was anywhere they could rest. Angela gave him a sharp look at the question.

Cline gave them directions to a home that welcomed guests. Dodge wasn't even large enough to support a proper inn. Tomas bowed to Cline, then they took their leave and wandered out.

They hadn't gone far when Angela stopped and put her hands on her hips. "Are you giving up so soon?"

"It's less giving up and more knowing when I've been beaten."

"They haven't won yet!"

Tomas looked around the small town. "You sure about that? There will be believers waiting to help him wherever he goes. Likely knights and inquisitors, too. They knew we were going for the train, and they were prepared for us. Even if I did track him and somehow found him alone, we can't beat him. I'm not strong enough, and you're not yet used to your abilities."

"So, what do you want to do?" It was a question, but a challenge, too.

"Honestly? It depends a lot on you."

Her stance softened. "What do you mean?"

"Angela, you're free. As far as anyone is going to know, you're dead. The sagani gives you several extra years of life, but it's a temporary gift. You can use it however you like."

Her eyes narrowed. "You want me to run away with you."

He didn't deny it.

"I can't. I made promises to the people of Razin. Becoming a host doesn't change that."

Tomas grimaced as she dashed his hopes across the ground. "What do you want to do, then?"

She put her hands back on her hips and looked around. "You're telling the truth about tracking Ghosthands?"

He nodded.

A long sigh escaped her lips, and some of the fire left her eyes. "Then I suppose I want to return to Razin."

She looked him up and down. "You'd be welcome to return with me if you like."

Tomas didn't want to return to Razin. He'd seen enough of that city for the rest of his life. Unfortunately, he was trapped by his own promises. He'd told Angela that he would guide her, and he'd promised himself he wouldn't leave her side. Promises were worthless if they were only kept when convenient.

He took some small measure of comfort in knowing that she had invited him. She wasn't pushing him away. It wasn't much, but perhaps it could grow into something more, something worth the sacrifice of spending his last days in a city.

"I would like that," he said. "Let's go to Razin."

3

Quinton stopped looking over his shoulder a week outside of Dodge. Rachel mocked his habit, but she underestimated Tomas's true nature. In her limited experiences with him, she'd fooled him like a naïve child. She'd only seen their last fight on the train, in which Quinton had defeated the rebellious host with ease. She scoffed at the idea that he was their greatest threat.

After a week on the road without so much as a whisper, Quinton forced himself to consider the possibility that she was right. Tomas hadn't been at his peak when they'd last fought. Madness had surrounded them both, but Tomas had suffered worse. The most damning evidence of all was the silence behind them. If Tomas was alive and well, he would have pursued.

Quinton couldn't completely let go of his doubts, though. Persistence defined Tomas. The cursed host didn't know when to die or when to surrender. He was certain the fall from the train hadn't killed the host, and he wondered if it wasn't a mistake to let madness kill Tomas.

What was done was done, though, and it made little

sense to turn back. He tried to soak up some of Rachel's confidence.

Prior to meeting her on the train, Quinton had only heard of Rachel in passing. The church devoted an enormous amount of its funds toward research across a variety of domains, but even among a crowded field of peers, Rachel stood alone. She studied the nexuses and was the principal designer of the weapon first tested at Kimson. Her research might finally solve the mysteries surrounding the demons. It was an honor to escort her to safety.

When she wasn't mocking his cautious glances south, she asked him endless pointed questions about his experience as a host. Her questions required him to dig up memories long buried, but he was glad to answer them. He couldn't guess what clues his past held, but if his life contributed to her work, it was worth the unpleasant taste of the memories that rose in the back of his throat. She had no way of recording his answers, but he suspected she forgot nothing of what he told her.

In the brief intervals when she wasn't interrogating him, he inquired about her work. He was curious about what she had learned, but most days, her answers were short and vague. It wasn't until a severe thunderstorm forced them into the hollow of an old tree that she opened up.

"Have you ever touched a nexus?" she asked as the rain pounded down like cannon fire.

"I'm not a fool. I know that touching a nexus means death for a host. Although I saw Tomas touch a nexus outside of Chesterton and live to tell the tale."

Rachel made a grumbling noise. "Tomas. Twice we've had him in custody, and twice he's escaped. What might we have learned if we'd kept him locked up?"

Quinton didn't think the question had been meant to cut

at him, but one of those failures had been his. He grimaced. "Do you know why hosts die when they touch a nexus?"

She gave a bitter laugh. "It's one question I want to answer, too. I've done a dozen autopsies on dead hosts who touched a nexus, but I've never found the cause of death, and none of my subjects have ever returned alive to tell me."

Quinton had hoped she would have known that answer, but he pressed on, not wanting to waste this brief window. "How did you first become interested in nexuses?"

He'd asked before, and she'd shrugged the question off. Tonight, she answered. "My father was a scholar for the church when I was little. I was always inquisitive, asking more questions about the world than I think either he or Mother were prepared for, and one day he took to see a nexus. He only meant to encourage my curiosity, but he accidentally sparked an obsession."

"What led to that?"

"When we visited, I touched the nexus. It was the most beautiful thing I'd ever seen, and as I ran my fingers over the stone, I felt something powerful within. Father said I imagined it, but I was certain. From that day forward, I vowed to learn all I could. I read Father's papers and formed my own theories. I like to think I've come closer than anyone else to understanding the nexuses, but there's still so much we don't know."

"You knew enough to create Kimson's weapon."

She brushed the comment away. "Child's play. We've known for years that the nexuses contain incredible power. All the weapon does is provide a basic mechanism for harnessing a fraction of that power. Its original aim was to help us understand the nexuses better, and in that, it failed."

Her nonchalance caught Quinton off-guard. When the first reports from Kimson had crossed his path, he'd thought the church sources had overstated the power of the weapon. The initial reports had since been corroborated, though. A few blasts from her "failure" could wipe out an entire army.

"A host is the key to the mechanism, right?" he asked.

"Correct. There's no mechanical process I've discovered that has any effect on the nexuses. It requires a human infected with a sagani, but one of my most important findings is that once we connect a host to the nexus, we can exert some control over the stones. It's a rough science now, but my research was proceeding smoothly before I was arrested. I'm eager to resume. I want to understand why we need an infected human to utilize the power. Hells, I want to know everything."

"Such as?"

"So much! For one, the nexuses and the sagani are connected, but I don't know how or why. My research into the nexuses has necessitated a considerable study of the sagani, and they're eternally mysterious."

"How so?"

She laughed bitterly. "I'm not even sure where to start. We've never witnessed the birth of a sagani. We can barely study their bodies, as they deteriorate so quickly after they die. They are unlike any other creature on this planet. They can shift their shape, which should be impossible. All other animals live in specific habitats, but the sagani are everywhere. And don't forget their mysterious link to the nexuses. A human barely has any reaction to the stones, but hosts report being drawn to the nexuses, and when they touch them, they die."

Rachel leaned her head back against the trunk of the tree. "When I first met Tomas in Razin, I hoped to figure out a way to capture him. He's an anomaly in more ways than one. He's lived so much longer than any other host, and as your own reports have noted, he's the only host we know of who has touched a nexus and lived to tell the tale. But then I overheard him telling Angela about his madness, and I cursed my poor luck. If I'd gotten my hands on him a year earlier, I might have learned so much more."

This time Quinton felt like the sting of the remark had been directed at him. He didn't defend himself because he deserved the blame. He had failed outside of Chesterton.

She shifted so she could face him more easily. "You're an oddity, too. You were the first host to willingly serve the church. Father started the host-knights because of how useful you've been. But all I know about you is that you're untouchable in the church, and you're probably the best sword the world has ever seen. Why would you, a demon-infected host, seek the Father like you did?"

Her question thrust Quinton into the past, a time when he'd been lost and dying in the mud. "When the sagani found me dying, I rejected it at first. I wanted to pass through the gates. But then it showed me a vision I believe came from the Creator."

They were already pressed together inside the small hollow, but she still leaned forward. "Tell me."

Quinton hesitated. He'd always considered the vision something private, shown only to him. He'd told the Holy Father without hesitation, but Father already spoke with the Creator. That had hardly seemed to count.

But Rachel was also a servant of the Creator, and he thought his story might help her.

"It showed me a vision of the world, with every human connected by thin strands of power. It was like a spider's web but infinitely more complex. And in this weaving, I felt the barest hint of something more. The Creator, moving across his web like a gentle breeze, steering us all in His direction. I had been suffering, but at that moment, I understood that my suffering had a reason. My life had a purpose. I was part of His plan."

Quinton's retelling didn't do the experience justice, but he didn't know how to put the sublime revelation of those few moments into words. It had been nothing more than a glimpse, but that glimpse had washed away his doubt and left him clean.

Rachel thought in silence for several minutes. He'd seen this look on her face before when he said something that made her reconsider one of her theories. If history was any guide, she'd soon fire at least a dozen new questions at him.

He wasn't wrong.

"Have you ever had a similar experience since then?" she asked.

"No."

She chewed on her lower lip. "No other subject has ever reported a vision when they accepted the infection. Why?"

He wasn't sure if the question was rhetorical, but he wanted to help. "It could be because I rejected the sagani at first. I was approaching the gate when it showed me the vision."

Her eyes shot up. "You've seen the gate? Does it look like a nexus?"

"It does. It's an arch that has the same glow as a nexus."

"So you died, and the sagani pulled you back?"

"Yes."

Her eyes flicked around their cramped space, but they looked at nothing in particular. He could almost see the theories created and discarded as he watched. Eventually, she reached a conclusion.

"I want you to touch a nexus for me while I'm studying you. If you want, I can hook you up to one of my machines.

It creates a bit of separation between the infected and the nexus, allowing them to live for a few minutes. We can take you out of the machine before you die."

Quinton didn't have to think about it. "Never."

She looked surprised by his answer. "Why not?"

"Father promised I would die a warrior's death."

She dismissed his concern with another wave of her hand. "I promise I'll take you out before you die."

"Have you ever done that before? You said you've never found a cause of death. What's to say simply entering the machine isn't lethal?"

"I've never pulled an infected from the machine before they die, but that's an experiment I'd be willing to run for you. It's possible you're like Tomas, that you have the key to understanding the nexuses."

"I'm nothing like Tomas!"

He pulled himself out of the tree. The storm wasn't over, but it had lessened, and the rain felt cool on his skin.

She called after him but didn't chase. "You want to serve the Creator, don't you? This is how! I'll do everything to minimize the risk, and you might just be the one who changes the course of the future."

Her offer tempted him. He'd vowed, long ago, to serve the Creator as best he could.

But he still held onto a bit of his pride. Father had promised him a warrior's death. A death on Quinton's own terms. It was all he had asked for when he'd pledged his sword to the church.

Death was death, but the manner of his death mattered. He couldn't say why, but he knew it to be true.

He paced outside the tree, torn between his desire to serve the Creator and his wish to die as he pleased. Twice he stopped to tell Rachel that, yes, he would be honored to serve as one of her subjects. But the words couldn't escape his lips. Both times, he returned to pacing.

Rachel swore and retreated deeper into the shadow of the tree.

It was a slight gesture, but it settled his decision.

Maybe she believed in the Creator. He couldn't say for sure, but it didn't seem that way. All she cared about was the nexuses, and the church was the vehicle through which she satisfied that curiosity. He would die for his Creator, but not for her.

The storm ended, and there was still daylight left. The nearest mission with knights was only a day or two of travel away, depending on how many miles they put behind them.

"Come on," he growled to the tree, knowing she could hear him. "Let's get you back to your research."

4

———————

Tomas woke in a familiar bed and took a moment to appreciate his life. Early morning sunlight streamed through the cracks in the curtains, casting sharp-edged lines of light through the bedroom. It was early yet, so no sounds came from the streets outside. Angela's slow and even breaths told Tomas she would sleep for a while yet.

He rolled out of bed and prepared breakfast. He wasn't as silent as he'd intended, though, and his cooking woke Angela up. She rolled out of bed and leaned against the doorframe. She ran her hand through her hair, loosening a few of the tangles.

"What's for breakfast?" she asked.

"Nothing special. The eggs we bought on the way in yesterday."

They'd arrived in Razin last night. Angela had considered marching straight to the prison to meet with her marshals, but the hour was late, and they were both sore from too many long days of walking. They'd returned to Angela's house after a brief stop to pick up food. Most had disappeared into their stomachs last night, but some odds and ends remained.

Tomas finished the meal and carried two plates to the dining room table. They dug into their food silently, devouring the eggs before they cooled. Angela pushed her empty plate away first. "Thanks for the meal."

"Least I can do."

She fixed him with a questioning stare. "Aren't you going to say something?"

Tomas picked at imaginary scraps of food with his fork. "I wasn't planning on it."

"You still don't think I should do it?"

"No. Life gets a lot harder when people find out. If you're not going to use your sagani often, you're only making unnecessary trouble."

Angela's steady gaze never wavered. "They're my marshals, people I expect to fight beside. How can I ask that of them if I can't be honest with them?"

"It's a noble thought but misguided. Your way has been tried. There's a reason command separated the unnamed units from the rest of the rebels. People can't trust what they don't understand, even if they want to."

Angela stood up. "But if we hide what we are, what will change?"

Tomas shrugged. He'd lost count of the number of times they'd argued on their return to Razin. Angela maintained an idealism Tomas envied. She didn't doubt the bitter lessons of his experience, but she believed in trust and honesty. She wanted to believe her marshals could accept her as a host.

Tomas wanted to protect her from the inevitable heartbreak, but her belief swayed him, too. Her relentless idealism sparked something in him he hadn't felt since he was much younger. Her efforts were likely doomed to fail, but he wanted to believe. And she was willing to gamble everything. She advanced despite the risk, a mark of her courage and character.

He stood up, too.

"You really don't need to come," she said.

"I know, but I want to be there." He wanted to support her with his presence, but he also wanted to observe her marshals' reactions.

He feared her idealism would blind her to the subtle reactions that would reveal her marshals' attitudes. And a part of him, he admitted, truly wanted to be proven wrong. He wanted to be there when she announced she was a host and her marshals welcomed her with open arms.

She didn't pressure him to change his mind, which made him think she was grateful for his presence. He threw on his hat and boots as she pinned a marshal's badge to her shirt.

She walked without hesitation to the prison, marching through the open front door without so much as a pause.

The industriousness of Razin impressed Tomas. It had only been a few weeks since the Family and the church had destroyed the old prison, but already a small substitute building stood in its place. The squat square structure was far too small for the city's needs, but it was better than nothing.

Angela's initial return was a triumphant one. The three marshals in the prison bowed deeply and smiled with relief. Tomas guessed that the last few weeks had meant long hours in a city troubled by unusual chaos. If nothing else, her return meant one more marshal to share the burden.

Once the initial excitement about her return dissipated, Angela asked after the other marshals. The report was better than Tomas expected. Two of the marshals had completely recovered from the attacks and were on patrol, and another two were at home resting after their overnight shifts. Angela ordered the marshals to gather, and while the youngest went to run around town and serve as messenger, she spoke with the two more veteran marshals.

News of the disaster on the train had already reached them. Angela deftly avoided the inquiries, saying she would tell all once they were gathered. She steered the conversation toward recent events in Razin. They'd left after a bout of violence, and she was curious how the city had fared in her absence.

The marshals confirmed that the fighting had inspired a brief uptick in petty crime. Public intoxication and vandalism had been the most common offenses. Minor by the standards of most frontier towns, but more than Angela tolerated in her city. The marshals had worked night and day to return the city to normal. From the sound of it, they had largely succeeded.

The older of the two veterans was a tall man named Adam. He carried himself with a confidence born of experience, and Tomas noted he didn't show the same deference to Angela that the others did. He had assumed command of the city in her absence, and although he had cracked down hard on the various crimes and misbehavior, it sounded like his harsh methods had worked.

As evidence, he pointed to the two small cells that were, at the moment, entirely empty. "Been a quiet two days," he drawled. "I'm hoping today makes it three."

"Me too. Thank you for all that you've done," Angela said.

The genuine gratitude in her reply turned one corner of

Adam's lips up. He tipped his hat in her direction. "Anytime, ma'am."

By the time Angela felt like she was caught up with events in Razin, the other marshals had arrived. They packed into the small office, and Tomas desperately wished for a window to let some fresh air in. Angela wasted no time in calling the meeting to order. "I'm sure you all have a lot of questions about what happened, and there's a lot to say, so thank you for all coming here so quickly."

Her appreciation earned a handful of nods around the room. Bodies settled deeper into chairs and leaned against walls to get comfortable. Once the room fell silent, Angela began. She was a better storyteller than Tomas had expected. In conversation, she was direct, almost to the point of brusqueness. But when she told this story, she filled in the main points with vivid details that even had Tomas leaning forward to hear what would happen next.

Some of it was new to him, too. He hadn't been around for everything Angela had experienced, and he hadn't asked about them on the journey because they hadn't seemed important. He was on the edge of his seat as Angela described the arguments she had fought with the army prior to their advance into Porum. They'd almost turned around when Tomas didn't return when he promised. He'd never known how close the mission had come to failure while he'd been battling his demons inside the town.

Then Angela came to the train, and her retelling of Rachel's betrayal sent off a wave of shocked anger. Tomas appreciated the loyalty the marshals displayed.

Angela ended the story with her being thrown off the train, a fatal wound in her stomach. "It's the last thing I remember."

The room fell silent. Adam was the first to speak, to ask

the question on all their minds. "If you don't mind me saying, you're looking pretty healthy for someone stabbed in the gut and thrown off a train."

Angela swallowed hard and nodded. "That's the reason I wanted to gather you all today. To survive, I became a host."

Her announcement was greeted by an oppressive silence, and it felt like someone had moved all the walls of the office about a foot in, squeezing them all together. Some marshals looked down at their boots. Others glanced around, silently asking their colleagues how they should react. No one muttered anything against Angela, but no one came to her defense, either.

"I know it's a lot to take in, but I want to be upfront about it. I'm not going to hide what happened, and if it makes you uncomfortable, I'd rather know now."

Adam tilted his chair onto its back two legs. "Are you going to fire anyone who speaks up?"

Angela looked hurt by the question. "Of course not."

Adam looked around the room, judging his fellow marshals' reactions. "I can't speak for everyone here, but personally, I've got mixed feelings. I'm glad you're alive, but I've never served with a host."

"I'm the same person who left a few weeks ago," Angela said.

"But are you?" Adam asked. "I don't mean no offense, ma'am, but how can you tell? I want to believe you're right, truly, but I need some time to watch you and judge for myself."

A few of the other marshals muttered their agreement.

Angela stood tall, but Tomas could tell the chilly reception of her announcement hurt. She took the hit on the chin, though. "I suppose that's fair. Starting tonight, I'll put myself into the patrol rotation. That'll give me a chance to work with each of you, and we can revisit the matter in a week or two. How does that sound?"

Her offer to help with patrol won the skeptics over, and there were nods around the room.

Tomas spent a little more time with the marshals, but he'd seen what he wanted, and remaining longer only hindered Angela from returning to the routine of her life.

He left the prison and turned toward Ben's place. Thanks to the marshals, he knew Ben and the kids had remained in the farmhouse well outside of town, but he longed for the comfort of the place. He meandered through the streets until he came to the wide gate, which was standing open.

Tomas chuckled and shook his head. Of course, Ben had left the gate open when he fled. The fool's heart was twice the size of his brain.

He walked through the gate and stood for a minute in the trampled dirt of the front yard. Without the constant noise and movement of the children, the poor state of the home captured his attention. Paint peeled everywhere, and one window was broken and boarded up. The walls blocked much of the noise from the city, which Tomas appreciated. He sat on the edge of the front porch and looked out over the empty yard.

Elzeth stirred. He felt like an old animal these days, barely moving unless it was necessary. He was still there, watching through Tomas's eyes, but he didn't speak often. "You think she'll win them over?" the sagani asked.

"I hope she does, but it feels like she won't."

"For all your advancements, humanity doesn't deal well with change."

"True. Though their questions make me wonder how much I changed after we joined."

"I'd always assumed not much. Unless my presence made you more charming," Elzeth said.

Tomas smiled. It had been far too long since he'd endured one of Elzeth's pointed comments on his many shortcomings. "I wish I knew. Like you, I always assumed it wasn't much, but it wasn't like there was much chance to find out. Most of my friends died in battle soon after I returned, and then they sent me to the unnamed units. Everyone I know today I met after becoming a host."

"You're thinking about what Ulva said, aren't you?"

Tomas nodded, then caught himself. It was such an instinctive reaction, yet there was no one on the property to see it. "Just thinking that if I don't know how much I changed back then, and I've had no cause to complain since we've been joined, maybe I'm worrying too much about what would happen if we followed Ulva's path. What would happen if we figured out how to live in permanent unity."

"It's different for you, though. You still have a body. A physical anchor to your past. I'm scared that if we were to try, everything that I am would disappear," Elzeth said.

Tomas took one last look around the yard and stood up. "I know, old friend, I know. I'm not pressuring you. It's just something that's on my mind."

Elzeth didn't answer, but Tomas didn't feel any displeasure coming from the sagani. He couldn't guess if Ulva's path would prevent the madness that threatened them, but it was nice to discuss it calmly.

It wasn't much, but maybe there was some hope for them yet.

5

The longer Quinton traveled with Rachel, the more uncomfortable she made him. On the surface, their trip proceeded much as it had before. She interrogated him as they walked, an endless barrage of questions he eventually tired of answering. But he sensed a tension between them that hadn't been there before the storm, and that tension made him aware of qualities in her he hadn't noticed before.

The best way he could describe it was that she didn't have a soul. Pain and suffering were nothing more than data, and her willingness to sacrifice *anything* in the pursuit of knowledge chilled his blood.

He feared, too, that he might become yet another in the long line of victims her research had left behind. She made it clear she wanted him in one of her machines, and he worried that when they reached Corrin, she might try to force his hand. He was friends with Father, but if she presented a case that she needed him to solve the mystery of the nexuses, it would put Father in a difficult position.

Quinton hoped it wouldn't come to that, but he wasn't sure what he could do to prevent it.

His worries eased when they finally reached a mission with knights. A group of ten joined him and Rachel, and their presence allowed Quinton to put some space between him and the eager scholar.

The last weeks of their journey refreshed him. They broke through the ever-shifting line that divided army and government land from church territory. Between the complement of knights and the growing distances that separated them from the army, Quinton had little to fear. He saw more sagani than he was used to seeing farther east, but the demons left the Creator's children alone.

Eventually, they reached another train, this one built only to ferry the Creator's children farther west. Quinton stepped on like any civilian and took a seat. It pulled out of the station on time, and soon he watched the endless miles pass without him having to lift a finger. The train attendants even served chilled refreshments.

The church had already accomplished so much. How much more would they achieve once they put these squabbles for independence behind them? He contemplated that question often on the uneventful journey.

They arrived in Corrin a mere two days later, farther west than Quinton had ever dreamed of traveling.

The sight of the city filled him with a child-like wonder. When not serving the church, he'd mostly remained in his small farm home. Time stood still there, a quality Father claimed to appreciate. As much as Quinton appreciated the advances of the church, he was more familiar with the ways of old.

Time moved much faster here, leaping into a future Quinton barely comprehended. Lanterns with no flame lit extravagantly large rooms. Clocks hung on every other wall, time a constant companion to the citizens here. He saw more suits than swords. Those who passed him gave his dusty clothes and battered sword sheath wary looks. A young boy pointed, and his mother pulled him away, whispering fiercely into his ear.

The knights led him through a maze of hallways, giving Quinton no time to stop and stare at the mundane miracles that surrounded him. They didn't give the lanterns or the suits a second glance. They seemed more intent on the clocks than on noticing potential threats.

Quinton imagined there weren't many threats in Corrin. This city was a grand experiment, the heart of the new church lands. And it was already far larger than Quinton had expected.

Rachel seemed more at home here than anyplace they'd traveled before. She took the marvels that surrounded them for granted. She looked grateful when they reached a blocky building with large windows. The knights gestured for her to enter, and she did, without even offering gratitude to Quinton for his service.

He shook his head but pushed the feeling down. He hadn't retrieved her for her thanks. They all served the glory of the Creator.

Most of the knights followed her into the building, but two remained to escort Quinton to his destination. He memorized their route carefully, but the wonders of the city prevented him from absorbing its layout the way he usually did when visiting unknown places.

Corrin was more uniform than most cities, betraying its

planned nature. Many of the buildings they passed looked the same, differing only in the numbers painted on their doors. All the streets were straight and well-maintained despite the heavy traffic. Men in suits and women in dresses bustled from place to place, but the streets lacked the sounds and smells Quinton associated with markets.

It would be easy to lose oneself here, Quinton decided. There was too much sameness and not enough landmarks. He appreciated the beauty of conformity, but it was difficult to navigate. The only landmark he saw was the enormous mission near the center of the city.

Fortunately, the mission, or some place nearby, appeared to be their destination. When the building came fully into view, Quinton had no choice but to stop and stare, much to the annoyance of his escort. He'd seen tall missions before, but the scale of this one dwarfed all the rest. It inspired the same awe in him he received from long contemplations on the Creator.

If today was the day that he died, it would be a good day. He saw the future now, and he took pride in knowing his hand had shaped the course of this city, however indirectly.

The bells of the mission rang out the hour, and Quinton saw the displeased look the two knights shared. He took one last, long look at the mission, then apologized for the delay. The knights led him to an enormous house across the street. Outside of the mission, it was the most unique structure he'd seen since leaving the station.

A servant greeted them at the front door of the house. The knights introduced Quinton as "Father's three o'clock," and the servant looked at Quinton like he was a piece of trash that needed to be thrown away.

"Perhaps you could escort him to the gardens around

back. I'll have someone open the side gate for you," the servant said.

The knights bowed deeply and said that 'of course, they would,' in a manner that suggested they were ashamed for not having thought of it themselves. They beat a hasty retreat and brought Quinton to a side gate. As promised, another servant opened the gate, and the knights left Quinton in her care. She led him through a beautifully manicured garden, filled with a wide variety of bushes that would never grow in the same place in the wild.

The servant led Quinton to a small table surrounded by chairs shaded by a gazebo. Quinton took the indicated chair and carefully considered how he might phrase his request. He'd thought of little else on the journey. After a lifetime of service, it was time for his reward.

Father appeared within minutes of Quinton sitting down. Quinton's eyes narrowed briefly before he bowed his head. Father looked younger and healthier than before. He walked with a spring in his step that had long been absent, and when he spoke, his voice was stronger than when they'd last met.

"Quinton, old friend, it's good to see you. Sit up, sit up. I keep telling you, there's no need for formality between us."

Quinton rose. "It's good to see you, too, Father. You're looking well."

Father grinned as though he was a child with a secret. "Thank you. When I heard word that you'd safely recovered Rachel, I was overjoyed. I had faith in you and in the Creator's plan, but I didn't expect Tomas to poke his nose into Razin again. As always, I'm impressed by your tenacity and want to hear everything."

Father's praise was like a balm, soothing all the small chips and dings Quinton's heart had suffered over the past few months. He told his story, leaving out nothing. Father was an attentive listener, his gaze only leaving Quinton when the mission bells sounded the half-hour. Quinton paused when he reached the moment he kicked Tomas off the train.

"Was I wrong, Father? That decision has haunted me."

"You're sure he was on the cusp of madness?"

"I am. I saw it with my own eyes."

Father rubbed his chin and considered for a moment before answering. "I do think you made a mistake, my child. It is not for us to deliver punishment. Your work, specifically, is to send souls to the gate so that the Creator may judge them and punish them as their sins demand."

Quinton felt tears gathering at the corners of his eyes. He'd known it! Guilt was a sign of error, and he should have paid it closer attention. "I'm sorry, Father."

"Fear not, my child. Though it was a mistake, it was a small one and easily overlooked."

Quinton's despair turned to relief at the words, and he wiped his eyes. "I live to serve."

"Indeed. And you've never disappointed me. Now, for—"

"About that, Father..." He hadn't meant to interrupt Father and bowed his head in apology.

Father's smile was gracious. "Go on."

All his preparation was for naught, and he blurted out, "Father, now that I've delivered Rachel, I would ask for your blessing. Please allow me to take my life."

A long moment of silence hung in the air, but Quinton couldn't read the expression on Father's face. Finally, Father asked, "You are that concerned about the madness you claim to feel?"

Quinton nodded rapidly. "It's—frightening—to feel the demon's grip tighten on my mind. Given what I am capable of, I fear what chaos I might sow if I'm allowed to live. With Tomas out of the way and this mission complete, I ask that you finally fulfill the promise you made to me all those years ago."

Father sighed. "I had hoped that it would never come to this, old friend. There was a part of me that hoped I would pass before you, so the burden of your life would no longer fall on my conscience."

"You are kind, Father, but I am not for this world. I've never been as sure of anything as I am of that. Everything I've seen today is a wonder, but I feel like an ancient, legendary beast wandering among civilized people. This city is more than I dreamed it would be, and I'm overjoyed by that, but there's no place for me here."

Father leaned back and closed his eyes. His lips moved silently as he tilted his face to the sky. Quinton had never seen Father converse with the Creator, but this was certainly what he witnessed now. He kept a respectful silence. What was it like, being able to speak to the one who controlled the world? Quinton had experienced the Creator's touch only once, but that moment had transformed his entire life.

Father enjoyed the privilege of speaking with the Creator on command. He basked constantly in the Creator's glory, an enduring taste of heaven on this fallen world. Soon, Quinton could die, and then he, too, would live on in the endless glory of the Creator. His fingertips tingled at the thought.

Father sniffed, breaking the train of Quinton's thoughts. His eyes watered, and it looked as if he held back tears. "I'm sorry, old friend, but I'm afraid I must deny your request."

Had the denial come from anyone else, Quinton would have burst from his chair in anger. But this was Father, and they'd known each other for over a decade. Still, Quinton's voice cracked when he asked, "Why?"

"There is more that must be done before you pass through the gate. A task that I wouldn't trust to anyone but you."

Quinton clutched the arms of his chair so tightly they creaked under the pressure. "Father, I'm not sure you understand. I can't promise you I'll remain sane long enough to carry out your task."

It was the closest he'd ever come to rejecting Father's requests.

Father reached across and laid his hand on top of Quinton's. "I understand. You have proven yourself, time and time again. You sense your rest drawing near, and it pains me to ask you to add one more sacrifice to your long list, but I must."

Quinton didn't want to argue with Father, but he couldn't bring himself to agree. The demon within him kicked the bars of its cage and ceaselessly prowled, waiting for him to make the smallest mistake. It was coiled like a snake, ready to strike. Father didn't understand how little room for error remained.

When Quinton didn't respond, Father continued. "May I tell you what I believe, Quinton?"

Quinton nodded.

"I believe the Creator brought you to me for a purpose. When you first found your way to me and shared your vision, I was certain the Creator had sought you out specifically. It is because of you that the church stands as strong as it does today. It is because of you that this town will grow and prosper."

Father's words were like drinking cold water as the sun

scorched his skin. They took the pain of Father's denial away.

Father continued, "I also believe you haven't yet completed your service to the Creator. The burden you bear has never been light, but your last trial will be your greatest. Not because of your enemies but because you'll need to fight the demon within you. I believe that if you triumph, your place by the Creator's side is guaranteed."

Quinton bowed his head in shame. Father had the right of it, and Quinton cursed his weakness. For one who carried as much sin as he did, the trials necessary to cleanse his soul would be crushing. "I'm sorry, Father, for my lapse in faith."

Father lifted his chin so Quinton could see Father's gentle smile. "There's nothing to apologize for, my child. We all stumble. That is why we have the church so that we can support one another in times of trouble. Your faith inspires me and gives me the strength to carry on."

"What would you have of me?"

"A few miles west of here, we've built a research station specifically for Rachel. It looks like a fort and houses several units of knights, but I'll take no chances, not when we're so close. She claims she'll finish her work in the next few months. I'd like you there, too, in case anyone arrives with hostile intentions."

Quinton didn't think he'd ever been asked to guard something in all his years of service. And now his request to end his life was denied for this? "Father?"

"I know, Quinton. You must understand, this project is everything. It's a weapon that will keep this city safe from the army forever and bring this foolish fighting to a close. And if Rachel achieves her most ambitious goals, it will also be the end of the sagani. You'll live to see a world cleansed of demons before you pass through the gate."

The claim left Quinton speechless. Every assassination he'd carried out for the church had been in the service of a dream he had never thought to see finished. He fought for the children of the church. Now he understood why he needed to prevent his fall into madness, why he needed to live for a few more months.

A world without demons was finally within their grasp.

6

───────

Tomas and Angela wandered together down Razin's Main Street, talking as Angela walked the city. She'd patrolled two of the last three nights and had volunteered for another shift today. Tomas was surprised she was awake, much less wide-eyed and enthusiastic. He didn't doubt she was glad to be back in Razin and patrolling like she once had, but her enthusiasm came across as a little forced.

She clutched at the past, hoping it could guide her future. But the more Tomas observed of Razin and its reaction to its returned marshal, the less sure he was of Angela's plan.

As large as Razin had grown, word still traveled faster than a stampede. Conversations ended abruptly when they passed. People looked away when Angela tried to catch their gaze. Those whom Angela stopped to speak to looked like they had other, more important places to be. No one spoke against her, and everyone was polite, but the message was clear. She wasn't one of them, not anymore.

Angela kept her smile plastered on her face as though

she could bridge the chasm that had opened up between her and her city if only she served them with every bit of her strength.

Tomas knew where it ended, and it was almost too painful to watch. He'd already tried to warn her away, though. No point wasting his breath in pointing out the obvious. Some lessons could be taught, but others had to be experienced, and this was one of the latter.

Angela entered a shop to speak with the owner, but Tomas elected to wait outside. It was a beautiful day, and he'd already spent too much time indoors. No one in the streets spoke to him, but he didn't mind. Razin wasn't his home, so there was no need to befriend anyone. He halfway expected he'd be gone again before too long.

Angela exited the shop with a farewell, then stopped when she saw the expression on Tomas's face. "Something wrong?"

"Just thinking about how much different my life has been from this. I've never stayed in one place for long, so what you're trying to do is something I've never done. I've always just moved along to the next town whenever things got uncomfortable. It's strange, staying in one place. I'm not used to it."

She laughed. "No kidding."

Tomas feigned mock outrage. "What's that supposed to mean?"

"Eventually, you're going to need to find a job or a hobby. You're quickly going to get bored wandering around town every day."

Tomas had been thinking the same, but he hadn't broached the subject. Truthfully, he didn't think they'd last long here, but he didn't want to say that. "Not sure what I'd do, though. It's foolish to look for work. I'd be the most help as a marshal, but I don't want to risk putting myself in a situation where I might need Elzeth."

"Why don't you go see Ben? If nothing else, it'll give you something to do. He might have some guidance for you."

Tomas almost protested, claiming that she could use his company. But that wasn't true. She had a good grasp of her new strength, and she'd served as the chief marshal of Razin long before he'd shown up. Walking around with another host probably didn't help her convince the concerned public that she was still one of them, either. "I suppose that's a good idea. Meet you at your place for supper?"

"That's a deal. Now get out of here."

Tomas tipped his hat in her direction and jumped to obey.

He felt better as soon as he broke free of Razin's busy streets. He'd spent so long wandering the west alone that he felt sensitive to the cacophony that accompanied civilization wherever it spread. So often, the noise felt like a weight, an unwanted burden life made it difficult to shed. Once he'd gotten a few miles beyond the outskirts of the city, the only sounds were the wind through the grass and the occasional chirp of a songbird as it flitted past. He was almost in a good mood by the time he reached the farmhouse.

The sight of a dozen children scattered across the field brought a smile to his face. Some of the oldest looked to be working in the garden while a handful of younger children chased each other around the expansive yard. They shouted and waved when they recognized Tomas, and he waved back. Two young girls raced toward him, and soon he had his own personal guard to accompany him to the house.

Ben emerged from the front door and greeted him on the porch. They both bowed deeply, and Ben offered him a quick tour of the place. Tomas accepted and let himself be led into the farmhouse, one girl pulling on each hand.

Memories of his first experience here lingered. This farmhouse had once bunked a group of Family serving as mercenaries for a church research station nearby. Tomas had led a bloody assault on the house, and when he'd been here last, signs of the violence had been plentiful. Blood and gashes had decorated the walls.

Those memories made Tomas's first impression of the new place that much stronger. When they had left for Porum, Ben had talked about buying the property and fixing it up for the children, and he'd acted quickly. The walls smelled of fresh paint, and while there were toys scattered around the living areas, the hallways, and kitchen were so clean Tomas imagined that dust fled in fear before it could settle.

"Incredible," he said.

"I thought you might like it. Olena did more of the work than I care to admit. And the kids were helpful. But it feels like we turned this place around in no time at all."

"You did. It feels like a home now. A good one."

Tomas meant the compliment. In just a few short weeks, Ben had brought that same sense of peace Tomas had enjoyed in the abandoned yard in Razin here. It felt sacred, a place set aside from the everyday cares of the world. He shook his head. "You're a remarkable man, Ben."

"You should tell me that again when Olena is around to hear."

Tomas smiled. "Somehow, I suspect she already knows."

Ben asked if he would like to sit inside or out on the porch, and Tomas chose the porch. They stepped outside and took a pair of chairs next to one another.

Ben opened the conversation. "It's good to see you again.

Especially after the rumors from Porum, but I'm guessing this isn't a social call."

"Actually, it mostly is."

Ben laughed. "Mostly?"

"Sure. Angela and I have been back in Razin for a few days, and she told me I needed to get out of her hair. So here I am."

"Pushing you off on me now, huh?"

"You're a lucky man," Tomas said.

They caught up on the events of the last few weeks. Ben's life, fortunately, had been far less exciting, but Tomas enjoyed listening to the stories from the remodel. Even Ben's stories radiated that same peace Tomas associated with his homes. The former inquisitor spread it wherever he went.

After, the two men sat in companionable silence as they watched the youngest children play. Out of the blue, Tomas chuckled.

"Care to share?" Ben asked.

"It's a funny life. You're the closest thing I have to a friend, and we met when you captured me and tortured me for several days."

"I consider myself your friend, and it's not so funny. The ways of the Creator are beyond human comprehension."

A few years ago, that comment would have enraged Tomas. Today it slid off of him like rain dripping off his hat. "You still believe, don't you?"

"I'm not sure exactly what I believe, but I think the saying captures something true. I've often felt like there's something out there guiding my life in ways I don't understand. Call it the Creator, call it fate, but it's something. And whatever it is, it's beyond my comprehension. All I'm sure about is that there is more to this world than what I can touch."

Tomas held out his left hand. "You think that this has some greater reason behind it?"

Tomas couldn't quite keep the bitterness out of his voice.

Ben watched the slight tremor. He nodded, and Tomas put his hand back on his lap. The tremors weren't constant, but they were almost a daily occurrence now.

"I don't know," Ben answered. "I wondered if it would ever get you or if there was something about you that made you special. Something that kept you safe from the madness."

"Looks like I'm not that special."

"What are you going to do?"

"That's the reason this isn't entirely a social visit. It's the same question I've been asking. No matter how many ways I try to attack it, I don't come any closer to an answer."

Ben stretched his arms up high, then leaned his chair back on its rear two legs and interlaced his fingers behind his head. He rested the back of his hands and his head against the wall of his new house. He thought for a moment, then said, "I don't think my advice has changed since we last spoke. You've chased one thing after another for as long as I've known you. If you don't have much time left, the best thing is to commit to how you want to use those days."

"What if I don't know?"

Ben clicked his tongue and shook his head. "It's not about finding something perfect. Any choice brings trade-offs, advantages, and drawbacks. There are no perfect solutions in life, so let go of perfect. Let worthwhile be enough. Maybe it means living quietly in Razin with Angela. Or, if that's too crowded, you'd be welcome out here, both of you. We could always use an extra hand, and I'd watch you if you're worried about madness. Or you could go off on one last quest, one last adventure. You could help

Hardin and Ulva. I wouldn't judge you unkindly for any of those choices."

Ben had said much the same before, but Tomas hadn't listened. Now he did, and he recognized the wisdom in the advice. "Thank you, Ben. I'll think about that."

"Don't think. Just choose and do. Every minute you spend debating is a minute you aren't living this precious gift of time that you still have." Ben leaned forward so his chair rested on all four legs, then he leaned over and glanced through the kitchen window. "Speaking of wonderful gifts, will you join us for lunch? Olena promised a feast."

"I'd like that very much."

(###)

The meal lived up to Ben's promise and more. Several of the children had a sense of humor that made Tomas laugh out loud. Seeing them all together with Ben and Olena was almost enough to make Tomas forget the trials they had suffered to get this far.

It was the sort of meal where the memories lingered longer than the taste of Olena's excellent food, and it was over all too soon. Tomas said his farewells and promised the children he would return sometime soon. He left the farmhouse with a much lighter heart than the one he had carried when he arrived.

He'd barely gotten half a mile back to Razin when movement drew his eye to the sky. A bird, larger than an eagle, soared high above in slow circles. He looked up and squinted and swore he saw flashes of color. Elzeth confirmed his suspicion. "It's a sagani."

A while back, such a sight wouldn't have elicited any comment from Tomas. Sagani freely roamed the western frontier and, so long as a traveler was wary, posed no particular difficulty or danger. But the mysterious creatures were no longer a common sight, at least in the portions of the west Tomas had recently wandered. Tomas watched the bird and couldn't shake the feeling that he was being watched in return. He waited for a minute to see if the bird would change its habits or fly off, but it continued to circle. Tomas shrugged and continued toward Razin. A mile later, he looked up, and the bird was still overhead.

"Are we being followed?" he asked Elzeth.

The sagani shifted in Tomas's core in a manner that Tomas associated with a shoulder shrug. "Beats me."

Tomas studied the bird some more and waited for several minutes to see if it would approach. It made no move to do so, content to circle far out of reach of even the most powerful rifles. "Any ideas?"

"Leave it be. If it wants something, it'll ask on its own terms. Nothing we can do anyway unless you've figured out a way to fly while I've been resting."

Tomas waited for a minute longer, then accepted Elzeth's advice. The eagle was still following them when Razin came into view. The sun dipped toward the horizon, and Tomas felt better than he had in several days.

The pain came without warning. Tomas's stomach twisted, and it felt like someone had reached into his gut and pulled out his stomach and intestines in one vicious yank. He wrapped his arms around his abdomen and dropped like a stone to the ground. A moment later, a familiar piercing shriek shattered his eardrums. It sounded like a thousand high-pitched voices, all crying out together in agony.

Tomas rolled onto his side as he vomited, the pain worse

than any wound he'd ever taken in battle. As he lay on his side, he watched the mysterious sagani plummet toward him at breakneck speed.

7

Quinton clutched at his stomach with his left hand and used his right to pull himself back to standing. A dozen knights watched him struggle without lifting a finger to help. If there was one consolation, and it was a small one, it was that two host-knights walking the walls were in no better condition than he was. It had been Rachel, not madness, that laid him low.

He bit back a curse.

Rachel would deny it to her dying breath, but he was certain she had waited until he was surrounded by knights to run her latest test. Maybe she hadn't known what would happen, but she had hoped. By the end of the day tomorrow, she would have a dozen reports on his collapse. She'd pick through each one for extra details, and then she'd corner him with another set of specific questions.

Once she'd squeezed every drip of information from him, she'd send the reports into Corrin, where they'd eventually reach Father. Her goal, never stated but always clear, was to keep him as a test subject. She wanted to steal his death from him.

Her relentlessness annoyed him and, if he was being honest, frightened him a bit. She had Father's ear, and if she persuaded him that Quinton's death under her studies could better serve the church, Father might grant her request.

Despite that, Rachel impressed him. He'd come across few people, either civilian or military, that possessed the same dedication to their calling. She had sworn herself to a cause: to be the first to understand the nexuses. It was no fair-weather oath, either. He didn't think an army of hosts would slow her.

Quinton gripped the wall with both hands until he was steady. The demon in his core felt small and weak, like a fire that had died down to an ember. The battle for control of his body ceased, like both sides had put down their weapons, signed a temporary truce, and retreated for the day. He was grateful to Rachel for weakening his sagani, even if she hadn't done her test for him.

When strength and balance returned, he continued his circuit of the fort's walls. In many ways, this fort was a mirror of the one outside Chesterton. Its wooden walls were thick and sturdy, sourced with lumber from the enormous forest that grew a few miles to the west. Like the fort outside Chesterton, the church had also built the walls around the site of a discovered nexus. The scenery beat Chesterton, though. If he stood on the western wall and squinted, he could see the mountains rising in the distance. It was a beautiful and quiet area, a suitable place to die.

Just not at Rachel's hands.

Ironically, it was her research that gave him the most reason to live. She claimed his insights were useful, and when they spoke, she kept him updated. With every passing day, she grew closer to understanding the nexuses. One day, she expected she would control them. And then, when she'd solved every mystery they contained, she would kill them. That day would mark the completion of her lifelong quest. It would also mark the day when Quinton could finally lay his own burdens to rest.

As though the thought alone had summoned her, Rachel emerged from the complex subterranean chambers below the fort. She found Quinton and marched toward him. She wasn't smiling, exactly, but her frown was less severe than usual.

"I take it your attempt was a success," he said.

"I haven't been able to discuss the details with the other test subjects, but they're all in their cages groaning, so I assumed it worked."

There was little joy in her observations, though that was part of her character. Quinton had never met someone as indifferent to success or failure as Rachel. To her, both were data that pointed her toward her next experiment.

"It worked. Even now, the demon within me is quiet." A new brief wave of pain washed over him, and he couldn't keep the grimace from his face. Rachel was too observant not to notice. She pulled out a pencil and a notebook. "Tell me everything that you experienced, down to the smallest detail."

By now, Quinton was familiar with the process and obliged willingly. Sometimes Rachel seemed inhuman, sympathy a concept she couldn't solve with her scientific mind. Quinton would have found it more off-putting, except that she applied the same disinterest to herself. The fort commander had assigned several staff to remind her to eat and sleep. If not for their efforts, Quinton suspected she would be close to wasting away. The only nourishment she craved was more knowledge.

He shared everything, from the feeling of having the demon ripped from his body to its current demure attitude. She made no comment nor offered sympathy for the pain she had inflicted. She scribbled notes in the secret shorthand she had developed, her pencil scratching against the paper at incredible speed. At times, she interrupted his story to ask a clarifying question, but that was all. When she had extracted every piece of useful information from him, she closed her notebook and nodded.

"Several subjects died operating the machine. Even though I had wired them in parallel, they didn't last as long as I had hoped. I want the bodies gone by the end of the day so that I can work on rewiring the pods into a new configuration."

"Yes, ma'am."

She left without another word, one of the host-knights in her sights. Quinton almost felt sorry for them.

He felt a little sorry for himself, too. Cleaning up Rachel's messes wasn't why he was here. But this stretch of frontier had been so quiet it might as well have been abandoned. Quinton wasn't bored, but Rachel's orders gave him something to do for the rest of the day. He found two young knights to help him, and they descended into the maze of passages below the fort.

Quinton didn't come down here often. He wasn't particularly welcome, but the greater reason was that the area made him uncomfortable. Wires, pipes, and tubing ran along narrow tunnels, and the temperature was often several degrees warmer down here than it was on the surface. The spaces were cramped and dark.

If that had been all, Quinton could have stomached the space. What truly bothered him was the machine Rachel built. He knew its purpose was noble, and his resolve to protect it from harm never wavered, but there was still something about it that made his spine tingle and his stomach clench. He hadn't been able to put his finger on why, though.

Most of humanity's creations inspired him. He saw the trains and the flameless lanterns and marveled at human ingenuity. All of Corrin was a monument to inventiveness.

But this machine didn't inspire the same awe. The closest comparison he could think of was that of weaponry. Rifles and cannons were both inventions that were objectively superior weapons to the sword Quinton had carried since he was a young man, and yet they both seemed like progress in the wrong direction. There was a skill required to wield a sword well, a perfection of the human spirit that shooting a rifle couldn't match. The analogy wasn't perfect, but it came closest to capturing Quinton's thoughts.

He ignored his unease as he entered the chamber where most of the pods stood. Quinton would have called them cages, but he wouldn't quibble over terminology. He unlocked the devices and then undid the manacles connecting Rachel's latest group of hosts to the machine.

Quinton tried not to think about the fact that Rachel would have been ecstatic to get him into one of these cages. These were hosts that inquisitors had captured over the years and had ferried across the nation from one cell to another. All three of today's infected showed ample evidence of their time in the inquisitor's care. All had missing fingers, broken teeth, and one had a limb freshly severed.

It was what they deserved for turning their bodies over to demons, so Quinton felt no pity for their trials. He pulled them roughly from the cages and passed them over to his helpers. They dragged the bodies up through the narrow tunnels and into the light, where they tossed them on a cart stained with old blood.

One knight fetched a horse for the cart, and after it was attached, Quinton dismissed both knights. The rest he was willing to do alone. There was a deep pit about a mile to the south where he would dump and burn the remains so that nothing in the wild would feed off the demonic flesh.

It was grisly work, but it was the Creator's work, and Quinton found it a worthy way to spend his remaining time on this fallen earth.

8

Tomas watched the sagani fall, unable to move. It struck the prairie no more than three feet from him, throwing up dirt and grass like a small cannonball.

Tomas lay in the grass after the initial wave of agony passed. The need to clutch at his stomach had passed, and the faint glimmer of Elzeth's presence deep in his core reassured him. All the same, the world felt very wrong. Colors didn't seem as vivid, and the feeling of the summer breeze felt less sharp than before.

He heard a cry that sounded like a wounded animal, and it motivated him to push his aching body into a sitting position. Where the sagani had crashed, the grasses stirred. It flapped its wings and launched itself into the sky, almost scaring Tomas back onto his side. Tomas braced himself with an arm and watched. The sagani looked unharmed at first, gaining elevation quickly, but then one wing stopped flapping, and the bird almost plummeted back to the ground. It recovered, spreading its wings out wide and swooping across the tops of the grass before climbing once again.

Elzeth rumbled to life, "I'm not sure, but that felt like Kimson to me."

"Agreed. Are you hurt?"

"Nothing I won't recover from, but that was scary. I'm not sure how you experienced that, but it felt almost the same as when you touch a nexus. It was that same pull calling me home." Elzeth couldn't hide the hurt in his voice, the longing that he had sacrificed on Tomas's behalf for so long.

Tomas chewed on Elzeth's comparison for a minute. It hadn't felt like that to him, and it seemed significant that he and Elzeth had unique experiences. "Do you think you could have? We weren't touching a nexus."

"That's the worst of it. It was all the desire with none of the ability. It was like being out here on the open prairie with endless vistas and complete freedom in every direction, except that I was locked in a cage and unable to move a foot."

Elzeth's metaphor hit Tomas hard. He thought he'd understood what his companion sacrificed every time they touched the nexus, but now he reconsidered. "When I touch a nexus willingly, it's like that for you, too, isn't it? Except the cage door is open, and the guard is asleep."

"Just about."

"I'm grateful, you know. Probably don't say it as often as I should. But I appreciate you keeping me alive."

"You're welcome. But if you feel like you can move, we should get down into the city."

Angela. He'd been so preoccupied with his own thoughts and Elzeth's suffering he'd completely forgotten about her. Whatever had happened had affected both the sagani in the sky and him, so it stood to reason she would suffer as well. He pushed himself to his feet and half ran, half stumbled into the city. Evening was falling, and she should be home preparing supper for them. Tomas hurried that way, ignoring the curious stares of onlookers.

It took him three tries to get the key into the lock and turn it, and he slammed the door open as though he were raiding the house. "Angela!" he shouted.

"In here." The answering call was weak, and Tomas feared what he might find.

Angela was sitting up against the wall in her small dining room. Her eyes were glassy and unfocused, as though she'd had too much to drink. He took some small comfort in her even breaths. "How do you feel?"

"Like someone punched a hole through my stomach."

Tomas helped her to stand and escorted her over to the chair. The movement seemed to help, and some of the focus returned to her eyes. She fixed her gaze on him. "What happened?"

"We're not sure. Whatever it was, it affected host and sagani alike."

"Rachel."

Once again, his companion had leaped ahead of him. He hadn't thought of the scientist, but she was as good an explanation as any. She'd been important enough for the Holy Father to send Ghosthands after her, and now Tomas understood why. He collapsed into his own chair, took off his hat, and ran his fingers through his hair. "Seems a likely explanation, I guess. Damn."

He stood, grabbed a pitcher and some cups, and poured water for both of them. Then they compared notes. They'd both had similar experiences, but Angela hadn't developed the ability to speak with her sagani, so she couldn't say if Elzeth's experience matched hers.

They talked until the sun went down, supper forgotten. They both worried about the event happening again, but as the hours dragged on, they felt a little more comfortable. It was a foolish comfort. They had no way of knowing when the church would strike again. It could be hours from now, while they were sleeping, days from now, when Angela was out on patrol, or years from now, after Tomas had passed through the gates. But what was the use of worrying?

One other question troubled Tomas. What would he do about it?

He had no official duty to solve the problem, but he felt as though the responsibility was his. He was one of the few alive who could stand against Ghosthands and one of the few alive who knew enough of the church's secrets to track Rachel down. The specter of madness hung over his deliberations, though. He had little time and not much strength to give. Did his actions even matter?

As they talked, he looked around the dining room. He had something good here. It wasn't a relationship he had planned for, but what in his life was planned? He could ignore this problem and leave it to someone else and maybe die with some measure of contentment.

He went to bed with the question unspoken, and his mind churned over the problem. It wasn't until hours later, with Tolkin high in the sky, that he fell asleep.

Elzeth woke him too early. Tomas's eyes snapped open, and he glanced out the window. It was still dark, and judging from the position of the moons, there was a fair bit of night left to go.

"Someone's outside," Elzeth said.

"Trouble?" Tomas asked.

"Not sure."

Tomas rolled out of the bed silently, pleased that the movement didn't wake Angela. He threw on his pants, crept out of the room, and let himself out the back door. He snuck around from the back of the house to the front, checking his surroundings for ambushes. The night was quiet, except for sounds he couldn't place coming from the front of Angela's house.

Tomas poked his head around the corner, and he saw a young man scrawling a message with red paint across the front of Angela's house. Tomas stepped out so he could read what was being written. His fist clenched when he saw it read "Demon whore."

He kept his voice cold, though. "Classy."

The young man yelped and almost jumped halfway out of his boots as he turned. Tomas caught the symbol of the church stitched into the man's tunic.

The boy made to run, but Tomas was faster. He grabbed the boy by the lapels and shook him hard. "What the hells do you think you're doing?"

The young man glared but said nothing.

The commotion woke up Angela. She came out the front door and took in the scene in a moment, including the message on her door. She sighed, "Let him go."

Tomas wanted nothing more than to give the boy a beating he would remember but listened to Angela. He threw the boy down hard, though. Before the boy could get back up, Tomas took the can of paint and poured it over the boy's head. The boy ran off, cursing them both, but Tomas made no move to follow. Once the boy was out of sight, he turned to Angela.

"I'm sorry," he said.

Angela stared at her door. "Nothing for you to apologize for."

She stared at the words for a while longer, and Tomas wished he had his own can of paint so that he could clean them off her house so she would never have to see them again.

She reached out and took his hand. "Come on. Let's go back to bed."

(###)

Tomas woke the next morning to Angela attempting to sneak out of bed. He scrunched his eyes shut against the glaring light of the late morning sun and groaned. "I think the sun rose too early this morning."

She laughed. "Fall back asleep if you want, but you'll miss breakfast."

Tomas sat up so fast it was like he had heard cannon fire nearby. "Breakfast, you say?"

Angela laughed again, and Tomas scratched the back of his head. He'd expected this morning to be a more somber affair after the events of last night. He fell back into bed as she made for the kitchen but rose again when the smell of bacon hitting the frying pan reached his nose. It was hard to stay in bed when bacon waited in another room. He threw on his clothes and joined her.

They sat down to eat, and Angela surprised him for the second time that morning. "I've decided to resign my position as the chief marshal in Razin."

Tomas put his pinky finger in his ear and dug around with exaggerated gestures. "Come again? I thought I heard you say you're going to resign."

"You heard right. I think it's for the best."

Tomas grew serious. "What changed your mind? It wasn't what that kid wrote, was it?"

"No. Not exactly. The chief marshal is supposed to be a servant of the town. It's not about me. If my presence is going to lead to more problems, the best way I can serve the citizens of Razin is by letting Adam take charge."

Tomas wasn't sure if she was certain or if she was seeking a debate. "Are you sure about this?"

Angela nodded. "I think so. I've noticed the way everyone has treated me since I returned. It pains me to admit it, but I can't be as effective as Adam can. And I have something more now."

Tomas's heart skipped a beat at that. "Oh, is that so?"

She leaned forward. "I'll help you fight the church. Together, we can stop them from whatever evil they're planning."

"How do you know that's what I was going to do?"

She gave him a knowing smile. "I know you better than that. You were going to tell me this morning that you had to leave, weren't you?" Tomas heard no hint of judgment in her voice, and he was amazed by the woman who sat before him. He found it hard to believe that someone could understand him so well and still be willing to spend time with him. A wide grin broke out on his face. "I might have had some thoughts along those lines."

"Then let's do it," Angela said. "I'll wrap up my life here, and then we'll hunt Rachel down and stop her."

9

Quinton hadn't felt well since Rachel's latest experiment. The blast from the machine had quieted the demon inside him, which Quinton was grateful for, but the demon hadn't regained the strength Quinton expected. It simmered quietly in his core like an ember that refused to be snuffed out but also refused to burn brighter.

The first few days had been a pleasant change after the prolonged struggle to keep the demon under control. The sagani's weakness allowed Quinton to focus on other, more meaningful work. He volunteered to train the host-knights, a task he hadn't expected to enjoy as much as he did. They were young, newly infected, and rough around the edges. He expected the demons to give him problems, but the knights' training and faith helped them stand strong against the demons' influence. They were humble, attentive, and willing to learn.

As trained knights, they were already among the strongest and fastest swords the church commanded, but

Quinton saw weaknesses in their techniques. He'd once suffered from the same ones. When they trained, they performed the same techniques they'd learned as knights, only faster. What they failed to realize was that becoming a host opened the gates to greater possibilities, moves, and strategies that would be suicidal without the inhuman speed and strength the demons provided. He set about correcting the error.

The training didn't just serve the knights. It also revealed how weak Quinton's demon had become since the blast. He lashed at it and exhorted it, but his efforts were rewarded with the barest of flames. The demon offered enough strength to instruct the host-knights, but barely.

After two days of fighting his demon to burn brighter, he let the knights train on their own. He had more to teach, but the constant struggle wore him thin. The bitter irony of the situation wasn't lost on him. For years, he'd fought to keep the demon tamed, and now he fought to get it to burn. He ate an enormous meal that left him hungrier than when he sat down, then shuffled to his private room, where he collapsed into bed without taking his boots off.

Time escaped his grasp. Sometimes he slept, other times, he tossed and turned, seeking any bit of meager comfort. It felt like the bed was filled with rocks. Cramps often kept him doubled over in agony. Sweat soaked through his pillow and sheets. His demon flickered and sputtered like a candle at the very end of its wick. When he closed his eyes, he wasn't certain he'd open them again.

He woke to Rachel standing over him. For a moment, he feared that he'd died and passed to the three hells, but he shook the suspicion off. He knew what it meant to die, and he hadn't passed through the gates yet.

Her icy hand on his wrist focused his attention. She pressed her fingers gently against his skin.

How could flesh be so cold?

"Do you know how long you've been here?" she asked Quinton.

He tried to answer, but his lips wouldn't obey his commands. He shook his head.

She glanced toward the door. "When was the last time anyone saw him?" she asked.

Someone answered, but the words were indistinct. Rachel nodded and turned back to Quinton. "I'm going to take you to my lab."

His heart pounded in his chest, trying to escape like the demon used to. His skin felt clammy. Fear gave him the strength to speak.

"Just let me die," he croaked.

"Father wants you to live. He says so every time I write to him. He wants you to stand by his side when we reach the end."

All lies. She spoke like a believer, but the Creator was nothing more than a tool to her.

"Leave me," he said.

She stood. "No. Your life is too valuable, and I have orders from the Holy Father. Your trials aren't over yet."

He tried to grab at her as she walked away, but he was too weak. She reached the door and issued orders. Quinton strained to hear, but it was as though someone had stuffed cotton in his ears. A pair of knights came into the room and picked him up like a child.

They were the same two knights he'd recruited to dispose of the bodies from Rachel's last experiment.

The sudden motion made him feel sick. He held the vomit in, but his head lolled to the side, and he passed out.

When he woke up, they were laying him down on the operating table in Rachel's lab. Quinton tried to struggle, but his strength was gone. The cold metal of her table felt delightful against his back. One of Rachel's aides brought him a ladle of water and tipped the refreshing liquid down his throat.

He'd never tasted anything more delicious. He imagined the water spreading through his body like a river suddenly unleashed upon a desert. His hearing returned with his voice. "What are you doing?"

"Saving your life, despite your insistence I do otherwise," Rachel said.

"But *what* are you doing?"

"I haven't decided yet. What can you tell me about what's happening to you?"

Quinton had never considered lying to Rachel before, but he considered it now. He watched her gathering her instruments, then decided to trust her. "It started with your last test."

"You said you were feeling weak, then."

"I never recovered. The demon has felt weak in me ever since. I used it a little training the new host-knights, but it was hard."

Rachel probed while the aide brought another much-welcomed ladle of water. She never settled for vague explanations. She made him tell her everything about the past few days, and she reached her diagnosis quickly enough. "It sounds to me like your sagani is dying."

"Is that even possible?"

"It's happened before. We've documented a dozen cases in the last ten years. It's rare, but my test was designed to hurt the sagani, so it seems more reasonable here."

Quinton groaned as another series of cramps nearly

doubled him over. Once the pain passed, he asked, "Why only me?"

Rachel shrugged. "A question I want to know the answer to, too. My first hypothesis is that your sagani was weaker to start. You've been a host for a long time. Those host-knights are babies in comparison."

He hated to ask, but he needed answers. "Is there anything you can do?"

"I think so. I need to hook you up to the machine."

"No." Quinton's answer was flat.

"Not like the subjects. I truly think that all you need to do is contact the control pads when the machine is turned on. That will establish a connection, of a sort, with the nexus."

"Which will kill me."

"No. At least, it shouldn't. Most subjects can last for several minutes, and that's with a different type of connection. You'll get the least intense one I've designed."

Quinton wasn't convinced. "What's that supposed to do?"

"Several subjects have reported that brief contact with the nexus can have a restorative effect. You've even said the same about Tomas, that he was stronger after touching the nexus outside Chesterton. I believe that contact strengthens the demon. Normally, that poses a problem for a host, but it sounds like it's exactly what you need."

Quinton's thoughts felt as though they were crawling through mud. Did he trust Rachel? She claimed she had orders from Father to keep him alive, but Father was far away from this lab. In the end, necessity won out. If he fought, she would just summon the knights again, and he wasn't strong enough to resist. Better to cooperate and hope he'd live to fight another day.

"Let's do it, then."

"Good. Can you walk?"

"Not without help."

She gestured to her aide, who got himself under one of Quinton's arms. Together, they stood, and the aide guided Quinton into one of the next rooms. In the center of the room was a small metal platform. It was circular and raised about a foot off the ground, a mess of wires and pipes visible underneath it. The aide helped Quinton onto the platform and made sure he could sit without falling over.

Quinton waited while Rachel and the aide prepared the platform for him. Several tubes were positioned around the room, leaning up against the walls. They were similar to one another, but each had slight differences. Some were taller or thicker, while others had exposed wires dangling from open holes. Quinton couldn't make anything of them.

They consumed Rachel and her aide's attention, though. They huddled over a pair of tubes and debated in hushed voices. The aide jabbed his finger at a tube, but Rachel shook her head and pointed to another set on the other side of the room. Normally, Quinton would have heard their whispers without problem, but today their voices seemed impossibly distant. He held his head in his hands and settled for not vomiting.

The aide seemed to triumph in their argument, and the pair each grabbed an identical tube and rushed over to the platform. They wasted no time screwing the tubes onto the platform. Once the work was completed, the aide and Rachel both reached under one of his arms and helped him to his feet.

"Can you stand?" Rachel asked.

"For a bit," Quinton said.

"You only need to stand on your own long enough for us to turn the machine on."

They stood him next to the tubes and guided his hands so that one was on each pillar. He leaned his weight on them and was grateful they were sturdy. Rachel took one tentative step back, holding out her hands as though she was afraid he'd tip over.

She waited a moment, then nodded. "Good. Just stay there. One minute."

She hurried from the room. The aide remained. Quinton noticed he was careful not to approach the platform. Before he could be worried about that fact, Rachel turned the machine on.

A wave of pure energy ran up his hands, burning his arms as though they were on fire. His hands locked onto the pillars. The demon, near dead, suddenly came alive and burst from its cage like Quinton had built the cell out of toothpicks. Muscles bulged from his calves all the way to his neck. His skin turned porous, and to his sight, it appeared as though he was leaking light like sweat.

His demon danced with joy, and a sense of relief and freedom flooded Quinton. He couldn't tell if the joy was his or not. The demon was in control, and Quinton didn't care.

As quickly as the energy surged through him, it was cut off. The restorative effects lingered, though. He felt stronger than he had in years. Faster and more flexible, too. The machine had stripped years off his age.

Quinton reasserted his control over the demon, rebuilding the cage so it was even stronger and tighter than before. He slammed the cage shut and pocketed the key, whistling as he did.

The demon raged, but it couldn't so much as make the bars of its reformed cage rattle.

Quinton pulled his hands off the pillar and stared at them in wonder. This, this was beyond anything he'd expected.

Rachel ran into the room, eyes wide. "Did it work?"

Quinton nodded, a smile widening across his face. "Oh, it worked, and I want more."

10

———

Tomas waited until Tolkin was high in the sky before leaving Angela's house. He stepped over half-packed crates and slid between out-of-place chairs. They'd been working through her possessions for the better part of a week, but there was still much more to do.

It amazed him that she had collected so much. Her house was small and tidy, but once the process of moving began, it was as though the house kept vomiting possessions. He'd always thought of a home as little more than the place where one slept for more than a week at a time, but he was coming to understand it was more than that. It was the paintings hanging on the walls, the furniture welcoming weary family members, and the pantry stuffed with hard-earned food and supplies.

He was glad to leave the house. When he shut the door behind him, he closed his mind to the subject of moving. Angela was leaving Razin because of him, and a lingering guilt bothered him. He was a tumbleweed, blown here and there by a shifting wind. She was more like a tree, deeply rooted in the soil and connected to her surroundings.

Traveling was in his blood, but not hers. He hadn't meant for this to happen when he saved her life.

She patrolled the city tonight, serving as a marshal even after announcing her resignation. From her daily accounts, the transition proceeded smoothly, but Tomas didn't miss the barely concealed emotion that cracked her voice when she related the mundane details of the changes.

One more week.

Then they'd be gone, and she could look forward to what came next instead of focusing on everything she had lost.

Tomas helped how he could, but he didn't fool himself into believing he'd accomplished much. From the day he'd first stepped into Razin, he'd done little but destroy Angela's life.

"You've been moping more than usual," Elzeth said. "You're not going to be too distracted tonight, are you?"

"Not sure there's much to worry about, but no, I won't be distracted."

"Because it would be a shame if you end up in prison a few days before you're supposed to leave. Especially after she gave her copy of the cell keys to Adam."

"I said I'm fine!"

Elzeth chuckled. "You're almost too easy to rile up."

"Speak for yourself. You're silent for days, and when you wake up, I'm never sure which Elzeth I'm getting. Some days you sound content, like now, and other days you're a nightmare."

Elzeth didn't deny it, but Tomas's accusations didn't stir the sagani's passions, either. "Sorry, I've been resting so much. I think it helps, though. My thoughts are clearer after a long nap."

Tomas's frustration with Elzeth burned itself to ash

quickly. They were both suffering, and it did little good to antagonize one another. For the moment, they remained stuck together. "I'm glad you're feeling better."

He turned a corner, and Razin's mission came into view. It was large, the spire dominating the local landscape, but not as big as some missions Tomas had seen. Its windows were dark, and Tomas assumed it was unoccupied. According to Angela, the inquisitor he had killed on the train had been recently installed as the priest for this mission. With his death, the mission was without a leader. Another priest would soon be on the way, but for now, a handful of laypeople ran the mission in their spare time.

There was no one about, so Tomas tried the main entrance first. The heavy wooden door didn't budge when he pulled, so he walked around to the side of the mission. The other door was less intimidating, but it was no less tightly locked. Tomas shook the door, but it was thick enough that he didn't think he could break it with brute force. He glanced around, then threw a stone through a window. Then he used his elbow to clear out most of the remaining glass. He climbed through before his commotion drew any attention.

The inside of the mission was dark and still. Tomas crouched by the window, listening for any sign his entrance had been noticed. Hearing nothing, he crept into the main hall of the mission.

The space sent a shiver down his spine. Most missions had a priest present most, if not all, of the time, and he couldn't shake the feeling that the empty building was a trap. A lone candle flickered near the altar, but most of the light came from Tolkin, its pale light colored as it passed through the stained-glass windows. At times, Tomas caught the scent of incense.

He wasn't interested in the main hall, though. He strode from end to end to ensure he was alone, then sought the priest's office.

"What are you expecting to find?" Elzeth asked.

"Nothing specific," Tomas admitted.

Elzeth had been so quiet the past few days that they hadn't even talked about tonight's endeavors. He'd hoped they wouldn't have to. Tonight's criminal activity was half motivated by boredom, half by a slim chance he'd find something useful.

"So, why are we here?"

"Angela said the inquisitor hadn't been here long, and I'm suspecting Ghosthands pulled him into the train attack. He wouldn't have had time to clear his desk. There might be some useful information here."

Elzeth scoffed as Tomas found the priest's office. "You're that bored, aren't you?"

"Maybe," Tomas said.

Thankfully, the door to the priest's office was unlocked, so Tomas let himself in. The office was devoid of any personal decoration, evidence of the rapid turnover in priests over the last few months. A large but cheap desk sat in the middle of the room, and a spacious window behind the desk looked out upon Razin's quiet streets.

Tomas took the chair behind the desk and flipped through files. In the past, he would have asked Elzeth to help sharpen his vision, but tonight he relied only on the light from the moon. Most of what he found was more likely to put him to sleep than provide him with a solid lead. There were church ledgers, as well as notebooks filled with details about church members.

The information wasn't salacious. It consisted of birthdays, connections, likes and dislikes, and fragments of conversation. Tomas had briefly hoped he could tarnish the church's reputation by bringing to light extortion attempts, but all he found were notes from a priest who cared for the people he served.

He also found plenty of communication from the church, but nothing that surprised him. They encouraged willing members to move west into church-controlled lands. Other letters detailed the support the church settlers moving west needed. It was all interesting but was nothing useful.

His first surprise came not from the papers within but from Elzeth. "I've been having dreams lately. Of my previous hosts, and the times between."

Tomas stopped flipping through the papers for a moment, then resumed. "Oh?"

"Not sure 'dreams' is right, actually. Visions, maybe, or memories."

Tomas set the papers down. He breathed out slowly. "Tell me."

"There's not much to say about the other hosts. They led delightful lives, but nothing you'd be particularly concerned with."

Tomas wondered if that was true or if Elzeth was trying to protect his feelings. He'd never quite come to terms with the revelation Elzeth had been hosted before. Hosting a sagani was intimate, closer in some ways than having a lover. The knowledge Elzeth had shared a similar bond with others tainted his relationship with the sagani.

Maybe it was foolish. The previous hosts had died, and Elzeth went through, well, whatever he'd been through. He tried to keep the bitterness from his voice, even though it was pointless with Elzeth. "So, what did you want to tell me about?"

"The times between. What happened after my hosts touched the nexus and I fled."

"What happened?"

"At first, it felt like when you and I have touched the nexuses. The power is overwhelming, and as you so aptly put it, the door to my cage opens, and I can escape. Once I'm free, it's as you've described it. I'm floating on a web of connections, infinitely complex. But then I'm pushed out," Elzeth said.

"Out?"

"I don't have a better way to describe it. One moment I'm drifting along the lines of power, then there's a shove, a time of nothingness, and then I'm a sagani once again, always reappearing in the same area out east, not that far from the range where you stumbled upon me."

"Where you meet with the other sagani?" Tomas asked.

"Yes, though my memories there remain vague and uncommon. Sometimes I wonder if it's easier to form memories when I'm hosted."

Tomas couldn't contribute to that inquiry, but something else Elzeth had said piqued his interest. "When you say you were pushed, that implies something or someone was doing the pushing."

Elzeth didn't answer right away, and Tomas guessed they'd come to the crux of what Elzeth wanted to say.

"I know how mad this sounds, but I think there's even more to the nexuses than what we guess. I don't know if I'd call it a person or a consciousness, but there's *something* acting within the nexuses. At least, that's what it feels like to me."

Tomas was grateful he was sitting. He gripped the edges of the desk tight. If Elzeth was right...

His mind tried to grasp the enormity of the implications, but he failed.

If there was some sort of intelligence, or consciousness, within the nexuses, what did it want? Why did it offer humanity strength through the sagani if the price was madness? Tomas had never believed in coincidence, but he believed in chaos. Elzeth's assertion challenged the foundations of his beliefs.

He looked again at the papers on the desk. Taken one at a time, they were boring evidence of the church's mundane tasks. Taken as a whole, though, they represented the goals of the church, a goal they had suddenly granted Tomas a new perspective on everything the church did.

The church sought the Creator.

Tomas wondered if Elzeth had found Him first.

11

———————

Tomas left Razin without looking back. His pack was heavy on his shoulders, but his step was light. He considered one last rude gesture as a parting gift to the city, but he was in too good a mood. He and Angela had put in an enormous amount of work over the past few days, and it was time to reap the rewards.

The only addition that would have made the departure better was Angela herself, but circumstances had demanded they leave the town separately. She had a stack of papers to sign at the sheriff's office, and he had a friend he wanted to visit.

Some of her papers dealt with the sale of her house, while others dealt with the official transfer of the chief marshal's title to Adam. The process sounded tedious and would only become more so as Angela said her last goodbyes to friends and neighbors. He'd intended to remain by her side, but she'd encouraged him to leave. Tomas suspected the decision was partly for his benefit but mostly for hers. She wanted the time to say farewell as she pleased, without Tomas sulking in the corner.

He wished he could accompany her out of the city, but this way was better. This gave him time to speak at length with Ben.

The walk to the farmhouse passed quickly, and as soon as Tomas was within sight, children raced toward him. He enjoyed their stories and laughed at their antics. He didn't know how Ben handled them. Their tales were grand entertainment, but he couldn't imagine being the adult tasked with caring for such rambunctious youngsters.

They stormed onto the porch of the farmhouse like a summer gale. The kids tore into the house like a tornado while Ben and Tomas bowed and sat down. Ben wasted no time in formalities.

"What changed?" he asked.

Tomas grunted. He supposed it was too much to ask a former inquisitor not to notice, especially after their previous conversations. "I finally found a purpose."

"Is that so? May I ask what it is?"

"We're going to discover the truth of the nexuses."

Ben laughed, then noticed Tomas's expression. "You're serious?"

Tomas's nod silenced the last of Ben's mirth. His face fell, and he weighed his next words.

"I want to be encouraging because you look more like the Tomas I once knew, but are you sure? Church scholars have explored the problem for decades, and I'm not sure they're much closer than when they started. And if you don't mind me saying, it's not exactly like you're our generation's greatest scholar," Ben said.

"Fortunately, it's not me leading the inquiry. It's Elzeth."

That caught Ben's attention. "Really?"

Tomas told Ben everything. He and Elzeth had talked more since breaking into the mission than they had in the past month. The regular conversation alone had done wonders for Tomas's mood. Although he'd spent most of the last decade wandering from place to place, he'd never felt alone, not until Elzeth had gone silent for longer and longer periods.

Tomas had missed him like a close friend who had moved away.

But now they were reunited. Their troubles hadn't disappeared, but Tomas hoped time would heal the scars that lingered.

Ben listened with rapt attention. When Tomas finished explaining Elzeth's intuition, Ben was silent for a long time.

The silence surprised Tomas. He'd expected a more encouraging response.

Ben apologized. "It's just that your story reminds me of something, but the source of it is slipping from my memory. It was a high-level document that circulated among a select few, a testimony from a host that claimed something very similar. They'd felt a guiding hand among the nexuses. They named that guiding hand the Creator."

"Are you saying the church already knows about this?"

"Some do, but it's a heretical idea. The more common interpretation among the highest clergy is that what Elzeth felt is the heart of the demons. The church's greatest enemy."

"They want to kill it?" Tomas asked.

"They want to kill all the nexuses. It's been the guiding principle behind almost all their research into the stones."

Tomas rubbed the edges of his eyes. "That might have been true when you were an inquisitor, but do you think that's changed now that they've developed the new weapons?"

Ben shrugged. "I'm skeptical. The church is enormous. It can't change direction quickly."

"Either way, it doesn't change what Elzeth and I feel we need to do."

"And what exactly is that?"

"We're going to head north to meet with Ulva. They've got a nexus there we can use."

"Don't you have a nexus in your pocket?" Ben asked.

"Sure, but we don't have Ulva. She knows more than she's told us. Her guidance helped us before, and we're hoping she can help us again."

Ben smiled.

"What?"

"This might be your first plan that doesn't sound stupid. I'm unconvinced that you can crack the secrets of the nexuses, but there's always been something different about you two. Maybe you can find something no one else could," Ben said.

"I'm glad you think so."

Ben chuckled. "Yeah? You would have turned around and marched the other way if I told you that you were being a fool?"

"No, but your opinion matters. You were the one that got me thinking about this."

"Well, I'm glad you saw reason, even if it took a near-death experience. It's nice to see you with a helpful goal for once. It makes a difference."

"Time will tell, I suppose. Thanks again for everything."

"You're very welcome." Ben glanced back at his house. "You planning on staying long?"

"Until Angela gets here. Then we'll be on our way."

"You should spend some time with the kids, let them know you're going."

"Would they actually care?" Tomas asked.

"More than you might think. Although the ones you've rescued have mostly moved on, the story of what you did has become something of a legend in these halls. They'd be stung if they didn't have time to say goodbye."

"I'm no good with kids."

Ben waved away the concern. "Trust me, I've seen worse. Go on in."

Tomas did, and he found them gathered in the living room. They mobbed him as soon as he entered. Some had questions, others wanted him to play with them, and a few wanted to tell him stories. He threw children over his shoulder and spun in circles. He answered some of their questions but avoided others. Several were curious about the night he'd rescued the children who'd lived with Ben a few years ago, but Tomas decided those were questions better left for Ben and Olena.

At one point, he glanced through the door and saw the couple standing in the kitchen. They held hands and whispered to one another as they watched, and Ben had a grin that stretched from ear to ear.

Then a young girl was pulling on his face, and he had no choice but to turn and listen to her story about the dream she'd had the night before. The next time Tomas looked up, Angela had joined Ben and Olena in the kitchen, and they were all having a great deal of entertainment at his expense. He broke free of the circling storm of children and entered the kitchen.

"None of you are much help," he grumbled.

"You'll stare down the entire church without blinking but can't handle a roomful of children?" Ben asked.

"I think I'd have better luck surviving a day with an inquisitor," Tomas said.

Olena wrapped herself around Ben's arm. "I've been surviving with one for more than a decade. It's not that impressive," she said.

With Ben's help, Tomas told the children he would be leaving. One of the young girls cried when he admitted he'd probably not be coming back. The farewells lasted longer than Tomas expected, but eventually, the four adults stood on the front porch alone.

"Once, I thought I'd never see you again. Now it's hard to believe that I'll never see you again. I appreciate your visits," Ben said.

"No more than I. They've meant a lot," Tomas said.

Ben wrapped Tomas in a hug, and once Tomas recovered from surprise, he embraced the older man. "I'll miss you," he said.

"And I you," Ben replied. He turned to Angela. "Take care of him because he's not good at caring for himself."

"I'll try my best."

Tomas was off the porch by the time he realized something. He'd felt no chain around Ben's arms when they embraced. He turned. "You're not carrying your weapons anymore."

Ben smiled and pulled up one of his sleeves, revealing his bare forearm. "They aren't too far out of reach, but it was time to put the past behind me for good."

Tomas nodded and waved, and soon Ben's house was well behind them.

"I didn't think you'd be any good with kids," Angela said.

"Not sure that I am, but it was good to see them."

He didn't miss the way she looked away from him. He didn't know what her thoughts were about starting a family, but that door had closed forever when she became a host.

Most only lived for five, maybe six years after they joined with a sagani. Becoming pregnant as a host would be cruel to the child.

Tomas reached out, took her hand, and squeezed it.

She squeezed his in return, and they traveled north.

12

———————

The host-knight's sword darted toward Quinton's throat faster than the tongue of a snake. Quinton turned the cut aside and lashed out with his own blade. Against any other enemy, his response would have opened a fatal wound, but the knight danced away with impossible speed.

The sight thrilled Quinton. Everything from the knight's attack to his defense relied on his demon-granted speed.

Quinton stepped away, ending the training with a sharp bow. "Incredible," he said.

The knight returned the bow. He tried to keep the flash of pride from his face, but he only partially succeeded.

The knight had every right to be proud, though. Only the best swords and the quickest learners survived the training to become knights, so it shouldn't be a surprise that the host-knights picked up his training with the ease they did.

Quinton remembered his transition from skilled sword to host, and it hadn't been a simple matter. He hadn't benefited from a guide like the host-knights, but there was only so much one could teach. The rest had to be mastered, and they'd approached mastery faster than Quinton had expected.

As Quinton returned his training sword to the fort's quartermaster, he caught sight of Rachel taking notes on their training. Instead of avoiding her like he might have a few weeks ago, he approached. She would have tracked him down if he tried to hide, but he found he no longer minded their conversations. She might not be as faithful a believer, but she'd pushed back the madness.

He owed her a debt he couldn't repay in the life he had left, but he hoped to make the balance as small as possible before he traveled to the gates.

She didn't look up from her notebook as he stood beside her. "It's hard for me to tell, but you were moving faster than you did during yesterday's training session, right?"

"I was."

"Could you move faster still, or was that the limit of your speed?"

"It was not my limit."

Rachel furiously scribbled notes. "How do you feel today?"

"Better than I have for many years."

"And what about the madness?"

Quinton hesitated for a moment. "It's still an issue, though it feels more distant than before."

"How so?"

He wondered how to best explain to someone who had never been infected by a demon. "One secret to my ability is how I've learned to master the demon within. Almost since the beginning, I've accepted nothing less than complete obedience, and the demon has had little choice but to acquiesce. As the madness developed, some degree of that control slipped. It is back now, though not as complete as before."

When Rachel finished her notation, she looked up. "Are there circumstances where you might consider returning to the machine?"

Quinton had spent a considerable time asking himself that very question. "Yes."

Rachel's eyes lit up, and she licked her lips as though he were a tasty morsel of food.

Shouts from the wall interrupted their conversation. Someone approached, which was a rare occurrence these days. Quinton didn't bother rushing to the wall. There'd been no alarm in the guard's shouts. Rachel looked upset, though.

"You know who's coming?" he asked.

She grunted and turned away, stomping into the tunnels underneath the fort like a child told they had to put their toys away.

Now Quinton *was* curious. He climbed the stairs to the wall and understood. A decent-sized caravan approached the fort, but the wagon in the center was familiar. The flag of the Holy Father flew above it.

Had he been given more warning, Quinton would have cleaned up, but Father was only minutes away, and he'd never insisted on the propriety Quinton considered his due. Quinton splashed some water on his face to clean off some of the sweat, then joined the guards at the gate to greet the caravan.

There were warm greetings all around. The caravan carried not just the Holy Father but fresh supplies from Corrin. The knights organized without anyone taking command, jumping to help wherever they saw a need. Perhaps it was a small thing, but Quinton saw it as a confirmation of the knights' upstanding moral character. In the army he'd served in long ago, almost no one had done anything unless a superior ordered it. Here, everyone pitched in without a word of complaint.

Everyone took a knee as Father descended from his carriage. It had been weeks since Quinton had seen Father last, and if such a thing were possible, the old man looked even better than before. Quinton wasn't the only one who'd had the clock pulled back.

Father gestured for everyone to rise, and the fort quickly returned to the hive of activity it had been a minute before. Father spotted Quinton and made straight for him. Quinton offered a deep bow, even though he knew Father didn't demand one.

"Quinton, it's good to see you again."

"And you, Father. You're looking well."

"I'm feeling well. But this visit isn't about me. You know I've been in contact with Rachel, and she told me about your close brush with death and your nearly miraculous recovery. How are you feeling?"

Father's quick summation of Quinton's experiences made his stomach clench tightly because it called attention to a troubling fact. The sagani were evil because they polluted the pure bodies of humans. The nexuses were evil because the sagani were connected to them. And yet, it was a nexus that had healed him and given him another chance to serve the Creator.

His answer to the dilemma was the same as the one he'd used when he'd first become both a host and a believer. The nexuses and the sagani might be evil, but that didn't mean the Creator didn't use them to further His purposes.

"I've been feeling well, thank you," Quinton told Father. "I owe it all to Rachel."

Father laid a comforting hand on Quinton's shoulder. "I'm simply grateful that you were here so she could help."

Father led them toward a quiet corner of the fort. "Unfortunately, I have another purpose for my visit today."

Quinton wasn't surprised, though Father's tone implied he should be. Father never traveled without the visit accomplishing at least two objectives. "Of course, Father."

"I need to ask you this again: how are you feeling? Are you capable of carrying out a laborious task?"

"Rachel and I were actually just discussing this, Father. Physically, I'm feeling better than I have in years, but I don't believe the madness has gone away. It's retreated a bit, is all."

"Are you capable of carrying out a new mission?" Father's eyes bored straight into Quinton.

"I'll do my best for you, no matter my condition," Quinton answered.

Father shook his head. "I know that, my son, and I'm sorry if you took it that way. I'm asking for your objective evaluation. This task is among the most difficult I've ever given you. Are you well enough to complete it?"

Quinton collected his thoughts before answering. "So long as it isn't something that will take too long."

"Define 'too long.'"

Quinton squirmed under such a direct line of questioning. "It's hard for me to say. This isn't something I have any experience with."

"But you still know better than anyone else."

"Only a month, maybe two. That's my best guess."

Father rubbed at his chin as he thought. "That should be more than enough time. I was thinking of sending you alone, but perhaps I'll send some host-knights with you. They'll be useful support, and they can watch you."

"What would you have of me, Father?"

"We finally caught a break. Do you remember how Tomas brought other hosts with him to Kimson?"

Quinton had read that. The church had been desperately trying to find where Tomas had found allies, though Quinton had never understood exactly why it was so important. A handful of demons was a problem, but hardly one worth dedicating so many resources to.

Father said, "One of our informants finally found a lead, thanks to orders currently floating around the army. The situation is even worse than we thought. East of here and a little north, there are two settlements being built just for hosts. I want you to lead a small contingent and attack them."

"I'd be honored, Father. Do you want me to kill all the demons?" Quinton asked as a formality, certain the answer would be yes.

"No, actually. Rachel's research demands more hosts, and this is the greatest collection we've ever come across. We can't waste the opportunity. Of course, kill the demons if there's no other option, but your mission is to capture as many as possible and return them here. While you're gone, Rachel will prepare for their arrival."

"Do we know the population?"

"I wish we did. Our best guess is a few hundred at most, but you'll need to scout it yourself. This place is cloaked in secrecy."

"Not that secret, if the army knows about it," Quinton said.

"Ah, yes. Thanks for reminding me. That's the other part. General Gavan has been pressuring the army to send recruiters to the settlements. The discussion among the generals is how we discovered this information."

"I thought the army had soured on the idea of bringing

hosts into battle. They've been focusing more on rifles and cannons."

"They are," Father said, "but Gavan's experience with Tomas outside Kimson made him believe that hosts still have an important role to play in military operations. He wants to create something similar to the unnamed units, and he wants them filled with warriors from these settlements."

Quinton didn't roll his eyes, but he was tempted. "Humanity refuses to learn the lessons of the past."

There was no denying the impressive feats the unnamed units had accomplished during the war. But their benefit was balanced out by the risks the army assumed in using them. Quinton compared an unnamed unit to lit dynamite: a powerful tool that could cause significant damage but almost as likely to explode in your hand.

Father agreed. "What's most important, though, is that Gavan has convinced others in the army. He and the 34th are being sent toward the settlements in the hope that they'll be able to recruit a significant number of hosts. They believe that with the conflict raging across the frontier, their efforts will be quite successful. You need to reach the settlements before the 34th does."

Quinton's fingers tingled. The opportunity to attack and capture two settlements' worth of hosts? A fight to capture and steal hosts from right under the nose of their enemy? He wanted to draw his sword and ride away immediately.

"I'll do it," he said.

Father smiled. "I was hoping you would. Of all the missions you've completed for the Creator, Quinton, this might be the most important. Rachel is close to cracking the secrets of the nexuses, and with more subjects, we'll understand everything. You'll be stealing demons from the army and helping them serve the Creator."

Quinton heard his excitement mirrored in Father's voice. Father said, "When I heard from Rachel that you were feeling better, I was certain it was a sign from the Creator. This is what you're meant to do, Quinton. Your greatest feat in a lifetime of tremendous service. Bring me those hosts."

Quinton bowed deeply. "The Creator's will be done, Father."

13

"Is your life always like this?" Angela asked.

The trail they followed branched into two paths. Tomas chose the one more well-traveled. Sweat dripped down his spine, and he desperately wished the breeze would pick up and cut through the tall trees.

"What do you mean?" he asked.

"Just—walking, wherever you want, all the time."

"Mostly. I occasionally have a destination, but I was content to wander west. Why do you ask?"

"I'm still not used to it," Angela said.

"You're doing fine."

"It's not the walking. I got plenty used to that serving in the army. It's the lack of responsibilities. There's no house to keep clean, no reports to file with the governor, no inane citizen complaints to endure. I keep feeling like I'm forgetting to do something, but it's only because there's nothing to do."

Though she couldn't see his face, Tomas smiled. Her concerns reminded him of his own when he'd started wandering. "I felt the same at first. Took me a while to understand that life is a lot simpler than most people make it out to be. All we need is food to survive and shelter when the weather turns."

"I'd argue we need company, too. Humans aren't meant to be alone."

"Maybe. It wasn't something I ever dealt with. I've had Elzeth with me since I started wandering."

"You two were already talking by then?"

"Within a few weeks of us being joined, yeah." He understood the true meaning behind her question. "Still nothing from yours?"

"No. I can feel its presence, and I think I can understand its emotions, at least in some limited sense. It responds when I ask for it to burn. But there's no actual communication."

"It hasn't been that long."

"What if it never happens? You said it wasn't uncommon."

Tomas shrugged. "I'm sorry. I don't have any better answers. Turns out, I haven't actually talked with many hosts over the years. Most of what I'm telling you I learned from Narkissa."

They lapsed into silence, allowing Tomas to listen to the music of the forest. They were a little more than a week north of Razin, but it felt like they had stepped into a different world. Endless plains had surrendered their vistas to densely packed trees. Birds and chipmunks made the canopy their home, and deer darted nimbly away whenever the two hosts approached.

Traveling with Angela was a joy. She was more observant than most, pointing out sights and details even Tomas had missed. Their journey had sparked a latent curiosity, which led to a series of stimulating conversations.

Thankfully, she was just as content walking silently, absorbing the world with the openness of a child.

Not only that, but her skill with a rifle made the problem of hunting trivial. Tomas typically contented himself with meager fare on the road, but she'd easily brought down all the game they needed to eat. Adam's parting gift had been a few boxes of bullets, a treasure more useful than gold. Angela never needed more than one to fill their packs.

He almost hated that they had a destination. There were days when he believed this was good enough. They could travel until the day he couldn't, and he'd grab the nexus in his pocket, release Elzeth, and that would be that.

Not a bad way to go. Probably better than he deserved.

"Do you hear that?" Angela asked.

Tomas paused and focused on his hearing. "No."

A moment later, he did. A low rumble snuck through the trees, close to the limits of his hearing. It grew more pronounced as he listened. It was lower than thunder, and more continuous. Besides, there wasn't a cloud in the sky. It wasn't a storm.

Angela recognized the sound a second before he did. "Stampede," she said.

Tomas agreed but didn't understand how. They hadn't come across herds of any type for at least two days, and the sound was coming from the south, where they'd just been.

Whatever stampeded was coming their direction, though. Tomas now felt the rumbling through his boots. He looked around.

"I think they're heading straight for us," Angela said.

Tomas wasn't so sure of that, but they would pass close enough that he wanted to be someplace safe. He listened closer.

The stampede had to consist of hundreds of animals,

but he was reassured by what he didn't hear. "Let's climb," he said.

They found a tree with low-hanging branches and clambered through the limbs. Tomas ended up about twenty feet off the ground on a comfortable perch, with Angela right below him. He saw less from up high, his line of sight blocked by the expansive canopy.

Less than a minute later, the stampede arrived. Most of the animals looked vaguely like deer, but Tomas saw the way their eyes glowed. They danced around the trees, running north with bounding leaps.

Tomas and Angela's position below might have been safe. The bulk of the herd passed a few hundred feet to the west, but a handful passed near where they had stood. The sagani didn't so much as brush a tree, which made Tomas think he would have been safe on the ground, but he was perfectly content up high.

After another minute, the herd was running away from them, and the forest quieted. Angela descended, but Tomas called for her to stop. "Might be worth staying up here until we see what was chasing them."

She saw the wisdom in his advice and remained where she was.

A few minutes later, she looked up. "Are we sure something was chasing them?"

They descended together. Tomas warily looked around but saw nothing that alarmed him. The rush of excitement passed, and he shook out his arms.

"I've never seen anything like that," Angela said.

"I have," said Tomas.

He explained, though the memories weren't particularly welcome. He'd been out west in the mountains when hordes of spider-like sagani had attacked. They'd been under the influence of another sagani, though, a monster the like Tomas hoped never to cross paths with again.

"Do you think they're being controlled?" Angela asked.

He held up a finger and asked Elzeth. Back in the mountains, Elzeth had felt the influence of the monster. "Anything?" he asked his partner.

"I'm feeling a pull, but it's not like back then. It's faint, but I'm pretty sure it's a nexus."

Tomas frowned. After seeing the stampede, he'd been almost certain they had another monster on their hands. A nexus sounded almost mundane.

He saw Angela barely restraining her questions. "Elzeth says there's a nexus nearby."

"Should we investigate?" Angela asked.

Tomas was about to say "Yes," but then thought twice. "You haven't been around a nexus, have you?"

"Not a real one, no. I sometimes feel the urge to reach into your pocket and grab that one, but I know not to."

"The pull of a full nexus is much stronger. At first, you won't recognize it. All you'll know is that you want to touch it, and you can't think of a good reason why you shouldn't. You'll think I'm exaggerating about the danger."

He noticed her hesitate. Maybe she was already having some of those thoughts. As a younger host, she might be more sensitive than him. "That's coming from my sagani?"

He nodded.

She considered for a bit, then took a deep breath. "I still think we should investigate."

Had it been almost anyone else, Tomas might have argued. But if he wanted her to accompany him as he and Elzeth tried to crack the secret of the stones, exposure to the nexuses was necessary.

"Let's go, but be careful."

Tomas could have asked Elzeth to guide him to the nexus, but the stampede had left a trail even a distracted child could follow. They threaded their way through the trees, heading north with caution.

"Any idea how close we are?" Tomas asked Elzeth.

"Not really. It doesn't feel that close, but I'm wondering if it is a nexus."

Tomas froze. "Why?"

"The pull feels the same, but nexuses are constant. Their song is like a singer stuck on one note for eternity, unable to take a breath. This doesn't feel like that. It pulses louder and softer. It's not quite a regular pattern, but close."

"Do you think it's a monster?"

"No. It's not that. My best guess is that it's a nexus, but there's something wrong with it."

"That's not a reassuring thought."

"Sorry," Elzeth said.

Tomas turned to fill Angela in before she bombarded him with questions. He finished with, "Do you still want to check it out?"

She nodded, so Tomas resumed tracking the stampede.

About a mile later, they came across the herd and the nexus. The herd seemed almost nothing like the animals that had stampeded earlier. For one, they seemed smaller. Tomas wasn't sure if that was because he was on their level now or if they'd shrunk.

Even more odd, though, was the nature of the sagani. They stood around calmly, reminding Tomas more of cows than bounding deer. He and Angela kept a safe distance, but the animals just shuffled around, uninterested in their visitors.

"Elzeth, can you talk to them at all?" Tomas asked.

"You know that's not how it works."

"Could you try?"

Elzeth gave a dramatic sigh and shouted at the nearby sagani. Angela winced, but the herd appeared like they couldn't care less.

"Told you that wouldn't work," Elzeth said.

As Tomas watched the herd, he noticed their movements weren't as random as he'd first assumed. They were shuffling around like grazing cows, but the herd kept moving north. "Is that the direction of the nexus?" Tomas asked.

Elzeth confirmed it was. Tomas chewed on his lower lip as he thought.

"I want to get closer," he said.

"To the sagani or to the nexus?" Angela asked.

"To the nexus, but that means going through the sagani."

Elzeth scoffed. "Are you serious? They look peaceful enough now, but if something upsets them, they'll turn on you in a heartbeat."

"Then we probably shouldn't upset them," Tomas said aloud.

At Angela's questioning look, he said, "Elzeth isn't thrilled by the idea of walking among the sagani."

"He's not alone in that," Angela said.

Tomas looked again at the herd. Even when they'd stampeded, they had paid no attention to the travelers. "It'll be fine. Probably."

Angela shook her head, but that was the end of her complaints. Tomas stepped out from behind his tree and advanced toward the herd. A handful of sagani looked up, but Tomas didn't sense any ill intent from the creatures. He kept his hand away from his sword and crept closer.

Then he was among the sagani. Their breath was hot

against his arms. He slid between the tightly packed animals, careful not to bump into any. He joined in the slow current and drifted north. It wasn't too long before he felt the pull of the nexus himself. He couldn't see it, though.

A thick clump of dark clouds passed between Tomas and the sun, temporarily darkening the forest. Tomas saw a faint flash of light, then another. He squinted, but the clouds passed, and the forest brightened. The flashes disappeared.

"That's the direction they're heading. The nexus is there."

Tomas shivered even though warm sagani surrounded him. They were deep in the herd now, guests among the mysterious creatures. He didn't want to speak to Angela, afraid the sound of his voice would spook the sagani. He caught her attention and pointed to the west. The change in direction would push them gently against the herd's movement, but Tomas wanted as much space as possible between him and whatever drew these sagani here.

Angela nodded and followed, and they broke from the flow of the herd and circled around the nexus. As they circled, the herd thinned. Tomas wondered if some sagani had broken off from the rest. There should be more.

A few tense minutes of slipping through the sagani brought them to the north side of the nexus. The herd was almost nonexistent here, but enough were crowded around the nexus that Tomas still couldn't see it. He climbed a few feet up a tree, then almost fell right back out.

He held on to a branch tight and watched, certain that he was imagining the sight. Perhaps the madness was striking in a new way.

Angela's gasp confirmed it, though.

Impossible as it seemed, it was real.

The nexus was embedded deep within the trunk of a

tree. Only a part was visible, like an enormous glowing knot of wood.

Tomas hadn't seen a nexus in a tree before, but that wasn't what captured his attention. That honor went to the sagani, who were queued up around the tree, taking turns.

One by one, the sagani flung themselves into the nexus.

When they made contact, the nexus flashed briefly, and then the sagani disappeared.

14

Quinton always considered it an honor to serve the church, but he rarely appreciated the benefits his service granted him. For example, no matter where he traveled, it was likely that the church had a place that would welcome him for the night. Whatever he needed to complete his missions, the church provided. Such benefits meant little to him, though. He was as content with the stars over his head as a roof, and his own needs were so little it rarely took much to meet them.

He was blessed, but he rarely realized how much.

The trip to Jonasson reminded him how fulfilling it was to be part of something larger. The journey would have taken weeks on his own two feet, but the church put him on one of their private trains, then provided horses and wagons once the miles of track ran out. He and the other two host-knights were soon in the deep woods surrounding the demonic settlement named Jonasson, well rested and well supplied.

According to the map provided by the informant, they were less than a day's walk away from their destination, and now they faced their first consequential choice. None of them felt comfortable bringing the wagons, filled with manacles and chains, into the settlement, but they disagreed on how they should proceed.

Quinton favored a direct confrontation. Every minute they waited was one he inched closer to madness. The demon fought against its cage, and Quinton swore he felt the bars weakening. The information they possessed also claimed that Jonasson strived to be a peaceful settlement, which was a noble but misguided sentiment. It left them open to anything he might try.

His companions, Bond and Fabian, felt otherwise. They argued that they didn't have enough information. They didn't know how large the settlements were, nor did they have any idea what defenses existed. Charging in with swords drawn was foolish.

Quinton knew they had the right of the argument, but he held to his position longer than he should have. Studying the settlement, even for a day or two, gave his demon more time to break the bars of its confinement. Eventually, he agreed, though he made the knights remain behind with the wagon. None of them carried anything that marked them as church, but the knights strutted through the world like most knights. Their training made them the strongest warriors in the world, but they too often acted like it.

They grumbled, muttering that their orders were to observe Quinton, but eventually, Quinton won them over to his way of thinking. He left the two knights behind with the carts and walked the last stretch to Jonasson alone.

He was glad that he did. Halfway from the wagons to the settlement, he ran into a patrol. It was a young man and woman. Scars covered the man from head to toe, but Quinton suspected the woman was the more dangerous opponent. They both carried swords at their hips, and Quinton guessed they knew how to use them.

"Welcome, stranger," the woman said. Her posture was open but wary. "My name's Myra, and this is Emerson. What brings you to this part of the world?"

Quinton had prepared a few stories. He kept his hands away from his sword and chose the one that seemed best. "My name is Quinton." He pretended to hesitate as though revealing a secret, then said, "I'm a host. I'd heard there's a place nearby that welcomes people like me."

"There might be. Tell me a bit more about yourself, Quinton, and why you made the trek out here," Myra said.

"There isn't too much to say. I've been working as a hired sword since the war, and I'm afraid I haven't made too many friends over the years. I tried to hide the fact I was a host, but word about my unnatural skill spread back east. The inquisitors caught wind of a mercenary who was a little too strong, and I decided it was time to start a new life somewhere out west."

Myra's wariness remained, but she seemed slightly more open than before. "We've got a few like you. We can test your claim about your strength later, but do you have any useful skills beyond the blade?"

"Not as many as I'd like, but if it's all the same to you, I'd like to do something that allows me to put my sword down. I'm a quick study and a hard worker, and I'm willing to help however I can."

Myra nodded. "There's always work for people willing. Why don't you join us, and we'll let you meet the founder of the place? Ultimately, it's up to her whether you stay."

Emerson grunted, the first sound he'd made since they'd met. He shot a glance at Myra, who suddenly looked sheepish.

She said, "Right. There's a good chance the founder isn't around at the moment. But we can still take a tour of the place, and we can get you settled in some temporary accommodations."

"I'd be much obliged. It's been a long journey."

Myra led the way to Jonasson, and Quinton noted Emerson took up position behind him. He'd been in army camps that had less wary guards. It spoke well of Hardin's warriors, but Quinton feared the task ahead would be more difficult than he'd expected. Generally, he found hosts to be exceedingly lazy. They became so reliant on the strength the demons granted they forgot the value of diligent effort.

As they walked, Myra dug deeper into Quinton's fictional past. He gave polite but short answers until Myra gave up and asked about his desire to lay his sword down.

Quinton didn't have to lie as he shared his answer. "I've seen a lot over the years. Enough for several lifetimes. I don't think I've got too many years ahead, and I'd like them to be more peaceful than the ones behind."

Myra nodded along as though she understood, but she had the look of someone preparing an objection. She silently accepted his answer for a few seconds, then said, "If your claims about your strength are true, my commander might speak with you. We're worried about our future, and your sword might be of use. We're looking for all the strength we can find."

Quinton fought to keep a snarl off his face. Of course these demons were searching for strength. Like Tomas, they spoke about living peacefully out of the corner of their mouth, then caused chaos wherever they walked. It made him sick. Not fighting was easy. Most citizens did it every single day. All Tomas, or any of these hosts, had to do was take their swords, put them down, and walk away.

Instead, they offered lip-service to the idea of peace while they prepared for war. The demons made hypocrites of them all. The day Quinton met a truly peaceful host was the day he put down his own sword.

They came to the shore of a large lake filled with crystal-clear water. Quinton took in the view. A cool breeze blew off the water, and Quinton had a sudden and unexpected urge to kick off his boots and go fishing.

"It's beautiful," he said.

"It is," Myra agreed, "and we'd like it to stay that way. We're hoping to negotiate an agreement with the army to allow us to officially own most of this land. It won't be too many years before settlers are common here, and we're hoping to have our claim honored by then."

"The army knows you're here?" Quinton asked.

"They do. We've had some contact with them in the past year, but you shouldn't need to worry. If Ulva or Hardin says you can stay, you'll be safe."

They followed a well-worn footpath that skirted around the edge of the lake. Soon Quinton caught his first view of Jonasson. He wasn't sure exactly what he'd expected, but it wasn't what he saw. The homes looked cozy and well-built, and the streets were clean and peaceful.

The three warriors walked around a small bay and came to the outskirts of the town. Quinton had expected a walled settlement, but the path they followed widened until it became a street, leading straight into the heart of Jonasson.

Quinton's first impressions were confirmed as he entered the settlement. The houses were even newer than in most frontier towns. They looked sturdy, cozy, and clean. Uncomfortably, the settlement put him in mind of some of the church-designed towns further west. The homes weren't as uniform, but the spirit of the place seemed the same.

Quinton hated it. It was like walking by a brothel with a fresh coat of paint. As nice as it looked on the outside, its very presence dirtied Quinton's soul.

Strangers greeted him as he passed, and he responded as kindly as he could. He'd never been good at pretending to be something that he wasn't, and he feared Myra and Emerson would see right through his ruse. If they sensed anything off about his act, though, they said nothing.

When they stopped to talk to another pair of warriors heading out on patrol, it took all of Quinton's self-control not to wash his boots. They'd seen hundreds of miles of mud, dirt, and blood, but the streets here were tainted. Sure, everyone smiled and was kind enough, but the smiles only masked the demons lurking within. When a family with a small child walked by and waved, Quinton reminded himself that everyone here was likely infected with a demon.

It would be so easy to kill them all. Only Myra and Emerson were armed. Everyone else walked around defenseless, relying on the strength of their demons to keep them safe. They didn't suspect Quinton had killed more hosts than any inquisitor.

Bond and Fabian's disapproval kept his bloodthirsty impulses in check. There was more to this settlement than was readily apparent. It was too clean and too orderly. Myra and Emerson, though weak compared to him, displayed a discipline that spoke of military training.

He would kill them all, but only when he had uncovered all of Jonasson's secrets.

Myra and Emerson ended this leg of Quinton's journey at a longer building that looked nothing like the houses they had passed. Quinton feared a trap until Myra opened the door and revealed a bunkhouse with several small private rooms. "Sorry it's not a more private place, but this is where all the new arrivals stay until we figure out something more permanent. It's somewhat quiet now. I think there's only one other family staying here, but they have a baby girl. They're near the end of the hall. Otherwise, feel free to claim whichever of the rooms you want."

Quinton stowed his pack in a room near the middle of the building. When he came back into the hall, he found Myra and Emerson waiting for him.

"Figured we could go see if Ulva is home. She's the leader of this town, and it's her that will have the final say. You'll have to leave your sword, though. She doesn't allow them in town," Myra said.

"You two are carrying," Quinton observed.

"Hardin's warriors are exempt. But we keep things peaceful here, so no swords. You don't need to worry about it, either. We haven't had a theft here since the settlement was founded."

Quinton ground his teeth at Myra's claim to peace but caught the retort on the tip of his tongue. He returned to his new room and left the sword. In case of an emergency, he was more than happy to borrow either of his escorts' weapons.

Satisfied, the two fools led the church's deadliest assassin deeper into the settlement to meet their leader.

15

Tomas stared openmouthed at the sight. He'd watched a dozen sagani vanish into the nexus, and each time it was as surprising as the time before. The silence from Angela made him think she felt much the same.

He asked Elzeth, "Have you ever seen anything like this before?"

"Never in all my lives."

"So you can't make heads or tails of it, either?"

"Not a clue."

Tomas watched yet another sagani disappear. Was it some sort of mass suicide? It seemed impossible, but his reason didn't stretch far enough to explain whatever this was. They were calm, too. Sagani made little noise by nature, but they behaved much like other animals, at least when they weren't stampeding toward their collective doom. Tomas saw no signs of panic or distress. Again, they reminded him more of domesticated cows.

The part that sent a shiver up his spine was the complete disappearance of the creatures. If carcasses had piled up in front of the nexus, he would have found it less disturbing.

But the moment they made contact, they simply disappeared. One moment there, the next gone without a trace. As if they'd never existed.

Animals weren't supposed to vanish, and yet they did, time and time again.

Eventually, he moved past trying to find an explanation. The herd had thinned, making the process easy to observe from the ground. He and Angela climbed down. Given the lack of attention the sagani paid to them, Tomas decided it was safe to pull out a meal and eat lunch.

It was a surreal meal, eating next to Angela and watching the herd of sagani gradually vanish. They never pushed one another. Whoever was closest went, then the next followed, and the remainder shuffled forward.

Amazing as the process was, even it turned monotonous.

Tomas finished his meal first and wiped his hands off on his pants. There weren't more than two dozen sagani left. "I'm going to go behind a tree for a bit. Do you need anything?"

Angela grunted and shook her head. Her gaze had been fixed on the nexus since they'd sat down to eat, but she'd possessed the control not to go anywhere near it.

"Are you sure you're good?" he asked.

She rolled her eyes. "I'm fine. Now go before it's too late."

He stood and walked away, searching for a suitable spot. Twice he glanced back at Angela, but she was sitting in the grass and eating the last of her lunch. Tomas grabbed a bunch of leaves, ducked behind a thick tree trunk, pulled down his pants, and squatted down.

When he finished, he stood up and pulled up his pants. He stepped around the tree as he worked on his belt, then froze.

Angela wasn't sitting in the grass. She was standing

among the sagani, her hand outstretched toward the nexus. The sagani parted before her as though she was one of them that had jumped the queue.

"Angela!"

She didn't flinch. That close to the nexus, it was possible that her sagani had taken over. That it was reaching out for a chance to escape.

Tomas ran, pants loose around his hips. Already, he knew he was going to be too late.

"Angela!"

Nothing. The sagani had taken control. Tomas was certain of it now.

"Elzeth!"

The sagani lit within Tomas, the first time he had burned since the train. Tomas's long strides ate up the distance between him and Angela. She was close but moving slowly like a curious child gradually approaching a fire. He thought he might just reach her in time.

He was about to catch her when she lunged forward, a marionette with its strings viciously pulled. Her hand touched the nexus, and Tomas didn't hesitate. He lunged at the nexus, making contact a moment after she did. The last thing he heard was Elzeth screaming that he was a fool.

He passed through the nexus quickly, the process now familiar. Finding Elzeth only took a second, but the sagani blazed with fury. "You damned fool! Do you have any idea how close you came to dying?"

"It doesn't matter. Can you find her sagani, help it find its way back to Angela?"

"Tomas—"

"We don't have time. Try!"

Elzeth stared for a moment, eyes raging. Then he vanished. Tomas took a deep breath and tried to center himself. He'd probably given Elzeth an impossible task, but he wasn't slacking, either. He let the power of the nexus flow through him, and he sought Angela's presence.

When he'd been in the nexus with Ulva, she'd shown him the connections that webbed everything related to the nexuses. If she hadn't already gone to the gate, he should be able to find her. He needed to find her. Even if Elzeth completed his task, Angela's spirit needed to return to her own body.

But how did he find her?

Ulva would know, but he had nothing to rely on but instinct. He imagined Angela as clearly as he could and felt an answering tug, the slightest pull on his spirit. He followed, keeping Angela in his mind. She was like one of the lighthouses far to the east, guiding him on a cloudy night. She was a pinpoint of light in a sea of stars, but when he kept her in his mind, she was by far the brightest. A moment later, she was close.

He stopped beside her, not sure what to do. He spoke, but she didn't react. Nothing happened until he reached out and touched her.

His surroundings immediately changed. He was back in her house in Razin, vividly recreated. Angela sat at the dining room table, flipping through the pages of a thick leather-bound journal.

"Angela?" he asked.

There was no response, so he took a tentative step forward. The vision wavered, like he'd thrown a pebble into a still pond. When it stilled again, she was looking up at him. "Tomas? I don't think you're supposed to be here."

"I'm sure I'm not. But I came to help you."

"Why? I think I'm beyond help now."

"You're not. I can help you find your body. Elzeth is

looking for your sagani. If we both succeed, you can come back with me."

Angela flipped another page in her book.

Tomas took another step forward, and the vision shook. He stopped. "Please, Angela, come back with me."

"It's peaceful here."

"You're only a step away from the gate. Please." Tomas reached out his hand.

She looked up from the table and smiled at him. "Maybe it's for the best. We've fought hard, and now it's time to lay our burdens down."

"I'm not ready, and I don't want to lose you."

He searched for a better reason, something that would bring her back. She needed something greater than his own selfish desires.

His search came up short. His hand dropped back down to his side. Outside her window, the town of Razin faded away, replaced by a darkness that knew no end. The gate appeared, its steady blue glow welcoming.

He supposed she didn't have to travel through the gate alone. He could join her, and together they could explore the mysteries on the other side.

Elzeth would be pissed. The thought of the sagani endlessly berating him made him laugh.

The sound echoed loudly in the space. Angela's eyes shot up.

Tomas held out his hand again. "Come on. There's a lot more yet you need to accomplish."

She held up the journal she'd flipping through. Within were drawings so sharp Tomas felt like he could step inside them. Angela was front and center of each drawing, and they wiped the smile from his face. Most were scenes from the war, of the blood she had spilled and the death she'd delivered.

They rarely spoke of those days. They'd fought on opposite sides, and both lived with memories they'd rather forget.

"I don't deserve another chance," Angela said. There was no great emotion behind the claim. It was an observation, spoken of no differently than if she had noted the weather. She flipped the page, and another drawing sketched itself. She seemed to shrink as she observed the fresh horror.

Outside, the world grew darker. The room around them dimmed and faded.

Despite Angela's misgivings, Tomas felt more certain than before. There was much about the world he didn't understand, but guilt?

He was the world's foremost scholar on guilt.

"Of course you don't. It's not about *deserving* anything. I don't deserve anything, either, but choosing the gates is the easy way out. There's no atonement there—only escape. And I want to atone. I want to do something better with my last days than I've done with those that have come before. I think you want the same. That's what I see when I look at the work you did in Razin."

"I'm tired."

"Then we'll take a nap. Now come on. Let's get out of here and learn more about the nexuses."

Angela set the book down on the table. Tomas wanted to step forward and close it for her, but he feared that any more movement would shatter the illusion and send her plummeting toward the gate. Thankfully, she shut the book on her own. But she made no move toward him. She sat at the table as the room darkened.

The pull of the gate was stronger now. Tomas listened to it as it whispered its promise of eternal peace. Its song was louder than ever, but Tomas wasn't interested. He and Elzeth had made their promises. His time would come soon enough, but not before they'd tried to understand the nexuses.

As if on cue, Elzeth burst onto the scene with another sagani in tow. They both took the form of birds, but Tomas would recognize Elzeth no matter his form.

"I see you found her sagani," he said.

"And you're welcome. One of the hardest things I've ever done. Now, let's get going."

Angela watched the exchange and frowned. "I can hear you," she said to Elzeth.

"Welcome to the party," Tomas said.

Angela turned slightly so that she was looking at her sagani. "And I can hear you, too."

Tomas had the wisdom to back away and let Angela have a moment with her sagani. Whispers passed between them, too soft for Tomas to hear. Angela reached out, and the bird landed on her arm. She brought it in close.

Tomas couldn't guess what had passed between her and the sagani, but it changed her attitude. She stood up straight and turned to Tomas. "You can find the way back?"

"I hope so."

"Then lead the way."

Angela dispelled her illusion, and Tomas sought the way out of the nexus. He'd pulled himself out before, but he'd never led another soul. Fortunately, it didn't seem to affect him. He found the darkness in the ether that was his body, and he slipped back into his flesh like putting on a comfortable pair of clothes.

He fell away from the nexus, as strong as ever but disoriented. Angela was still in contact with the nexus, and as Tomas stumbled, he feared Angela hadn't followed through on the last step.

Then she blinked and pulled her hand away. Her eyes rolled back in her head, and she stumbled back. Tomas caught her in his arms. The sagani resumed their march toward the nexus, but nothing was further away from Tomas's thoughts.

"You back?" he asked.

"I am. Thank you."

"Any time. Though I'd rather you not touch a nexus again anytime soon."

"Agreed. But it taught me something new."

"Yeah?"

"Yeah. Now I can talk with my sagani."

16

Quinton followed Myra and Emerson as they gave him a guided tour of Jonasson. The tour itself wasn't much because the settlement was still too small to be called a town. The pride they held for their pitiful excuses of shops sickened him, but he nodded and smiled as they spoke reverently about their baker's bread and the craftsmanship of their carpenters.

All lies. Demons couldn't create anything beautiful. All they knew was how to destroy. Rot ate at the foundations of this settlement, and Myra and Emerson were willfully blind to the fact.

Still, he appreciated the tour, though not for the reasons his gracious hosts would have expected. It gave him the perfect opportunity to memorize the layout of the settlement and get a feel for the place. He noted dead-end alleys and climbable walls. He paid particular attention to anyone carrying a sword, although there weren't many of those.

The lack of defenses confused him. Were they so

confident in their safety that they felt they needed none, or were there layers to their protection he didn't see?

Myra stopped outside a small home that looked much the same as any other. The paint was older, and the rocking chair on the front porch appeared well-used. Emerson knocked gently on the door, but no one answered.

"Where is she?" Quinton asked.

He didn't miss the quick glance that passed between the two warriors.

"She's been working on a private project lately, one that takes her beyond the borders of the settlement," Myra answered.

Vague as the reply was, it revealed several interesting details. The first was the secrecy surrounding Ulva's project. Myra hadn't hidden anything else from Quinton. In a settlement full of hosts, Quinton wondered what kind of project would demand such secrecy.

The second interesting detail was that Ulva wasn't far away. Emerson's grunt back when they'd first met implied Ulva was often gone, but Myra still thought it worth checking at the house. If Ulva led this settlement and was gone for longer than a few hours, these two seemed like they would know, which meant she came home most nights.

Perhaps tonight, he would need to explore the lands around the settlement.

"What would you like to do next? Do you want to meet Hardin?" Myra asked.

"Yes, please." If they were going to continue showing off the settlement's weaknesses, he wouldn't refuse their generosity.

Myra led him out of Jonasson. The settlement ended abruptly, as though someone had drawn a line in the wilderness and proclaimed it an impassable barrier. In just a few steps, Quinton went from well-worn dirt streets and cozy homes to a thick forest of tall trees. The sudden change was disconcerting, and he glanced back to ensure his memory wasn't playing tricks on him.

He'd expected Myra to lead him to the other half of the settlement, where he knew Hardin led his more militaristic followers. That didn't seem to be the case, though. The path they walked was overgrown, and his suspicions grew with every bush and broken branch he pushed away. He kept close track of Emerson's closeness, wary of a killing strike from behind.

He only relaxed when he heard the familiar chorus of practice swords clacking somewhere ahead. The forest thinned and then opened into a clearing that human hands had developed. A small group of warriors trained together, led by a larger man with a presence Quinton felt from across the clearing.

Myra confirmed that the large man was Hardin. He had a beard that fell to his chest and an amiable smile that was on full display as he trained a pair of swordsmen. Myra stopped their party before they reached the training grounds, giving Quinton an excellent chance to observe the proceedings. He couldn't have asked for a more gracious host.

Quinton watched and could find no fault with Hardin's instruction. The commander knew his sword and his students, and though Quinton never watched Hardin spar, he observed the man's effortless grace and smooth movements. Hardin was the first person in this settlement that appeared worth Quinton's time.

After giving the swordsmen a new drill to practice,

Hardin broke from the training and approached. His smile flashed through his thick beard when he saw Quinton. "Myra, you've brought me a warrior."

"Perhaps, though he wishes to lay his sword down."

Far from being bothered, Hardin's smile grew wider. "A conversation I look forward to having with him, then."

Hardin bowed, and though it pained Quinton to do so, he matched the bow.

They introduced themselves, then Hardin said. "Myra, why don't you take over? I'm sure they'd rather have you, anyway. I'll bring Quinton back and show him around Alliston."

Myra bowed. "He hasn't met Ulva yet."

Hardin waved away the concern as he glanced up at the falling sun. "We may run into her on the way. Regardless, no reason not to be hospitable."

Nothing about Myra's expression changed, but Hardin felt like she was rolling her eyes. When Quinton drew his sword, she'd have the final small pleasure of knowing her doubts about him were justified. Until then, he delighted at the unearned and generous welcome.

Hardin led Quinton away via a different, less overgrown path, and Quinton noted Emerson continued to follow. Quinton didn't think he could kill an armed Hardin with his bare hands, but Emerson's presence was enough to convince him of the complete futility of the idea.

"I assume, because you're here, you're a host. What brings you here?" Hardin asked.

Quinton shared the same story he'd told Myra. Hardin swallowed it whole, like a fish jumping onto a hook. When Quinton claimed he was looking for a new start and a chance to put down his sword, Hardin nodded, but he maintained the air of a man already marshaling his arguments against the decision. Quinton expected no less. The demons reveled in chaos and couldn't abide the idea of a warrior seeking peace.

The woods they walked through weren't as thick as the ones Myra had taken them through a few minutes ago. Clean cut stumps served as explanation enough, and the wooden wall they encountered in another quarter mile provided the last piece of the puzzle.

Alliston was much more like what Quinton had expected Jonasson to be, and for the first time, he was grateful his host-knight companions had dissuaded him from attacking. These walls would be a problem.

He set the problem aside as Hardin showed him around. The similarities between Alliston and Jonasson were fascinating, revealing that the two shared the same carpenters and builders. Quinton liked Alliston better, though. Not because it reminded him of the army forts he'd spent so much time in as a younger man, but because it wasn't a lie. Jonasson's peaceful appearances were nothing but a thin pretense. Alliston, at least, didn't pretend to be anything other than what it was.

He felt the same about Hardin. Twice more, Quinton repeated that he was interested in laying down his sword, and twice more, Hardin ignored the statement. Hardin was looking for warriors, and he made no bones about it.

Though Quinton preferred Hardin's fort, he didn't like what his observations revealed. Hardin ran the settlement well. The guards on the walls appeared alert, and the number of swords more than made up for their lack in Jonasson. The settlements were close enough that it wouldn't take panicked citizens more than a few minutes to run to the safety of Alliston's walls. Conquering the settlements would be troublesome.

Eventually, the three men ended up in Hardin's kitchen, where the large man put on a pot of water for tea. It wasn't very good tea, certainly nowhere near as good as he brewed back home. He still accepted it gratefully and sipped as they spoke.

It didn't take Hardin long to broach the subject he'd been thinking about from the moment he realized Quinton was a host who could handle a sword. He leaned forward as he asked, "So, just how serious are you about sheathing your sword for good?"

Quinton took a sip of his tea while he debated how best to answer the question. He didn't want to spar with Hardin before they attacked. It would be too easy to reveal too much about himself. Some of his techniques would be recognizably his. "Serious. I've done more than my fair share of fighting. It's time to move on."

Hardin spread his hands out wide. "Here you'll have someplace safe, a place where you don't need to worry about what you are. Isn't that worth fighting for?"

"Haven't been here long enough to say for sure, but maybe."

Hardin's eyes narrowed, revealing the steel behind his smile. "You're telling me you ran all the way out here to avoid trouble, but you aren't willing to help us defend it?"

Quinton set down his tea. He met Hardin's hard stare. "In my experience, most people who pick up a sword end up using it. I've been there, and I don't want any more blood on my hands."

Hardin ground his teeth together, but the moment passed, and some fraction of his smile returned. "Maybe we'll talk again in a few days after you've seen what makes these settlements special."

They spoke for a while longer, but it was clear Hardin wasn't interested in anything beyond recruiting Quinton. Once Quinton finished his tea, he claimed exhaustion, and Emerson rose to escort him back to Jonasson.

Hardin's last words as Quinton left were, "Think on it, at least. Some things are worth fighting for."

Emerson led the way to Jonasson, following yet another trail. This one was the widest yet, and Quinton noticed one well-worn track heading off into the woods. He pointed. "Where does that go?"

Emerson hesitated before answering, then said, "It's a logging path. There's a grove there we've been working in."

Quinton gave no sign that he knew Emerson was lying. "Do you have a need for any woodcutters? I've always preferred my sword to an axe, but it seems like something I might be useful at."

"Beats me. I'm not involved with anything like that. When you speak to Ulva, though, it's a good question to ask."

"Do you think she'll be home?"

"No idea." Emerson glanced toward the mysterious path, then looked pointedly ahead. Quinton pretended not to notice.

"You been here long?" he asked.

"Quite a while," Emerson conceded.

"What do you think about what Hardin said? Is it worth fighting for?"

"With every drop of blood I possess," Emerson said.

Quinton smiled. Soon, he'd make Emerson pay what was just promised.

(###)

Thankfully, Emerson left Quinton alone after returning him to the bunkhouse. They'd stopped by Ulva's house again, but it had been empty, and Emerson didn't seem surprised by the fact. Then they'd grabbed a bit of food, and Emerson had called it a night. Quinton watched him leave, heading down the street that would take him back to Alliston.

Quinton picked at his food while considering all that he'd learned. Alliston presented more of a problem than he had prepared for, but there were solutions. Any attack would have to start within the walled fortress. Properly done, Quinton and the knights might conquer it without word reaching Jonasson. If they accomplished that, the rest of their assignment would be simple.

Could he get all three of them within the walls to launch the attack? Myra was suspicious, but that seemed more her nature than anything specific to Quinton.

His plans coalesced, but he needed to know something more first. He needed to know Ulva, and he needed to know what was at the end of the path Emerson had lied about. He suspected the two answers were related.

Quinton saw little point in waiting. He finished the last of his meal, strapped his sword to his hip, and snuck out of the bunkhouse. The streets were empty. He hurried down the road, burning a little of his demon in exchange for sharpened senses. The whole town slept, and he imagined going from house to house, slaying demons. It would be so simple, but Rachel needed hosts. The simple routes were closed to him.

As he passed through the outskirts of Jonasson, he heard a young baby wail. The sound slowed his steps, and for a few moments, he listened.

The church had confirmed that when a demonic

mother, father, or both, became parents, the child was not born as a demon. The Creator wouldn't allow such innocent souls to be so defiled. Still, the baby's cry brought him up short. Here, it must have at least one host-parent, and maybe two. What kind of monster would bring a child into the world, knowing they wouldn't live long enough to see it grow?

Or were the hosts' plans even more demonic? Quinton shuddered at the thought of a child being sacrificed to the demons and hurried out of town.

The trail between the two settlements was empty, but in the distance, Quinton saw light from the top of Alliston's walls. He reached the trail he'd seen earlier and followed it. The path took him, thankfully, away from the walls and toward the lake.

The demon within him suddenly came alive and pushed against the bars of its cage. Quinton had felt the demon fight this way before, so he recognized what was ahead. What was Ulva doing with a nexus?

The trail went on for longer than he expected, but eventually, he found a small outcropping of stone. A tiny cave was hidden around the corner, but as soon as Quinton found it, he saw the familiar pale blue glow that confirmed his guesses. He stepped into the cave and stared at both the nexus and the oldest woman he'd ever seen.

Ulva had to be ninety or perhaps even a hundred. Quinton had been younger during the last war, but she'd been old during the war before that. She was standing with her hand against the nexus. It should have killed her like it killed all hosts, but her breathing was steady.

Quinton's barely was. He'd been near nexuses before, but his demon longed for them with a strength even

Quinton found hard to fight. The demon thrashed against its cage, straining to convince Quinton to touch the stone.

He was well aware that doing so would likely kill him. Only Tomas had survived touching a nexus, and now this woman made two. Tomas had definitely been here. Had he learned about the nexuses from this woman?

He nearly jumped out of his skin when Alva spoke to him. "I know I'm a sight for sore eyes, but didn't your mother ever teach you it's rude to stare at a lady?"

Quinton was about to reply that she was a demon and no lady, but he held his tongue. He wasn't sure where this meeting would lead, and he didn't want to act hastily. "You are touching a nexus. I thought they were fatal to hosts."

The old woman turned, but her hand never left the stone. She opened her eyes, and they were glassy, though they were pointed in his direction. He did not believe they saw him. A hint of a smile spread across her lips, and she said, "True enough."

Before Quinton could question her enigmatic statement, she asked, "Who are you?"

"My name's Quinton. I found my way to your town today, and I'm staying at the bunkhouse. Had a lot on my mind tonight and went exploring."

The old woman frowned. She cocked her head to one side as though listening to a call only she could hear. "My boy, what have you done to your sagani?"

"What do you mean?"

"It's screaming and crying out for help." Ulva closed her eyes as though she were focusing on the sound.

Could the demons talk to one another? It had long been a question that the church had studied, but the man who had gone out west into the mountains to research the question had never returned. What if the demon told Ulva all that he had done?

He couldn't take that chance.

He didn't dare summon his demon's power this close to a nexus, especially not with this woman's unknown abilities. Quinton stepped forward, drew his sword, and with one powerful cut, took off her head.

17

The sagani were long gone, leaving Tomas and Angela alone in the forest. They'd watched the last of the sagani disappear, and Tomas had no more answers than before. Had they committed suicide, or was there some other purpose he didn't comprehend?

As important as the questions were, they all paled compared to the concern he had for Angela. At a glance, she seemed unharmed. If anything, she seemed more interested in everything. She looked toward the nexus, but her attention was on the conversation she held with her sagani.

Although it was about the last thing he wanted, Tomas gave her the space to discover this new relationship alone. He tried to remember the days immediately following his discovery of Elzeth, but they were now blurred by the passage of time. A few memories remained clear, like the first time he'd heard the now-familiar voice in his head, as well as the first battle he'd fought in unity. The rest were indistinct, more impressions and feelings than facts.

Looking back on it, all these years later, it felt as though he and Elzeth had always been the way they were now, and he had to remind himself that wasn't true. They hadn't spoken at first, though for the life of him, he couldn't remember how long it had taken for their relationship to develop.

Instead of rushing Angela, he queried Elzeth. "Why do you think she can talk to it now?"

"I've been wondering the same. I figure it has to be one of two things. Either the contact with the nexus strengthened the sagani and gave it more abilities than before, or the ability to speak has something to do with separating from the nexus. It might be a bit of both."

"I'm not sure I get it," Tomas confessed.

"I'm thinking about the mountains where we found that monstrous sagani. It had touched a nexus but not been absorbed. We know now, from the memories the nexuses have unlocked, that I've been hosted several times and that, apparently, I cooperate with other sagani. That could be why you can touch a nexus without dying and why I can speak to you."

"And now that you helped the sagani return to Angela, she can do the same."

"That's my best guess."

Angela startled them both when she spoke out loud. "I want to touch the nexus again."

Tomas grunted. "If you want to kill yourself, a rifle is faster."

She glared at him. "You've touched nexuses several times before and lived to tell the tale. I'm aware of the risks, but I think we can survive."

"Why, though?"

"Because I can almost understand my sagani now. When we were in the nexus, I experienced a moment of clarity.

Since leaving, that clarity has faded. My sagani is speaking, but I can't understand." She gestured to the glowing stone embedded in the tree. "The answers are there."

"It could just be that you need more time," Tomas argued.

"I don't think so. I can feel my understanding fading," Angela said.

"If my guess about what happened is correct, Angela might have the right of it," Elzeth said. "My memories aren't clear, but I think it took me several passes through the nexus to think and speak like I do now."

Angela knew Tomas well enough to notice when he was talking to Elzeth. "What does he think?" she asked.

"He agrees with you. He thinks that the sagani having contact with the nexus, then breaking away, has something to do with his ability to speak."

"I think it's worth it," Angela said.

Tomas didn't have an answering argument. His concerns were more selfish. "I don't want to lose you."

"I'll come back," she said.

Tomas sighed and stood up. "Then I suppose we'll come with you. Elzeth saved you both last time. Maybe he'll be helpful again."

"I'm always helpful," Elzeth muttered.

They walked back to the tree, and Angela extended her hand. Tomas reached out, grabbed it, and gently guided it back to her side. "Let's wait for a minute or two."

"Why?"

"Because I want to make sure that you can resist the call of a nexus. I want to know that when you touch that stone, it's because you chose to, not because your sagani took over for a moment."

She looked irritated by the delay but didn't argue. They

stood next to the nexus for several minutes. Neither reached out, though even Tomas could feel the desire building. He wondered if there was a limit to how long he could resist.

Today wasn't the day to find out. Angela resisted her sagani's urges, but sweat had formed on her forehead, and she looked as miserable as a hungover drunk enduring the sound of nearby cannons. He nodded, took her hand, and they touched the nexus together.

The rush of power didn't overwhelm him the way it used to. He was prepared for it and kept his body relaxed. Once, it had felt like being overwhelmed by a violently crashing wave, but now it felt more like a slow but mighty river. He rode the power deeper into the nexus and sought Angela.

He found her thrashing like a child, tangled in both blankets and nightmares. Tomas reached out and made contact. She calmed, and he pulled her gently deeper. He constructed her bedroom back in Razin, and they appeared within.

She arched an eyebrow. "Interesting use of the nexus."

"Wasn't thinking about that."

He didn't think it was possible for an expression to convey more skepticism. He held up his hands in mock surrender.

"Honest. It's just the place of yours where I have the strongest memories. It was the easiest to recreate."

"Sure."

Elzeth and the other sagani appeared before long, looking worse for wear. "Glad to find you two someplace so cozy," Tomas's partner grumbled.

"Thanks for keeping them safe," Tomas said.

"You're welcome, though it wasn't as hard this time. I think her sagani is learning how to find her. He actually found you two before I did," Elzeth said.

"Were we in danger?" Tomas asked. He'd assumed Elzeth would have no problems.

"Maybe a little. I think I would have found you before my desire to rejoin the nexus overwhelmed me."

Tomas grunted. Then he turned to Angela. "Being as I'm here, I figure I should explore the nexuses a bit. Did you want to come with or stay here?"

"What does that even mean?" she asked.

"We're connected right now, allowing us to share a space like this. If you wish, I could separate us, and you'd be alone with your sagani for a while."

"No thanks. I think so long as my sagani and I stay close, we'll figure out how to develop what you and Elzeth have, so we might as well all stick together."

Tomas was glad she felt that way. Though he knew more about navigating the nexuses than she did, her presence calmed him. He let the bedroom vanish, then spread out his senses.

It was like when Elzeth sharpened his sight or his hearing, except the effect was several magnitudes more powerful. His awareness ran along the lines of force that connected the sagani, humans, nexuses, and the incomprehensible power beating at the heart of the planet. He couldn't keep every detail in his mind, but he could draw a rough map, and he did so.

Angela gasped. "What's this?"

Forming words proved difficult. How had Ulva done this so easily? "Our world. Everything connected. Humans, sagani, nexuses."

"And that?" she asked, pointing toward the bright glowing core.

"The heart of the planet."

He couldn't keep his awareness spread any longer. He

called it back to himself and let the crude map crumble into nothingness. "Sorry, that was harder than I thought it would be. Ulva made it look easy."

Angela looked down at her hands, then to the place where the globe had floated before them. "I know you've told me it's all connected, but I never imagined. Why are we tied to the nexuses like the sagani?"

Tomas shrugged. "I'm hoping to find the answers before I die."

Suddenly, the globe reappeared in exquisite detail. This time, Tomas and Angela gasped together. "How—"

"Don't know why you made this seem so hard," Elzeth said.

"You're doing this?" Tomas asked.

"I am, though I'm genuinely not sure why this was hard for you."

Tomas looked at Elzeth, who was in the form of the mountain cat Tomas had fought out east so long ago. For the first time, he truly wondered at the creature within him.

Strange that it had taken him so long.

Angela was lost in wonder. She walked around the globe, studying the intricate web of connections. "When I look at this, it makes me think this is the most important question in the world. It touches us all."

"And the church has a lead. If we don't catch up soon, I'm not sure that we ever will. It sounded like Rachel was close to a breakthrough."

Tomas joined Angela, though his awe was pointed more in Elzeth's direction than the globe's. How did his sagani hold this all so easily in his mind? After all their years together, Tomas had thought there was little left to learn of his companion, but now he wondered if he'd even scratched the surface. Elzeth didn't seem troubled by his feat at all.

The arrival of a fifth presence interrupted their examination of the globe. Tomas felt it before he saw it. It was familiar, yet he couldn't place it.

The presence solidified into Ulva. She looked as Tomas remembered her from the nexus outside Jonasson, younger than she was in the physical world, though still plenty old.

"What are you doing here?" Tomas asked. He started to introduce Angela, but Ulva interrupted him.

"I was probably working on the same problem as you, if this is what it looks like. But plans changed, and now I have little time. I've got a few things that need saying."

As always, being around the elder host threw Tomas off-balance. He always felt like he was one step behind her, following her lead in a dance he couldn't hear the music to. "Sure."

"First thing you should probably know is that I'm dead. I was—"

"*What?*"

"A new host came into town today, apparently. Severe man, but he cut off my head when we met. Didn't even have the courtesy to introduce himself."

Tomas's jaw dropped, and he struggled to speak. After a few stammered failures, he finally said, "How are you here, then?"

"I was exploring the nexus when he killed me. Fortunate, really. My spirit is lingering for a bit, though the gate's pull increases by the moment. It won't be denied, so I can't stay for long."

"Who killed you?" Angela, always a marshal at heart, asked.

"As I said, he didn't even introduce himself." But Ulva described whom she had seen and Tomas knew. Ghosthands was in Jonasson.

"From the look on your face, I'm guessing you've crossed paths," Ulva said.

"I have."

"Well, Hardin will probably gloat, telling himself he was right all along about needing more defenses. But I still say if you two hadn't gotten up to the trouble you had, I'd probably still have my head. What's done is done, though, and so now I'm going to ask you for a favor, Tomas."

"Anything."

"Return to Jonasson. I don't know what will happen now. You can't reach us in time, but I've warned Hardin before I found you, so they'll have a fighting chance. Keep my people safe however you can."

"Of course. We were heading there anyway."

"Good. Well, you take care. I think it's time to go. We're excited. My sagani is still a part of me, so we're going through the gate together. I think it's the first time a sagani will pass through."

The old woman faded, but Tomas held her back with a question. "What do you know about the nexuses that you aren't telling me?"

A deep, throaty chuckle came from Ulva's throat. It was so like her laugh, Tomas couldn't believe she was dead. "More than I have time to tell you now. But you're well on your way to discovering the same truths. Keep following Elzeth. He'll show you the way."

"Why can't you just tell me?"

"Almost no time left. The gate's got a pull like you wouldn't believe. But I'll tell you this. The nexuses were left here, a gift for humanity. How we use them will determine our future, and the church wants to kill them. They can't. They'll kill the world in more ways than one." Once again, Ulva began to wane.

"You can't leave it at that! What are they?"
But Ulva faded and was gone.

18

The corpse stood, one hand on the stone, angled toward Quinton just as it had been in life. The sight sent a shiver down his spine, which intensified as the body continued to refuse to fall. For the briefest of moments, he wondered if he'd killed the old woman or if she was somehow immortal.

He cursed himself for the foolish thought. She had no head. Not even the fastest-healing host could survive such a cut.

He couldn't tear his eyes away, though. He didn't feel alone in the cave. Her presence lingered even after her soul departed for the gate. He was tempted to put his hand against her chest to check for a heartbeat.

He shook his head but still stared.

His demon forced him to move. It fought and gnashed against its cage, drawing strength from its proximity to the nexus. If he remained too long, the madness might return. He sheathed his sword and looked around for any clue what the old woman had been doing.

He found nothing. She'd just been standing there, her

hand pressed against the nexus, waiting to frighten visitors. He finally left the cave but took one last glance back. The body remained still. He swore under his breath and put the cave behind him. He hurried back to the main trail while he debated what to do next.

Plans eluded him. His thoughts kept returning to the old woman, probably still standing there, refusing to die properly. But why should she? She was a demon, and a unique one, too. Her death would be as cursed as her life.

The thought calmed the turbulent waters of his mind, and he finally turned his thoughts toward his next steps. Myra and Emerson had seemed unconcerned about Ulva, but they knew where she had been and would certainly worry if she didn't appear soon. Speed now mattered more than secrecy.

He saw two routes forward. In one, he gathered the host-knights, and they attempted to besiege Alliston. That idea had less chance of success, but it carried the greatest potential reward. The other idea would be to ignore the fort and capture Jonasson. It carried less risk of complete failure but was the less productive of the two plans. They'd never catch as many demons as they could otherwise.

Alliston would be his target. If this was his last mission, let it be remembered as his greatest success. He picked up his pace.

Jonasson was as quiet as he'd left it, but he didn't stop at the bunkhouse. He walked straight through to meet the other host-knights.

Far behind him, a bell clanged. Quinton turned around in disbelief. They had left the old woman alone nearly all day, as far as he could tell. How could they have discovered her so quickly?

Jonasson came alive. Candles flickered in windows and

doors opened. The bell clanged like mad, and Quinton stood in the middle of the street with a bloody sword at his hip.

The outskirts of Jonasson were close enough that Quinton thought he could reach them before he was observed, but it would take him time to retrieve the host-knights. How would Jonasson react to the alarm?

He felt the success of his mission slipping through his fingers like water. He was Quinton! The Holy Father's sharpest blade. He growled and drew his sword. They couldn't take Alliston anymore, but Jonasson was ripe for the harvest.

A door to the left opened, and he darted toward it. A young man stuck his head out the door just in time for Quinton to strike him with the flat of his blade. The sword solidly smacked into the side of his head. The demon dropped with a meaty *thunk*.

"Dad?"

The voice belonged to a young girl standing in the middle of the living room in her nightgown. Quinton kicked her in the face, and she crumpled. He strode through the house, the sword of the Creator, but found no one else within.

Screams from the streets carried through the open door. Quinton stepped out in time to witness a commotion near the outskirts of the settlement. He nodded in satisfaction. The host-knights had arrived, and their swords were clearing a path through the citizens who'd left their homes.

Quinton jumped off the front porch, earning several frightened looks from the nearest neighbors. Their eyes traveled from his bloody sword to the open door of the house, and they ran.

Quinton darted among them, dropping as many as he

could. A handful escaped his rampage, as there was only one of him, and a few of the hosts could run very fast indeed.

The host-knights rendezvoused with Quinton.

"What happened?" Bond asked.

"I think they found a body I left behind, but there's no time to talk. This settlement is undefended, at least for a few minutes. Cripple or knock out everyone you can. Later, we can come by with the chains and load up the wagons. Beware of any warriors coming from that direction,"— Quinton pointed toward Alliston—"they'll be hosts, and they're well-trained."

The host-knights stuffed any questions they had away and obeyed Quinton's orders. He followed them, too, taking off in a different direction.

He encountered his first resistance when he caught a family trying to flee to Alliston's walls. Both father and mother were armed with spears, and they told their two young boys to run while they held Quinton off.

It was a noble effort; the demons pretending they were worthy parents, but Quinton slipped past their spears with ease. It took two hits with the pommel of his weapon to drop the mother, and he stabbed his sword through the father's stomach. Normally, such a wound would be fatal, but if the father was a host, he should live.

Then he caught the children, who weren't all that fast and too scared to duck into the woods for protection.

A few others put up a token resistance, but Quinton quickly realized none of the true warriors were in town. Even without the demon burning in his core, he could have defeated most of the traitorous demons who stood their ground against him.

The next few minutes were chaotic as Quinton raced

against the citizens of Jonasson. The alarm had spread to every house, and neighbors exhorted one another to run. Quinton raged at every demon that escaped down the path connecting the settlements, but there was only so much he could do. For every one he killed or captured, one ran away.

Hopefully the host-knights fared better.

When he cleared his street of demons, he angled toward the path that led to Alliston. If Hardin's warriors leaped to Jonasson's defense, they'd arrive soon, and Quinton planned to meet them. If not, he'd catch the stragglers making a break for safety.

His timing couldn't have been better, and as he had so many times before, he felt the gentle push of the Creator at his back. He reached the edge of the settlement as a couple rushed by. He struck them down, looked up, and saw Myra and Emerson leading a small squad of warriors from Alliston.

Myra snarled like the animal she was when she saw him and rushed forward.

He'd expected her to be skilled, but she caught him by surprise. She was nearly as quick as Tomas and not half as reckless. Quinton retreated a step before adjusting for her speed.

He burned his sagani brightly, reveling in its screams as he squeezed more out of it than it was willing to give. Myra's sword slowed as Quinton cut at her legs. She collapsed, her screams of anguish a beautiful confession of her sins. Quinton knew the Creator listened, accepting her offering.

Before Quinton could deliver the fatal blow, Emerson and the others reached him. The path filled with swords, and Quinton wasn't fast enough to deal with them all. He fell back, keeping the warriors at bay while he searched for openings.

Myra and Hardin's training was evident. The warriors fought well enough alone, but they cooperated better. Quinton was a dozen feet from the nearest home, and he thought he might need to lead them within to break their coordination.

Soft, quick footsteps behind him heralded the arrival of his allies. Quinton stopped giving up ground. For the space of a heartbeat, four swords flickered dangerously close to his heart, but he held them off until the host-knights arrived.

Skilled as their opponents were, the host-knights were stronger and faster. They disrupted the squad's coordination and picked them off one by one. Fabian's first duel was so lopsided that the knight knocked the warrior unconscious instead of killing him.

Quinton seized the opportunity to burst past the remaining members of the squad and toward Emerson. The scarred warrior stood guard over Myra while she tried to heal her worst wounds. Quinton looked forward to killing him, and he seemed eager to die. As Quinton approached, he broke away from Myra to meet him.

Quinton tested him first, attacking slowly and observing how Emerson reacted. Like all the others, he was good but not good enough. Worse, the demon was terrified. Quinton saw it in his eyes, in the way they darted back and forth, searching for someone to come and save him.

Emerson's fear sentenced him to death.

Their steel met, met again, and then Quinton was inside Emerson's guard. He stabbed through Emerson's throat. The demon barely spoke anyway, so he had no use for it. Quinton twisted as he pulled the blade clear.

Myra screamed, but she remained too wounded to stand. Quinton snapped his blade in her direction, splashing her with some of her friend's blood.

"Demons reap what they sow," he said.

He advanced toward her, confident the knights would soon kill the rest of the squad.

He heard the arrows a moment too late. They emerged from the darkness of the path and leaped at him. One caught him in the side, and the other cut across his cheek and took off the top of his left ear.

Quinton leaped away before another volley of arrows could bring him down. He pulled the arrow out of his side and snarled. "Archers!" The warning was probably superfluous, as the knights were already seeking cover.

A big man moved in the shadows, followed by dozens of smaller shadows. Quinton retreated a few steps. He couldn't see the archers among the mob of warriors. A host with a bow was more dangerous than infantry with rifles. He retreated a few more steps, never in a straight line. His muscles were taut, ready to carry him in any direction if he caught the whisper of an arrow.

Soon Hardin and the others passed through a break in the trees and were illuminated by Tolkin's light. Quinton still couldn't see the archers, a fact that was becoming more troubling with every passing moment.

Finally, he turned and ran. Hardin's soldiers let out a cheer, but they misunderstood his intent. He gestured for his knights to follow. They grimaced at the order but obeyed. They all took cover behind the nearest house before the archers launched again.

"How many warriors do you estimate?" Quinton asked.

"Two dozen, maybe," Bond said.

That matched Quinton's guess. Four or five squads. He hadn't expected Hardin to march from Alliston with so many. Twenty years ago, before rifles had become as widespread as they were today, Hardin would have commanded one of the greatest military forces in the nation. Now a well-armed infantry unit would laugh at their advance.

Quinton wasn't laughing, though. They had no rifles and were severely outnumbered. No matter how much faith Father had in his skills, Quinton couldn't perform miracles. For the first time, he wondered if it had been wise to kill that old demon.

"Ideas?" he asked.

Fabian was the first to speak, and his plan reflected the lack of thought he'd put into it. "Charge them. It will catch them by surprise, and the Creator will grant us a victory."

Bond nodded along, and Quinton wondered if these new host-knights were already succumbing to madness. Charging Hardin and his small army of hosts was a pointless suicide, and the church was relying on them. This didn't seem like a battle he could fight his way out of. Fortunately, he'd long ago realized there were other ways to win besides fighting. The idea sprang to his mind like a revelation from the Creator, and he had faith in the divine inspiration.

"Find two hostages. Children would be best."

The two knights blanched at the order. Quinton didn't understand why they were so eager to die for their belief but so unwilling to fight for them.

"Remember, they're demons, not people." Quinton honestly doubted any of the children were infected. None that he'd seen moved like hosts, at least. But he didn't think that would occur to these two, and he saw no reason to tell them.

It was the will of the Creator. Quinton was sure of it, and he knew better than to ignore the Creator's will.

The two knights swallowed hard, then ran off. Quinton

poked his head around the corner of the house. Hardin and his demonic army stood cautiously around where Myra had fallen. Hardin was down on one knee, speaking quietly with the wounded warrior.

Quinton was grateful for Hardin's caution, though he also understood it. Hardin did not know how small the forces attacking his settlements were. Little did the giant demon know that if he'd simply charged his army in, they would have forced Quinton to retreat empty-handed.

Their delay gave the knights enough time to return with two unconscious children. One was the girl Quinton had first encountered, the other a boy who looked about four or five.

"Knives to their throats, and keep them in front of you as shields. Those archers will be a problem."

The knights obeyed, though not quickly. They stepped back into the street, and two dozen swords suddenly pointed in his direction.

"Call your archers back and keep them where I can see them," Quinton demanded.

"Go to the three hells," Hardin growled.

"The Creator has greater plans for me, demon. But I mean what I say. I will kill these children if I don't see those archers soon." Quinton snapped blood off his blade and put it to the girl's throat.

"What happened to Ulva?" Hardin asked.

The question confused Quinton. Hadn't they found the body? "She's as dead as this little girl will be if I don't see some archers." He slid the edge across the girl's neck. A drop of blood traced a line down her neck.

Hardin's eyes darted back and forth as he searched for a solution. Quinton couldn't give him that time. He dug the sword deeper into the girl's neck. "Now!"

"Fine!" Hardin called for the archers.

They emerged from the forest. From their position, Quinton guessed they'd been angling for better shots. "Join your friends," he said.

They listened. Quinton strained his hearing for any sign of more ambushes, but for the moment, there were none. "Go back to your walls. We'll be leaving soon, and we're taking some of your citizens with us, including the children. If I catch even the slightest glimpse of you after you leave here, I'll kill them all. Do you understand?"

Hardin glared.

Quinton spoke louder this time. "I said, do you understand?"

"Yes," Hardin growled.

"So, what are you waiting for? Go hide behind your walls, and quick."

Hardin spit at Quinton, though the distance was much too great. He looked around, and Quinton was about to cut through the arteries in the girl's neck to encourage the giant. Hardin noticed Quinton tense, and he gave the order to retreat.

There were a few seconds where Quinton wasn't sure the others would obey. Hardin led the way, turning his back and vanishing into the shadows of the woods. One by one, the others followed.

Quinton watched with growing satisfaction. He'd have to be wary, but he didn't think Hardin could successfully move against him. Not if the big man wanted the children to live.

Quinton grinned. The sword of the Creator had struck again. He'd just conquered Jonasson, a settlement of hosts, with only three swords, and he'd beat the demon army. Father would be proud.

19

———

Tomas and Angela pushed hard toward the settlements. Strange as the method of delivery had been, Tomas didn't doubt for a moment the truth of Ulva's warning. That she had reached out after she had died awed him, but if he knew anyone capable of such a feat, it was the mysterious founder of Jonasson.

The journey chafed at Tomas because he was the one who tired first. He was the one Angela had to support. Since the war had ended, he'd prided himself on his self-reliance, the strength born of hard experience. He still thought of himself in that way, but every time he had to ask Angela to stop and rest, it was like his pride was being forced to swallow a nail. Angela never commented and was always patient, and in a way, that was worse, as it was another sign of her superior abilities. Even her patience surpassed his.

The scenery eased some of the sting. The forest was a mix of pines, birch, and maples, and as they drew closer to their destination, the land became more rugged. Rolling hills grew taller, and they frequently passed small lakes filled with crystal clear water.

Once again, Tomas complimented Ulva on the choice of her location. The land here remained pristine, unsullied by the hands of settlers. It was rich in water, lumber, and game. He wished Jonasson had remained untouched by the conflict. He wanted it to maintain that sense of tranquility he'd experienced on his previous visit.

Night fell on the fourth full day of their journey. As they had every night before, they continued through the darkness, Tomas trusting Angela's sagani-aided senses to guide them. Only a little moonlight trickled through the thick canopy, but she slid between trees and undergrowth like it was the middle of the day.

He was proud of how well she'd adapted to life as a host, but he couldn't deny the pangs of jealousy that threatened to sour his gratitude. She entered the time of her greatest strength as he lost his. It revealed itself in the details, from her endless endurance to her vision in the dark. Her sagani burned and spoke with her as Elzeth slumbered deep in Tomas's core.

Finally, his legs could take no more. "We should stop for the night," he said.

"Sounds good. It's been a long day."

They didn't so much make camp as they set down their packs, unrolled their bedrolls, and sat down beside one another. Tomas pulled dried meat and berries from his pack and divided them into two portions. Selfish as the thought was, he was hoping for an enormous hot meal soon.

They ate in silence, but when they lay down to sleep, Angela said, "It seems something's been troubling you the last few days. Care to share?"

"Besides the fact that Ghosthands found a town full of hosts, and who knows what's happened in the days since Ulva warned us?"

"Yes, besides that. It's easy to see that you're worried and that you're pushing yourself as hard as you can to help them. But there's something else lurking, and I have no idea what it is. I was hoping you'd tell me before we reach Jonasson."

She was right. Another set of questions had worried Tomas's thoughts, but he hadn't figured out how to articulate them yet. He stared through a hole in the canopy at the stars. "I'm not even sure I've figured it out for myself yet."

He paused again to order his thoughts. She waited patiently.

"It's something I've been thinking about for a bit, but something Ulva said has me thinking about it in a different light. Anyway, for a while, I've been wondering who I am without Elzeth. I've spent far more of my adult life as a host than not, and now that he's resting as much as he can, I'm realizing that most of what I considered to be 'me' was always 'us.'

"Then Ulva said I should follow Elzeth's lead, and it got me thinking that maybe we're not even 'us.' At least, we aren't equal partners in the endeavor. Now I'm wondering if maybe I'm like a dog on a leash being led around by Elzeth. It's my body, but he's the one issuing the orders."

"Is that how you feel?" she asked.

"No, but can I trust my feelings? Surely you've noticed by now that it can sometimes be hard to tell what belongs to you and what belongs to the sagani."

"What does Elzeth think?"

Tomas grunted. "He thinks I'm being a fool, too. He says that I'm thinking myself into knots, and I need to trust my feelings more."

"If nothing else, he sounds like the wiser half of your partnership."

Tomas laughed. "Yeah, that thought has occurred to me before, too."

"You should listen to him, and you should listen to your own feelings."

Tomas wasn't convinced, but he trusted both Angela and Elzeth, and neither seemed as concerned as he was. Perhaps they were right. Regardless, it felt good to discuss it. The question had been gnawing at him for days, but he hadn't known how to broach the subject. It was easier now that she was a host. He felt like he could share anything with her.

He extended his arm out to the side, and Angela used it as a pillow, curling in against his side.

Tomas slept better that night than he had in days.

(###)

The path Tomas found to lead them into Jonasson wasn't the largest one. That one was farther north and ran almost due east for a half dozen miles before slowly turning southeast. This was the path Tomas had followed the first time he'd been searching for the settlement.

It wasn't much wider than a game trail, but there was enough evidence of human passage that Tomas had suspected he was close to his destination the first time he'd visited. The trail had grown a little wider and more packed down since his last trip but was otherwise unchanged. Tomas was glad not to see any evidence of a military force passing, though he suspected the church forces would have come from the west.

Some surroundings were familiar, and when he came to the big lake that bordered one side of Jonasson, he worried. Hardin and Myra ran competent patrols of the area. Where were they today? Tomas had kept his own senses sharp, but he'd asked Angela to be wary, and she'd reported nothing. After an attack, he would have expected more patrols, not less.

Unless the attack had been worse than he'd thought. He saw no smoke, so he hoped the settlements hadn't burned down, though he feared even the embers might be cool by now. Ulva's warning had come too late.

They worked their way around the lake, Tomas's fears growing into a rock in his stomach. Jonasson came into view, and it was too quiet. Tomas stepped into the settlement, looked around, and feared the worst.

"Where is everybody?" Angela asked.

"That's the question I'm wondering, too."

Jonasson wasn't just quiet, it was dead. Nothing moved in the street nor behind the windows. They walked past a few houses and saw no evidence of life.

But they also saw no sign of death, so Tomas didn't know what to make of the scene. They passed another house, the door hanging open. Tomas stepped onto the porch and poked his head through. He saw the blood on the floor, but it wasn't enough to be fatal. A fight had happened, certainly, but maybe not a murder.

Angela joined him.

"Can you make any sense of this that I can't?" he asked.

Angela looked around the inside of the house for a minute before answering. "No. Lots of possibilities, though."

By the time they reached the center of town, Tomas was convinced the whole place was abandoned. A growing certainty replaced some of his fears.

"I think they're in Alliston," he said.

Tomas led the way but was brought to a stop by a wide stain in the middle of the dirt street.

"Looks like the fight claimed at least some lives," Angela said.

"Looks like." Tomas didn't want to imagine whose lives.

Tomas led them to Alliston so fast they almost ran. When they came within sight of the walls, loud voices ordered them to stop. Tomas obeyed, then shouted, "Tell Hardin it's Tomas."

Angela eyed the wall.

"What do you notice?" Tomas asked.

"There's many people inside. More than the walls were meant to hold."

They could both guess at what that meant, and Tomas desperately hoped that Hardin had protected most of everyone.

It took little more than a minute for the thick front gates to open and Hardin to emerge. The large man smiled when he saw Tomas, but there was no joy in his eyes. "Apologies for the rudeness, Tomas, but what in the three hells are you doing here?"

"Ulva called to me through the nexuses. She said you were under attack, and I think I know who was responsible."

Hardin's tone was flat. "The church did this. Just like I always warned Ulva they would."

"Not just the church. From the description Ulva gave me, it was the Holy Father's right-hand assassin, a man named Ghosthands."

"The man who gave you such trouble in Chesterton?"

"The very same."

Hardin pulled at his beard, but his thoughts seemed elsewhere. "Bastard seemed like the right type of asshole. Didn't make the connection, though."

"I'm sorry. I couldn't have gotten here in time to help. Ulva's message traveled a lot faster than I'm able to."

Hardin nodded, his mind on other things. "I kind of hate to admit it, but if not for her, we would have lost a lot more than we did. She woke me, too. Gave me enough time to prepare something, though it wasn't time enough."

"What happened? We've passed through Jonasson, but can't make heads or tails over it."

Hardin didn't answer Tomas's question, but studied Angela. "Who's this?"

Angela introduced herself, and Tomas caught the first hint of a genuine smile on Hardin's face. It still felt too empty, though, like someone had hollowed out the giant and forgot to refill him.

"Tomas talked a lot about you," he said and waved for them to follow him into Alliston.

The settlement was packed full of people. Tomas couldn't get an accurate count, but it felt to him like a fair number of Jonasson's citizens had retreated to the safety of the walls. Just like Hardin had always planned. Though he knew Hardin had hoped the walls would never be needed.

The contrast to Jonasson was startling. Every window here had someone moving behind it, and Tomas saw some bedrolls laid out on porches. They had pitched tents near the corners of intersections, and there were people everywhere. Hardin led them through the chaos, though their progress wasn't rapid. People kept asking him for help, and he listened to the requests patiently.

When they finally reached a quieter street, Hardin asked, "Did you see anything on the way in?"

"Nothing unusual, but we came from the south," Tomas said.

Hardin's shoulders tensed at the answer, but he relaxed them with what appeared to be a deliberate effort. He stopped one of his warriors as he passed and whispered an order. The young man bowed and went rushing off.

They reached Hardin's house a minute later. A young man was camped on Hardin's porch, and when the door opened, Tomas saw a new mother. She bobbed her head at them, then went to speak to the young man. Even Hardin, it seemed, had guests temporarily living with him.

Hardin led them to the dining room table where they sat. The enormous man didn't offer them tea, which gave Tomas a sense of how desperate the situation was. As soon as he sat, Hardin sagged in his chair.

He didn't make Tomas ask about the events of that night. The story came on its own. He talked about how he'd been asleep, and at first, when Ulva had appeared before him, he'd thought it had been some sort of nightmare. Instead, she had warned him of the threat, and he'd responded just the way they'd trained.

Their advance had ended at the border of Jonasson. Hardin and his hosts believed they had the upper hand, but Ghosthands had his blade at little Emily's throat.

Tomas remembered the young girl from his first visit. She had seemed nice, and Tomas clenched his fist under the table at the thought of Ghosthands using her as a hostage.

"What did you do?" Tomas asked.

Hardin went silent, and it suddenly felt like a storm was brewing in the house. "There was too much I didn't know. We'd only seen the three so far, but who knew how many more were within the settlement? We knew they'd injured or crippled dozens, and I couldn't guess what their plan was. I ordered us to hold, but then Ghosthands ordered the other two back into Jonasson."

Hardin put his head in his hands. "After a while, I couldn't take it anymore. I couldn't allow one man to prevent us from saving all those still in the town. I didn't give any orders because I figured Ghosthands would hear. Instead, I burned my sagani as bright as I could and charged when I thought he wasn't looking."

Tears formed in his eyes. "Don't think I'd made it more than two steps before he drew his sword across her neck from ear to ear. Then he picked up Andrew, as easily as if he was a sack of potatoes, and put his sword to the boy's neck."

Tomas slammed his fists on the table. Angela jumped in her chair, and Tomas stood, pacing the room quickly.

"I've seen plenty of violence in my years," Hardin said as he brushed the tears from his eyes, "but I don't think I've ever seen a man take a child's life with so little regard. Truthfully, it froze me in place. By the time I gathered my wits, he was safe behind Andrew."

Though Tomas had only known Hardin for a bit, their brief time together had exposed them to more trials than most people experienced in a lifetime. He'd seen triumph spread Hardin's smile wide, and he'd seen Hardin command his warriors calmly in combat. At a glance, he might seem a brute, but he was as competent a leader as Tomas had ever crossed paths with.

Hardin had met his match when he faced Ghosthands's cruelty, though. Tomas's heart went out to the man, for Hardin now endured the same agony Tomas had experienced in Chesterton.

Hardin held his head in his hands as he stared at the table. "I know what I should have done. Andrew might have died, but if we'd all attacked, we would have saved so many more."

Tomas frowned. He was about to ask for Hardin to clarify when Myra limped through the door. Her leg was bandaged, and Tomas raised an eyebrow.

"Sagani hasn't been healing me as fast since Kimson," she said.

"It's good to see you," Tomas answered.

"You, too. If we're leaving, I'm coming with. I'll be good to fight in a day or two."

"Why would we leave?" Tomas asked.

"Ghosthands and his knights kidnapped our citizens. Took them west, though we couldn't follow. Ghosthands made it clear he'd continue killing hostages if he saw any sign of us, and he had over two dozen with him."

Tomas felt sick at the thought. When he closed his eyes, he was back in the research station outside of Razin. If Ghosthands hadn't killed any hosts, those he captured had a fate worse than death waiting for them at their destination.

Hardin still held his head in his hands, and Tomas wasn't sure the founder of Alliston was still with them. His eyes stared past the table, looking into the past.

Myra followed Tomas's gaze. "He blames himself for not giving the order to charge, though no one who was there thinks he should. We didn't know how many knights they had, and Ghosthands was the most frightening swordsman I've ever seen. We might have defeated him, but he cut me down easily. Hardin's the only one who might have stood a chance, but he was already in shock. At the moment, there was no one who thought the order was the right one."

Tomas had come to Alliston to research the nexuses and to die. Once again, fate had thrown him onto a different path. At Ghosthands once again, when Tomas and Elzeth were at their weakest.

He leaned back in his chair and closed his eyes. "What do you think, old friend?"

Elzeth let out the longest exasperated sigh Tomas had ever heard. "We can't leave them to Ghosthands, can we?"

Tomas relaxed a bit. In the past, he wouldn't have doubted Elzeth's agreement, but after everything and knowing how weak they were, he wasn't sure. "Thanks. I can't do it without you."

Elzeth snorted. "Some days, I'm not sure how you get dressed without my help."

Tomas opened his eyes, stood, and walked around the table to put his hand on Hardin's shoulder. It broke Hardin from his reverie.

When he looked up, Tomas said, "Don't worry. We'll get them all back, and we'll make the church pay for their sins."

20

The first problem Tomas and Angela faced was finding a place to stay. Alliston was bursting at the seams. People were already sleeping on porches, couches, and living room floors. Myra offered them some of her floor space, but Tomas had hoped for something more comfortable. After some negotiation, Myra gave Tomas permission to use the bunkhouse in Jonasson. She wanted her citizens in Alliston for at least a few more days until she was absolutely sure the immediate danger had passed, but she made an exception for Tomas.

The two of them stowed their packs in the bunkhouse and returned to Alliston for the evening meal. Thanks to the sudden arrival of so many new citizens, Myra had organized enormous community meals. The meals weren't just an effective use of food, but the time together started the long process of closing Jonasson's and Alliston's open wounds.

Tomas became an instant supporter as soon as he ate the first meal. Granted, his stomach had been rumbling for hours, and he hadn't had a hot meal for days, but he swore the stew was some of the best he'd tasted. It was thick with chunks of meat, carrots, and potatoes. Freshly baked bread with a thick crust and soft center rounded out the meal. He ate until he was sure his stomach was about to burst.

Myra walked them back to Jonasson. Tomas got the sense it was less because she felt they needed an escort and more because she wanted to speak without a dozen listening ears around every corner.

"How do you think the settlements are doing?" Tomas asked.

"We're in rough shape," Myra admitted. "I'm not sure the extent of our wounds is even apparent yet. We're small enough that everyone knows everyone, which means we all lost friends and family in the attack. People are still in shock. You'll see adults suddenly stop and look around like they don't understand where their partner went."

Myra kicked at a loose stone that crashed into the underbrush off the path. "Added to that, we lost Ulva, and some days it's like we've lost Hardin, too. Ulva's loss hit us hardest. Kind of surprising, given that she was old enough that most of us half-expected her to croak getting out of bed in the morning. I think it's the nature of how she died, though. Ancient as she was, she had earned the right to die in peace."

"I spoke to her after she died," Tomas said.

"Really?" Myra didn't sound as surprised or as skeptical as Tomas would have expected.

"She said she was in contact with the nexus when it happened. If it's any consolation, she was excited. She and her sagani were going to pass through the gate together."

Myra stuck her hands in the pockets of her pants and stared at the ground. After a few steps, she chuckled. "Yeah, that sounds like her. You should share that story with others. I think it will help."

"Of course."

Myra drew up short on the outskirts of Jonasson. Tomas saw the shudder that ran through her body. "I'll leave you two here. You can find your own way back."

Tomas nodded.

"It's good to have you, Tomas. If anyone can get Hardin back on his feet, I suspect it's you. But I have to know, are you serious about getting our people back?"

"I am."

"Good." She swallowed hard. "That's really good."

She turned and walked away without another word. Angela reached out and took Tomas's hand. Once Myra was too far to hear, she whispered, "They're hurting so much."

Tomas squeezed her hand. "We'll do everything we can to heal them."

(###)

Tomas woke up first the next morning. Angela's torso was exposed, while her legs were tangled in the sheets. Tomas appreciated the moment, then slipped on his clothes and snuck out of the bunkhouse.

Jonasson was too quiet. Tomas still clearly remembered his last visit, when he'd heard hammers and saws building the future. The settlement had been alive, not just with people, but with purpose. Terrible as the loss of life had been, Tomas feared the most devastating murder was the death of the settlement's dreams. If he could return those to the citizens, it was as good a way as any to conclude his life.

He went through his forms just the way his old masters had taught him in the sword schools. Punches and kicks snapped in the morning air, his concentration tighter than it had been in a long time. The road to the end was finally clear. His stomach rumbled, ready for breakfast, but he continued until he completed the last of his forms.

When he finished, he noticed Angela leaning against the doorway. She had her arms crossed and had a smile on her face, but it looked like she'd forgotten to dress. "Haven't seen you that focused since we left Razin."

"Thankfully, I wasn't aware of the distraction behind me."

She turned around and led him back to the bedroom, breakfast temporarily forgotten. When they emerged later, the sun was already above the tops of the trees.

"So, what do you want to do today?" she asked.

"First, I want to eat, but then I want to visit the nexus."

"Are we going in again?"

"We are. The nexuses are still at the heart of everything, and to beat the church, we'll need them. It's important to Elzeth, too."

They were too late for Alliston's breakfast, but Tomas scrounged up some scraps, which were still better than most of what they'd eaten on the trail. With their bellies satisfied, they told Myra where they were going and left Alliston.

Halfway to the nexus, Angela said, "You plan to die against Ghosthands, don't you?"

Tomas sighed but didn't slow. It was a conversation he'd hoped to avoid, but she was too observant not to notice, too clever not to put the pieces together. "Not against Ghosthands, specifically, but against the church. How'd you know?"

"I saw something similar with soldiers I commanded during the war. You could always tell the ones who'd made their peace with death."

"I don't want to die, especially now that I'm with you again, but it seems foolish to prepare for anything else. In another battle against the church, if I try to live, I'm afraid I won't be strong enough to do what's needed."

Others might have argued, but Angela nodded. "I'd like you to live, too,"—she paused and kicked at the ground with her toe—"but I understand."

Her words brought Tomas to a stop. His throat was tight. "Thanks," he said.

They soon reached the nexus, and Tomas paused before the mouth of the small cave. It was odd, but he swore some part of Ulva remained. It felt less like he was stepping into the cave and more like he was stepping through her front door into her dining room. He halfway expected to find her there, a fresh cup of tea waiting for him.

Instead, he found only the bloodstain from her murder. He crouched down next to it as though it had something to teach him. He ran his fingers across the dried blood, but they came away clean.

"How well did you know her?" Angela asked.

"Not that well. She was an avowed pacifist and had little use for me. She actually tried to run me out of town before I met Hardin. Told me I would only bring trouble." Tomas stood. "I'm worried she was right."

"You can't blame yourself for what the church did."

"Sure, but Hardin and I ran risks that weren't necessary. I can't view myself as blameless."

He looked at the nexus. Its pull was strong, but he'd grown used to it, and he found it easy to ignore. He was surprised to learn how much Ulva's death affected him. It felt more like he'd lost an old friend than a woman he'd only spoken to a few times.

"She had a lot to teach me, I think. She found a new way to host a sagani, where the two of them became inseparable. Not unity, but something else."

"I would have liked to meet her," Angela said.

"I think she would have liked you a lot more than she liked me."

"Most people do."

Tomas laughed, grateful to banish the last of his depressing thoughts.

"So, do we have a plan here?" Angela asked.

"I was going to take Ulva's advice. Elzeth seems much stronger within the nexus than I am, so I was going to follow his lead. Hopefully, we can find the answers we're looking for."

She accepted the plan with a shrug. "I'll probably focus on understanding my sagani better. But I'll tag along if you don't mind."

"Not at all. We'll be glad to have you."

Tomas checked with Elzeth to ensure the sagani was ready. He took Angela's hand and they touched the stone together.

The transition was even easier than before. Tomas and Elzeth found each other on the other side only a few moments before Angela and her sagani appeared.

Tomas shook his head. He was still the better sword, but he thought Angela might be the better host. She picked up on new skills much faster than he had.

Although maybe it was only because she had such a great guide.

"What are you thinking, Elzeth?" he asked.

The sagani was in the same mountain cat form Tomas was familiar with. Tomas now thought of the cat as Elzeth's resting form. He appeared deep in thought, so Tomas didn't bother him.

Eventually, Elzeth answered. "Can you follow me?"

They floated in the void, so Tomas willed wide open plains into being. "Let's go."

Elzeth led the way. Tomas followed, and Angela and her sagani wandered a little way behind. Tomas caught whispers of the conversation that passed between them. Angela was curious but patient, and the sagani eager but uncertain. They were two strangers in the same body, slowly becoming friends.

With Elzeth guiding and Angela busy with her sagani, Tomas found himself alone in the middle of the group. He took pleasure both in the snippets of conversation he caught from behind him and in the sight of Elzeth following whatever mysterious threads he did. Here, lost in the nexus, Elzeth seemed more like a sagani than he did as a voice in the back of Tomas's head. His nose was to the ground, and he wandered back and forth, pursuing a scent invisible to all but him.

Tomas breathed easily. Madness didn't trouble him here, and the certainty of his impending death sharpened his senses, almost as if Elzeth were burning within. Despite the pains of his past, this moment was a good one. He was more fortunate than he deserved, but he refused to question his good luck. He was with a woman he loved and a friend who would accompany him right to the edge of the gate. What else could he ask for?

He was so lost in his own thoughts that he was slow to recognize the changing sky. His imagination and will had formed a relatively featureless prairie. But now the sky was brightening and changing from a familiar light blue to something darker. Tomas tried to change the sky back, but to no avail.

"Elzeth?" he asked.

"We're getting close now," the sagani said.

"To what?"

"To the heart."

"Of the planet?"

The feline head nodded. "Quiet, please. This isn't as easy as it looks."

They stopped, and Angela came to stand beside Tomas. Together, they watched Elzeth sniff his way forward. Tomas wanted to ask what the sagani was looking for, but his answer appeared first.

A gate, which hadn't been there a moment before, now stood in the middle of the prairie. The uncut diamond arch glowed with the otherworldly blue light that had become so familiar over the years. Instinctively, Tomas took a step back.

The space within the gate wasn't transparent. Inside the glow was a darkness blacker than black, a void that swallowed all light and returned nothing.

"Is that..." Angela began the question but couldn't bring herself to finish.

"I don't think so," Tomas answered. He didn't know how he was so sure, but he was. He'd felt the pull of the gate before, and this wasn't it. It was something else, related but distinct.

"It's the door to the heart. Our answers are on the other side," Elzeth said.

"You want to go in?" Tomas asked.

"Yes, but I think it's best if we go in together. I fear that if I go in alone, I won't be able to return."

Tomas looked again at the arch. Back when he'd been in the unnamed units, his commander had an idea for a daring ambush. The army had left a flank undefended, but that was because a sheer cliff protected it. Tomas's commander had the mad, but inspired, idea to use his hosts to climb the cliff at night and strike the enemy camp.

Tomas remembered looking up at that dark cliff face

and thinking the climb was impossible. That no matter his strength, the feat was beyond him.

The same fear seized him now. His spirit recoiled from the power emanating from the arch. No matter how strong he was, the heart would overwhelm him.

He'd survived that night long ago because partners had tied themselves to each other. Tomas's partner had caught him once when he slipped, and Tomas had returned the favor twice. They'd only made it up because they'd gone up together. He turned to Angela, shook his head, and she nodded. She wouldn't follow in his foolish footsteps.

He swallowed his fear, grabbed onto Elzeth's fur, and followed the sagani into the heart.

21

The carts bounced and jostled down rough trails. Few people traveled through this area, so the path they followed wasn't meant for carts. It was barely wide enough to walk on. After a short stint in the carts, Quinton decided it was more pleasant to walk ahead of them than ride upon them. Each of the host-knights drove one cart, and neither seemed pleased by the responsibility.

He didn't bother looking behind them often. The demons knew better now. Not long after they'd left, Hardin had sent pursuers after them, but the pursuers had turned back fast when he'd threatened another one of the demon children. As soon as they'd seen Quinton's sword at the child's neck, they'd turned tail and run the other way, and no one had appeared since.

He snarled at the memory. He hated when the demons pretended to obey human morality, even as he used that weakness against them. Demons wrapped themselves in lies and deceit. They knew they couldn't win in a contest of strength against the Creator and His servants, so they resorted to their dirty tricks.

Quinton hated how they worked and hated more when it proved to be effective. Even Bond and Fabian, knowing the truth about their prisoners, had wavered in their dedication. Quinton had caught each offering more aid to their prisoners than was necessary. Each time, Quinton had lectured the young knights, striking any of the prisoners who argued against him.

Thankfully, the prisoners had finally stopped complaining. Chains ran from wrists and ankles to steel eyelets secured to the floor of the carts. A few prisoners had tested their strength, but the church builders well understood the strength demons granted. Twice a day, Quinton and the knights offered the prisoners just enough food and water to keep them alive. When Quinton and the knights stopped each night to take turns resting, they left the prisoners in their chains. They had enough slack to move around a bit, and Quinton had no plans to let any of his precious gifts to Rachel escape.

This night was no different. Quinton volunteered to take the first watch, as he usually did. Bond and Fabian found comfortable places to lie and were soon fast asleep. By tomorrow, they would return to Saxton, the town where the train ended, and unload their prisoners.

He had few concerns about the rest of the trip. Bond and Fabian were too kindhearted toward the demons, but they were both competent and faithful. The demons might tug at their hearts, but they'd never betray the Creator. And once they were at the trains, they'd have support from local inquisitors.

His concerns were more for himself. It had been weeks now since Rachel had treated his madness, and the symptoms were returning. Quinton often found his thoughts traveling in odd directions, and he didn't recognize as much until it was too late. Worse, his hands were twitching. He didn't think the knights had noticed yet, but it was another reason he'd walked in front of the carts with his hands in his pockets.

The prisoners tried to get comfortable, but Quinton largely ignored them. So long as they weren't attempting to cause trouble, he didn't much care what they did. The long days of travel had made them filthy, which seemed fitting. They could hardly claim to be human in their current state.

He wandered behind a tree and held out his hands. All his life, they'd been dependable, but now they betrayed him. The demon in his core bashed against the bars of its cage, relentless in its assault.

Quinton clenched his fists to still the tremors. Deep breaths slowed his pounding heart. His skull ached from the constant effort to contain the demon. He pressed the back of his head against the tree trunk. Soon he'd be back in Corrin, this one last task complete. The moment he delivered the prisoners, he would go to Father and ask for the pain to be taken away for good.

He only had to hold out a few more days.

(###)

Quinton pressed his palms against his forehead and eyes. He rubbed them around, hoping to find some point that would ease the constant ache behind his eyes. No matter what he tried, the pain refused to relent.

He was no stranger to pain and suffering. A lifetime as a swordsman had guaranteed constant cuts and bruises. Years of service in the army had taught him other forms of suffering. He considered himself immune to heat and thirst, hunger and cold. Yet his demon's constant troublemaking was almost enough to make him beg for mercy.

It simply never stopped. A mad animal in a cage might

beat itself senseless against the bars or run out of strength. The sagani did neither. It raged day and night, demanding release. No single moment demanded much from Quinton. His will was firm as iron, and he'd contained the sagani for years. The creature might struggle, but Quinton was its undoubted master. But the constant, never-ending vigilance took its toll. He hadn't craved alcohol since becoming a host, but right now, he'd gladly drink a bottle of the worst whiskey if it would take the pain away.

Fortunately, there was no whiskey on the train. So he hid in corners, as far from people as he could, and waited for the pain to fade. It never did, but at least the others on the train left him alone.

He was on the platform outside one of the passenger cars, hoping the fresh air would ease some of his suffering, when one of the alarm bells clanged. He straightened at the sound. The alarm was from farther back, near the cargo car where the prisoners were being held.

An animal growl escaped from the back of his throat. He ran through the passenger car and hopped across the gap to the car where the prisoners were being held. One inquisitor rang the bell, his face pale.

"What happened?" Quinton asked, the pain in his head temporarily forgotten.

"One of the prisoners started a fight during the meal service. He had more strength than we expected, sir."

Quinton threw open the door and peered into a scene of chaos. Most of the prisoners were still chained securely to the wall, but two had escaped. Their wrists were manacled, but a chained host could still be a fearsome opponent. The inquisitors should have been competent enough to handle them, but if the inquisitors had grown lax and the demons had caught them by surprise, it might be enough to explain what Quinton observed.

The two escaped prisoners fought with a ferocity that surprised Quinton. He watched an inquisitor launch a chained dagger at one demon's heart. The demon willingly took the blade in his arm without so much as a grimace of pain. Then he grabbed the chain, pulled the inquisitor toward him, and delivered a crushing elbow to the inquisitor's face.

Quinton leaped into the fray. Two inquisitors were already down. The demons chained along both sides of the car kicked at their unconscious forms, cheering the insurrection. The third inquisitor, who'd just taken the blow to the face, was staggering back and about to fall.

Quinton stepped lightly around the fallen inquisitors, dancing around the kicks the chained demons aimed in his direction. He didn't dare release his sagani, but after observing the two escaped prisoners, he didn't think it would be necessary. The demons were strong, but they lacked any skill.

After the constant battle with his sagani over the past few days, it was almost a relief to have something physical to fight in front of him. This was a battle he could win.

The first demon saw him coming and spun around in an awkward twirl, attempting to land a powerful two-handed blow against the side of Quinton's head. Quinton leaned back and let the demon's manacled fists pass an inch in front of his face. The demon twisted and stumbled as the expected impact never occurred.

Quinton seized the advantage. He drew up close to the demon and delivered two quick punches to its kidneys. His fists felt like he was punching stone. The demon grinned at his ineffectual efforts and steadied itself.

Quinton stepped back as the demon regained its balance and lashed out with a quick kick at his shin. Quinton deflected it and retreated one more step.

The demon, perhaps flush with its victories thus far, raised its hands high over his head and stepped forward, clearly intending to bring them down and flatten Quinton like a pancake. Everything about the attack was pathetic, from the timing to the distance between them. It reminded Quinton that strength and speed alone did not make a warrior.

He stepped forward and punched hard at the demon's exposed throat. His fist connected, and had the host not been burning his demon like it was the center of a bonfire, he would have died in seconds. As it was, the demon coughed and choked, clutching at its neck like that would help. Quinton grabbed the demon's chains and yanked, sending it sprawling to the floor of the car. He motioned to the last inquisitor, still standing by the door, and the inquisitor hurried to re-chain the demon to the wall.

Quinton advanced against the last demon, who had retreated close to the rear of the car. Its eyes were wide, and it seemed to Quinton it was in the grip of madness. Perhaps in its bid to escape, it had burned its demon too fast. Quinton's shin still smarted from his last duel, and he saw no reason to waste time with honorable combat.

He drew his sword. "Submit or suffer the consequences."

The demon hissed, convincing Quinton that madness had consumed it. "You have no right. We were free families."

Quinton snarled. "You lost your rights the moment you accepted a demon into your body. Humans have rights. Animals are predators or prey, and only the strong survive. Our laws don't apply to you."

The demon rushed at Quinton. His sword made quick

work of the battle, and before long, the demon was crawling on the blood-covered floor. Quinton sheathed his sword. The chained demons jeered, and before Quinton knew it, he was straddling the injured demon, raining blows down on its face and chest.

The next thing he was aware of was an unnatural stillness. He blinked and looked down. The demon's face was a bloody mess, barely recognizable as something that had once been human. His own hands were bloody and scraped raw, but the wounds healed before his eyes. The jeers of the demons had gone silent, and when he looked up, Bond and Fabian were at the door, judgment written in their features.

He stood, his legs trembling. Slowly, he stumbled forward and left the cargo car. He stood on the platform and bent over the rail, certain he was going to throw up.

The vomit never came. The cool air refreshed both body and spirit, and he breathed in deeply. For now, the inquisitors left him alone. Bond and Fabian returned to the passenger car without a word.

He listened to the sounds of the inquisitors dragging the demon back to the wall and chaining it again. They helped their wounded to their feet. One inquisitor loudly announced, "There will be no water or food until we stop, not if this is the way you accept our hospitality."

There were complaints from within the car, but Quinton paid them no more mind than he would a cat meowing in hunger. Three of the four inquisitors went into the passenger car to lick their wounds, but the last one, the one who had rang the bell that summoned Quinton, stopped him.

"I'd recognize what I saw anywhere. What makes you different?" he asked.

"Than them?" Quinton asked. He was surprised the inquisitor was bold enough to ask.

The inquisitor nodded.

"They let the demon into their flesh and allow it to control them. I'm the master of my own. It does nothing without my permission, and that's what separates us. I remain human while the demons corrupt them."

"And what of the other host-knights?"

"They, too, are human, though the temptation to allow the demons deeper into our flesh is always present. They make a noble sacrifice on behalf of us all, but it also behooves all of us to watch one another to ensure we don't falter."

The inquisitor looked as though he was about to charge into battle. "Then, as one believer to another, I'll tell you that you've gone too far. Madness is consuming you."

Quinton's bitter laugh surprised the inquisitor. "I'm well aware. But have no fear. As soon as we reach Corrin, I will take my life."

The inquisitor nodded, satisfied. "See that you do. Otherwise, we'll have to do it for you."

22

———————

At first, walking through the heart seemed little different from wandering the strange plane of the nexuses. Tomas couldn't control his surroundings as he had on the other side of the gate. The power within the heart was too great for him to shape. Instead of the prairie, he and Elzeth wandered the eastern mountains where they'd first met.

"Are you doing this?" he asked Elzeth.

"Not intentionally, though I think the heart is pulling from my memories."

"Any idea where we should go or what we should do?"

"Not yet."

They wandered across a ridgeline with no particular destination in mind.

Tomas enjoyed the view, but not for long. As he walked, he noticed another presence pushing against his senses. It began as a whisper in the back of his head, soft like a trickle of sand sliding down a distant dune. It grew louder, into the hiss of a dozen angry snakes. There was a pattern within the noise, though, just beyond his perception. He stopped walking so he could direct all his attention toward listening.

The hissing became voices. First, two or three distinct whispers, then a dozen voices talking in hushed tones. They spoke different languages. Some were high-pitched and lyrical, like a musician playing only the highest notes on a harp. Others sounded crude and guttural, and others yet bordered on the edge of comprehension. Their volume grew until they were almost as loud as Elzeth's voice when they were in the physical world.

"Do you hear that?" Tomas asked.

"I don't hear anything, but I sense a disturbance. A ripple in the heart. It's growing closer."

Tomas didn't like the sound of that. "We should leave."

Elzeth turned in the direction they had come from and pointed with one of his front paws. It was a surprisingly human gesture from the mountain cat. "I don't think we can."

Tomas looked back and followed Elzeth's paw. "Oh."

Their tracks were easy to follow in the snow, and Tomas saw where they'd begun. No gate stood there.

"What about running?" Tomas asked.

"No point in wearing ourselves out. We're guests here, and I think the heart will do with us as it pleases."

"Not terribly comforting."

"The truth rarely is."

The voices grew louder yet. Tomas almost clapped his hands over his head before he remembered it wouldn't do him any good. They shouted at him, wanting something, but he didn't understand what. He took two steps forward, and the voices were louder. He retreated, but the shouting didn't diminish.

Two dozen voices shouted directly into his mind so loud he couldn't think. Useless as it was, he pressed the palms of his hands on top of his ears. He dropped to his knees, the noise physically painful. His eyes watered, and his head felt like it was about to split open. He thought he heard Elzeth call, but couldn't be sure over the cacophony.

The pain was unbearable. No headache compared. The voices hammered against his skull, relentlessly pounding at the shreds of his sanity that remained. With every breath, he thought he'd found the limit of what he could endure, only for the pain to double with the next breath.

Then Elzeth pressed up against him, his fur warm to the touch. The sagani shuddered as they made contact, and Tomas felt a wave of relief that wasn't his own.

The voices stopped growing, but they didn't diminish. Tomas gripped Elzeth's fur and held it tight. He took some measure of comfort in Elzeth's presence, even if it did nothing to save him.

Then Elzeth spoke, his voice drowning out the screams for one blissful moment. "Let them in!"

Tomas shook his head. He wouldn't surrender here. At the very least, he'd return to Angela one last time.

Elzeth shouted again, and Tomas sensed the strength and determination it required to reach him. "It's like when you touch the nexuses!"

The voices overwhelmed Elzeth, but Tomas understood. Any attempt to control the power of a nexus was suicidal. They could burn through a human body in moments. The power of the heart would burn through a mind in even less time. The only chance for victory came through surrender.

Tomas stopped fighting the voices. He welcomed them into his mind and his thoughts.

He gasped. It felt as if someone had thrown a bucket of cold water on his face, and he saw with unmatched clarity. The mountains he walked became translucent, and though the illusion supported the weight of his spirit, he saw through it. The space surrounding him was turbulent, like a spiral of dust kicked up by a sudden gust of wind. As he watched, it settled.

"Thanks. I wasn't sure how much longer I could have kept myself together," Elzeth said.

"It affected you, too?"

"It was tearing me apart. I don't think a sagani is supposed to be here alone. I'm not sure I would have survived if you hadn't come with me."

The thought sent a shudder down Tomas's spine. "Easy to make a mistake here that kills us, huh?"

"If the answers were easy, someone else would have found them already."

Tomas kept his hand in Elzeth's fur. "So, what next?"

"Can you still hear the voices?"

At first, Tomas thought the voices had disappeared, but when he listened, he could still hear them. They spoke a dozen languages, but their request was the same, and now he understood them. "They're asking for help. Can you pull up the map of the world again?"

Elzeth went silent for a minute, but soon they floated in the void next to the globe. Tomas admired the vast web for a moment before allowing the voices to guide his attention. The globe spun and grew larger, dropping Tomas and Elzeth toward the ground like two stones from the sky. They ended their descent in a field. In the physical world, Tomas might not have noticed anything special, but the heart revealed the underground bunker as clear as day.

The pair dropped through the door and floated along the corridors. Emaciated bodies rotted in cages, and Tomas was grateful the illusion didn't come complete with smell. The layout of the bunker was familiar—it was the same design as the research station he'd destroyed outside of Razin. In the darkest recesses of the tunnels, they found a nexus.

At least, Tomas thought it was a nexus. It was an enormous stone, but it didn't glow.

Tomas's perspective shifted, guided by Elzeth. He saw what had happened.

They had killed the nexus. The thick tendril that connected it to the heart was withered. Tomas followed the destruction of the tendril and saw it had reached about two-thirds of the way to the heart.

He asked the voices, "What would have happened if that reached the heart?"

The voices didn't answer, but Elzeth grunted. "I think it's trying to show me."

They floated up and away from the research station. Its inky stain was easy to spot now that Tomas knew where it was. The globe flickered and a shot of darkness traveled down the web, reaching the heart a moment later. The heart pulsed, a blinding flash of unbelievable power. Then it convulsed and went dark. Death spread through the tendrils, causing each nexus to wink out. Darkness consumed the world like a shadowy fire, consuming the nexuses dozens at a time. As each nexus died, the threads and lights that represented the sagani withered and died, too.

Tomas stumbled backward at the sight. Crops and humans didn't die, but the world did. The process took dozens of years, but if the heart died, so did all life on the planet.

Tomas closed his eyes and wished he could forget what he'd seen. In the quest to rid the land of the nexuses and the sagani, the church would destroy everything.

"So, we know what the church wants, but it still doesn't tell us what the nexuses are."

Elzeth was silent, and Tomas wished he could follow the direction of the sagani's thoughts. His partner looked back, and Tomas swore he saw a mischievous grin on the cat's face. "You ready to go deeper?"

"We can go deeper?"

Tomas gripped Elzeth's fur more tightly as the globe disappeared. They fell through an endless void. Their descent taught Tomas another difference between the heart and the nexuses. Entering the nexuses felt like plunging into a rushing river. Manipulating them successfully meant riding the currents. The heart was less a river and more a deep lake. It contained so much more power, but the power was at rest, a nearly infinite supply.

Tomas wondered what good he could do with such strength, but the mere thought caused the power to shudder and respond to his will. He stopped before he crushed himself with his own foolishness. He could barely direct the power of a nexus, so who was he to think he could do anything here?

Tomas sensed their descent stop. The void was the same, although the pressure against his spirit was stronger than before. It almost felt as though he was encased in power.

"Did you find an answer?" he asked Elzeth.

"Quiet."

Tomas obeyed, stretching his senses to their limit.

The boundary between Elzeth's spirit and the heart

wasn't as sharp as the one that divided Tomas and the power. It was fuzzy, connecting to the heart with thousands of tiny tendrils. Part of the heart was in Elzeth, just as part of Elzeth stretched through the heart.

"It was a gift," Elzeth whispered. "Left for us by those who came long before."

"What do you mean?"

"Look."

The world melted and reformed around them. Tomas found himself standing in a sea of wild grasses. Fire fell from the sky, like a torch somehow burning upside down. Something landed, burning the grass for hundreds of feet in every direction before the fire mysteriously vanished. It stood tall, like a building, but it was like no building Tomas had ever seen.

The sun rose and fell. A door in the building opened and a man stepped out. He was taller and thinner than any man Tomas had ever seen. His steps were uncertain. He held out his hands, as though trying to catch water from a waterfall. A stone rested in his hands, brighter than any nexus, but the same color.

The man knelt, and the stone vanished into the soil, as though the man had dug a hole and planted it like a seed.

But no hole had been dug.

Tomas saw through the illusion. He watched the stone sink through soil, through the rock below, and whatever was below that. It settled in the center of the world.

"The heart was planted," he said.

Elzeth nodded. "And look at that."

Tomas had a sense of time passing. The heart grew, and the nexuses grew from it, budding from its surface, then breaking away and floating to places near the surface.

The man disappeared, then reappeared on a new day,

once again emerging from the building that had fallen from the sky. A long table floated in front of him, filled with small creatures. He stopped, and the table descended until it was resting in the grass.

Tomas squinted. "Are those—?"

"Sagani," Elzeth finished. "We were brought here with the heart."

Tomas stepped closer to the scene, but as he did, he felt the power of the heart swirling around him and Elzeth. The voices that had been under control grew louder and more insistent. Elzeth recoiled until he was almost wrapped around Tomas's leg.

"It's time for us to go," he said.

"Show me the way, and I'll follow," Tomas said.

Elzeth's fur flattened under Tomas's hand, and the sagani tensed. A glowing gate appeared in the void, revealing Angela's dining room on the other side. Human and sagani ran for the gate together, pursued by the disturbance in the heart. As soon as they had passed through, it closed behind them.

"What was that? I thought we had it under control," Tomas said.

"I don't think it likes anyone asking questions about its origins," Elzeth said. The sagani seemed smug. "But we got some answers, anyway."

Angela was relaxing in a chair and drinking some tea. Her sagani had taken the form of a plump chipmunk and was nibbling bits of cracker from her hand.

"It's good to see you, too," she said dryly.

Tomas looked down at his feet. "Sorry, got distracted."

"I take it you found what you were looking for?" Angela asked.

Tomas turned to Elzeth to let him answer the question.

"Most of it. We also discovered what the church is trying to do. They've figured out a way to kill the nexuses, and now they want to kill the heart. If they succeed, they'll destroy the nexuses, the sagani, and eventually the planet."

"That sounds bad," Angela said.

"Agreed," Tomas said. He looked around. "Didn't like the prairie?"

"Liked it just fine, but when you and Elzeth stepped into the heart, it vanished. I had to learn how to make my own place."

"It looks good. Have you had a pleasant conversation with your sagani?"

"I have. I think we understand each other well enough for now, and I'm excited to return to the physical world to see how much of what we've learned carries over."

Tomas guided them back to their bodies. Before long, they were back in the cave. From the position of the sun, it didn't look like much time had passed. It had felt like hours inside the nexus, but Tomas doubted they'd been gone more than a few minutes.

His hand twitched when they stepped outside the cave. It wasn't as surprising as it used to be, but he stared at it all the same.

"I'd hoped our contact with the heart would help me," he admitted to Elzeth.

"I feel better, but I think the madness isn't originating with me. It's your body finally breaking down after hosting me for so long," Elzeth said.

Tomas sighed but was quickly over the disappointment. He'd been going mad when he touched the nexus and was going mad now. Nothing had changed.

Except that, while they'd explored the nexus, the world had shifted again. Halfway back to Alliston, they ran into

Myra, who hurried toward them. Her face was grim, and Tomas feared something had happened to Hardin.

Fortunately, the news wasn't so dire. Myra delivered it quickly.

"We've got visitors," she said. "The army finally showed up, and they brought cannons."

23

Tomas and Angela followed Myra back to Alliston. "How much do you know?" Tomas asked.

"Not too long after Kimson, Hardin reached out to General Gavan to discuss the possibility of negotiations. It looks like the 34th has responded."

Her explanation first infuriated Tomas. How could Hardin have been so foolish as to trust the army? Then all of Myra's words registered. "It's the 34th out there?"

"It is, but it looks like they've brought the entire army. I think Hardin was only expecting an envoy."

Tomas's throat tightened. He couldn't guess the army's goals, but there were plenty of possibilities he didn't want to consider. He couldn't let the worst of those come to pass, not after what Jonasson and Alliston had already endured. The fact that it was Gavan gave him hope, but Gavan was still an army general. He would follow his orders, even if he found them distasteful.

"What was Hardin thinking?" Tomas asked.

Myra had a ready answer. "That Kimson forced our hand. I know you never spoke of us to Gavan, but five trained hosts, all appearing at once? Questions were sure to arise. Settlers keep coming closer, and the church is building to the west. We always figured we'd have to reach out to the army. We just didn't think it would be this fast."

"Do you want me to talk to Gavan?" Tomas respected the general, even if their purposes didn't always align. If any army general would be reasonable, it was him.

Myra shook her head. "No, but I want you with us when we visit. Hardin's still not thinking straight, and I'm hoping you'll keep a level head."

"Is this the first time anyone has asked you to act as a peacekeeper?" Elzeth asked.

Tomas chuckled, then explained when Angela and Myra shot him looks. "Elzeth is pointing out I'm rarely selected to keep the peace between people."

Myra didn't think it was as funny as Tomas and Elzeth did. "You did more for us outside of Kimson than you realize. If not for you, I don't think Gavan would have let us return to our homes and families."

Tomas wasn't so sure but accepted the compliment gratefully. "I'd be happy to join you and Hardin if you think it will help."

Myra thanked Tomas. They stopped at the gate of Alliston, where Hardin was waiting for them. He stood straighter than before, and Tomas thought he saw some hint of the flame that had once driven him to found his own settlement. He looked the part of a commander, but Tomas wasn't sure he had the heart needed to face the 34th.

"Glad to have you here," Hardin told Tomas. "Are you ready to do this?"

"As I'll ever be, I suppose."

Tomas glanced at Angela to ask if she wanted to stay behind, but she had a stern look and she kept close to him.

The four of them left the main gate of Alliston. Guards closed the heavy wooden doors behind them, and Tomas heard the crossbeam fall into place. The scene reminded him of his days in the army when he'd leave the safety of the forts behind to scout deep in enemy territory. The thought broke some of the tension building in his chest. Hells, it was even the same army. All these years, and so little changed.

They walked through the empty streets of Jonasson and followed the well-worn trail that led south. Tomas heard the army before he saw it. The trees here were thick, but they didn't stop the sounds of camp from reaching his ears. Less than a half mile from Jonasson, they came upon the 34th's sentries.

The woman commanding the checkpoint recognized Tomas. "I didn't think we'd see you again," she said. She didn't sound entirely pleased to be proven wrong.

"Didn't think we'd cross paths, either, but here we are. How's Gavan?"

"Tired and cranky," the woman admitted. "We were supposed to be back home for months yet, but the army called us up for this. He wasn't too pleased about it."

"I can imagine."

The sentry looked at their swords, and Tomas could see her hesitation. But she waved them through and assigned them a guide. It was a small gesture, considering Tomas saw even more rifles among the 34th than before, but he interpreted it as a good sign.

His initial burst of optimism didn't last long. He'd traveled with the 34th long enough to know their numbers and their material, and they had reinforced both since Tomas had parted from them. There were half again as many warriors as Tomas had traveled with before, and every squad was armed with at least one rifle.

Unfortunately, the rifles weren't what worried Tomas the most. That honor went to the cannons. The church had destroyed most of the 34th's supply in the Battle of Kimson, but Tomas passed several new cannons, their metal gleaming where the sun struck them.

Tomas noted the differences but didn't mention them to his companions. Hardin wasn't blind. He'd seen all the same cannons. He understood the stakes of the coming negotiation.

Guards admitted them directly into the command tent. Gavan stood there with two of his commanders, but their discussion ended as soon as their company arrived.

Like the commander of the sentries, Gavan started when he saw Tomas, then he shook his head with a rueful grin. "Figures you would be here."

Gavan dismissed his commanders and gestured for them all to take a seat.

Tomas couldn't decide how much danger they were in. The number of warriors and cannons outside the tent implied Gavan had come prepared for a battle, but they were also allowed to enter the command tent armed and alone. Tomas wished someone would just explain the situation to him. He'd never been skilled at negotiations.

As if Gavan had heard his thoughts, he said, "Thank you for coming, and I apologize it couldn't be under more favorable circumstances. As you can imagine, news of Jonasson and Alliston has caused quite the stir back east. No small number of leaders are secretly calling for your destruction. They almost sent both the 3rd and the 34th out, but I was able to convince them the 34th would be sufficient."

Tomas nodded in understanding. He let himself relax

and breathe deeply. "I appreciate you coming out here, then. I know you were looking forward to being home."

Gavan rubbed at his eyes, looking older than ever before. "Eh, I was getting bored anyhow. Nothing back east to keep me anchored there. Starting to think the camp is my home, and the house I bought out east is more of a place to rest between campaigns."

The general leaned back in his chair. "But I know you didn't come here to listen to me complain. Before we get started, I'd like to get caught up. Tomas, why are you here?"

Tomas ran through the story as quickly as he could, relying on Angela to ensure he didn't forget any important details. He'd already written a comprehensive report telling of his failures escorting Rachel, so the process was quicker than it might have been. Gavan listened intently, then sat up straight in his chair when Tomas told him of Ghosthands's attack.

Gavan cut off Tomas's retelling with a wave of his hand and turned to Hardin. "Tell me everything."

Hardin did. The giant man's voice cracked in the retelling, and when it was over, a heavy silence pressed upon them all.

Eventually, Gavan broke the silence. "I'm sorry. I didn't know."

Hardin took a long breath and looked up, a man who had no time for sympathy. "Now you know everything that has happened here. You come with enough cannons to flatten my settlements in less than an hour and an entire army to chase the stragglers down. Why are you here?"

Gavan didn't mince words with his reply. "There are those among my superiors who begged me to create a reason to deploy these cannons against your settlements. They aren't believers, but they fear hosts nevertheless. I've fought by your side, and I'd like to prevent that, if possible, but you need to understand the pressure coming from the east."

The look Hardin gave Gavan wasn't exactly full of sympathy, but Gavan didn't retreat from the glare. He spread his hands out wide on the table. "I'm not really any more pleased than you, though I wish the timing could have been better. So, let's talk."

"What do you want?" Hardin growled.

"That you and every settler in Jonasson and Alliston swear their allegiance and that you'll allow a considerable army presence in Alliston."

Storm clouds darkened Hardin's expression. "The church came here less than a week ago. They killed my people and took others hostage. Now you're here, after I extended you a peaceful offer, to crush us under the heel of the army? I think not."

Gavan didn't rise to Hardin's provocation. He spoke calmly, without a hint of accusation. "What did you think was going to happen when you founded Alliston? That you'd be able to live free from the laws that govern this land?"

"Seems to work pretty well for the church these days."

"And you're no church. You have a force large enough to be a threat but not so large that the army can't come and crush you at any time. And today, the army will crush you if they believe it is necessary. The church has taught them not to ignore threats."

"Try it," Hardin dared. "You'll find it isn't as easy as you think."

Myra desperately looked at Tomas for help. Tomas didn't know what he could do, but he jumped in before Gavan could lose his temper. He spoke softly, mirroring Gavan's tone. "General, what do you *need* to bring back to your superiors?"

A disgruntled rumbling escaped from the back of Hardin's throat, and Tomas worried he might leave prematurely. Thankfully, he remained seated while he waited for Gavan's answer.

It was a while in coming. Gavan considered carefully, then said, "More than anything, I need to prove that these settlements aren't a threat. Oaths of loyalty would be helpful, especially if they were signed. They would reassure the politicians but wouldn't mean much in reality. You'd still be able to self-govern."

"What if the politicians use the oaths as a pretext for further action? Either by claiming the oaths were broken or by implying the oaths have greater reach than originally intended?" Tomas asked.

Gavan shrugged. "Like I said, in reality, they matter little. The politicians can point to them as a sign of success, but at the end of the day, they're only scraps of paper. If the government wants the settlements destroyed, there isn't a piece of paper in the world that will save you."

"So what prevents the politicians from ever wanting to destroy the place?" Tomas pressed.

"Same as with any negotiation. The price of attacking the settlements has to be too high. And no, before you object, it isn't yet. The 34th could destroy the settlements and be gone by tomorrow night."

Tomas batted the problem around, approaching it from different directions. "So, the government needs to lose something if they attack?"

Gavan nodded.

Tomas looked at both Gavan and Hardin. "What if, in addition to the oaths, Alliston committed some percentage of its warriors to the army for a set period? They complete a tour of duty, then return to Alliston."

Hardin started to object, then held his tongue. He considered the offer. "I'd need to talk with my people. There's a possibility there, but I won't commit until I speak with them."

Gavan pretended to think, but Tomas knew the general too well. After a period of silence, Gavan nodded. "We'd need to work out the details, but that would be acceptable."

They spoke for a while longer, debating those very details. Once they had something of a working plan in place, Hardin stood and announced he would take the idea to his people. Tomas couldn't be sure, but he thought they would accept it. It wasn't ideal, but it would keep their settlements safe.

They started to exit the tent together, but Gavan reached out and stopped Tomas before he could leave with the others. "Mind staying back for a minute?"

Tomas gestured at the others to go ahead. Myra and Angela looked doubtful, but Tomas shooed them on.

Once they were alone, Gavan said, "I really didn't think I would see you again. I thought the madness would have taken you by now."

He left the question unspoken out of courtesy, but Tomas answered it. "It's still a problem. Can't say if it's getting worse, but I don't think I have long left. It's what drove me out here in the first place."

"So you said. I'm glad you were here, though. Hardin looks like he's in rough shape."

Tomas nodded. "Ghosthands has that effect on people. But somehow, I have the feeling you would have reached the same deal without me. You want the hosts."

Gavan grunted. "Figured that out, did you?"

"You don't care much about the politicians back east. You just want to win any fight they give you."

Gavan didn't deny it. "We can't recruit any hosts back east. The unnamed units still have a stigma about them, but even if they didn't, I don't think it would matter. Sagani are almost impossible to find, so there are no hosts."

Gavan let his gaze travel over the camp. "More and more, we move to rifles and cannons, and I don't think that's all bad. But high command forgets that not all battles are a matter of flattening the enemy under a barrage of artillery. Some missions require more finesse, and for that, a host is still the best weapon there is."

"You want to recreate the unnamed units."

"Of a sort. There are lessons to be learned from the war, and I hope to take those to heart. But yes, I want to create something similar. Small units capable of completing missions that our cannons can't. And right now, the only place I can find hosts in any numbers is here."

Tomas couldn't help but chuckle. "A cynical man might think you had this all planned out before you came."

"They might be right. But I didn't lie to Hardin. I did not know the church also had its sights set on these settlements. If what you've told me is true, we can't let the church have those hosts. So if Hardin agrees to my terms, I'll be honor bound to help him retrieve his hosts. After all, they will be loyal citizens."

Tomas's throat tightened. As a rule, he didn't hold a high opinion of the army generals, but Gavan broke the mold. "I think I'm glad I ran into you that day so long ago," Tomas said.

"I am, too. Now go, tell Hardin what I've told you. We may live in the age of rifles and cannons, but we still need hosts. Maybe more than ever before."

Tomas thought about that in light of all he'd recently learned. The nexuses were vital to the health of the planet, and humans were connected to them. Maybe hosts were necessary in the new age. He wasn't sure, but he bowed to Gavan and chased after the others.

24

———

The train rumbled into Corrin on schedule, but that didn't surprise Quinton. The church's trains always ran on time. Despite the speed of their return, the train ride had dragged on for an eternity. The tremor in his hand wasn't constant, but it struck three or four times a day, a constant reminder of the fate that awaited him. It didn't matter, though. Rachel had given him more time than he'd expected, and he'd used that time to powerfully serve the Creator.

It was time to rest. Father couldn't deny him any longer.

Had he been alone, Quinton would have leaped from the train before it reached the station and run for Father's home. His sense of duty kept him from such dramatic action, though. Until the prisoners were safely under Rachel's supervision, he didn't dare.

Fortunately, when he poked his head out the window, he saw Rachel and a great number of knights waiting for their arrival. He unlimbered himself from the corner he'd tucked himself into and was the first out the door as the train shuddered to a stop.

"It's done," he said.

Rachel nodded as though she'd expected nothing less. Her lack of praise annoyed him as though she thought capturing the hosts was no more difficult than picking some basil from the garden. He shoved his frustration down. Her approval meant nothing. Father would recognize the difficulty of his accomplishments.

He took the knight commanders aside and warned them of the danger the hosts presented. Such warnings were probably unnecessary, and the pained expressions on a few of the knight's faces said as much, but Quinton would not take any chances. The hosts had gotten the jump on the inquisitors, and while Quinton suspected inquisitor overconfidence was more to blame than any special skills the hosts possessed, he didn't care. He'd risked too much to bring the demons here. He wouldn't let some foolish oversight rob him of his accomplishment.

His efforts paid off, though. The knights were exceedingly careful as they transitioned the demons from the filthy cargo car to the carts that would carry them to the fort. One demon tried to cause trouble, but a knight beat him senseless so fast that the others were cowed into submission.

Quinton watched the carts pull away, then put the bell tower of the mission in his sights. Bond and Fabian traveled with Rachel and the knights, and the inquisitors on the train melted into the crowd, leaving Quinton without an escort. Whether by intention or oversight, Quinton didn't question his good fortune. The escorts had always made him feel more demon than human.

He didn't condemn them for their caution. It would be difficult for anyone to understand what separated him from the prisoners chained to the carts bound for the tunnels under the fort. Still, it was freeing to wander the streets as he pleased, with no suspicious eyes judging his every move.

Not that there would have been much to see. Quinton made a straight line for the mission, turning only when buildings blocked his path. He reached the majestic building in short order, then walked around it until he found the Holy Father's residence. He marched up the front steps and was stopped outside the door by a knight standing guard.

"Who are you?" the guard asked.

"Quinton. I came to visit Father."

"You aren't scheduled for today," the knight replied. Quinton's name hadn't sparked the faintest recognition from the warrior.

"True, but I was hoping for a few minutes. I understand he's likely busy, but I'm willing to be patient."

The knight wasn't interested. "Get lost. Line up on seventhday at the church like everybody else."

Uncontrollable rage flickered to life in Quinton's chest, and the demon caged in his soul snapped at it like it was a treat dangled just beyond the bars of its cage. He gritted his teeth and clenched his fist, breathing his anger out. The bars held the demon firm, and the rage burned out as fast as it had sparked into an inferno. He reached slowly into one of his pockets and pulled out a piece of paper that was dear to him.

Written on the paper were orders from the Holy Father, granting Quinton whatever he desired. The letter carried Father's seal, and the knight paled as he examined the paper. "I'm sorry, sir. I didn't recognize you. Would you mind waiting here with my companions while I see if the Holy Father is home?"

Quinton's eyes narrowed slightly, but he nodded. The

commander of the guards should know Father's schedule by heart. How could he not know if Father was within the grounds or not? The commander handed back the paper, offered Quinton a bow, then disappeared within the building.

At first, the delay annoyed Quinton, but as reason reasserted itself, he calmed. If all went well, he'd be at the Creator's side by the end of the day, so his rush made no sense. He turned and took in the view from the top of the stairs. The mission was a gleaming beacon of hope in this dark, corrupted world, and Quinton wondered if he might tour it before taking his own life.

Corrin was a beacon, too, and though Quinton acknowledged all the development that had gone into the city, it wasn't for him. He didn't like the harsh lights that lacked a candle's soft glow. He didn't like so many people gathered together. But it was impressive to see a city built that honored the glory of the Creator.

He turned when the door opened behind him. The guard commander reappeared. "I'm sorry, sir, but Father isn't home today."

Panic nibbled at the edges of Quinton's awareness, but he ignored it. He couldn't remember a time when he'd been so emotional, and he wondered if the demon was to blame. He kept his voice calm. "Do you know where he is or when he might return?"

"I'm sorry, but I don't. Whatever he left on was private. I spoke to one of his chief aides, though, and she suggested you return to the fort. She'll pass on the message to the Holy Father, and she assures me he'll summon you as soon as he's able."

Something about the entire exchange left Quinton feeling wary, as though he was walking into a trap he couldn't quite see. He didn't know what he could do besides accept the news with as much grace as he could muster and walk away. He was tempted to charge into the home and see if Father was there, but doing so would erase all the glory of his work in Jonasson. They would brand him a demon and put him to death without dignity or hand him to Rachel and let her do as she pleased.

Quinton forced himself to bow to the guard commander and retreat down the stairs. He didn't know what thoughts were genuinely his and which were poisoned by the demon. His thoughts didn't feel any different, but therein lay the difficulty with madness. How would he know?

The question made his stomach churn. He'd always been competent, even before becoming a host. What remained when madness stole his skill and intuition?

With no place better to go, he left Corrin and returned to the fort with heavy steps. One opportunity remained, but the thought of pursuing it left a bitter taste in the back of his throat. Rachel had slowed the madness once before, so maybe she could do so again.

When he reached the fort, the knights had already secured the prisoners. The fort had absorbed the new arrivals and returned to the normal rhythms of its days. Quinton assumed Rachel would waste no time in experimenting on the demons, so he hurried down into her lair.

The tunnels had been unpleasant before, but now they sounded and smelled like something out of a child's nightmare. The prisoners were filthy from their transport, and they were shouting and screaming about something. Too many voices echoed too loudly in the confined space, and Quinton couldn't make sense of their demands. Something must have happened, though, because the demons hadn't even been this upset when Quinton and the inquisitors had fought the escapees on the train.

A handful of knights wandered the tunnel, bashing the hilts of their swords on outstretched arms and hands. Most prisoners had learned to stay near the back of their cages as they yelled, but a few pressed themselves against the bars as they reached for the knights.

Quinton ignored the chaos. One lady grasped at him, but he slid smoothly away and continued deeper into the tunnels. Thankfully, after he passed through two doors, almost all the sound was behind him.

He found the reason for the outrage soon enough. A young man was shirtless and strapped to one of the steel research tables. He was struggling against the straps, but they were too tight to allow movement. A thick gag muffled his cries.

Rachel looked up as Quinton entered. "What are you doing here?" she asked.

"I was going to ask you the same."

Rachel shrugged. "Our first step is to determine who is human and who is possessed. We've developed a set of tests that tell us, so we don't have to rely on their word."

Quinton nodded but realized he didn't care. "Would it be possible for us to talk in private?"

Rachel grimaced and looked at her new subject. Quinton felt her rejection coming and interrupted her before she could answer. "I promise it will only take a few moments. I have some questions about my demon."

As he'd expected, that was enough to catch her attention. "Only if it's quick. There's a lot of work to be done."

She led him into her office, where it was quieter yet. "Out with it."

He'd meant to ask about his madness, but another question suddenly seemed more important. "Have you received any new orders from Father since I've been gone?"

"Nothing that concerns you. But you said you had a question about your demon."

"Do you know if Father is planning to visit again soon?"

Rachel was visibly frustrated. "How should I know? If you're so curious, why don't you ask him? It's only a few hours' walk."

Quinton bit back his retort. Rachel clearly believed Father was still in Corrin. But she might not know, and she was one wrong question away from ignoring him in favor of her new subjects.

"Sorry. Is there anything you can do to help me hold back the madness? It's worse than before."

As he'd hoped, the question immediately transformed her attitude. She sat down at her desk, grabbed a nearby notebook, and looked up at him. "Tell me everything," she said, the experiment in the next room temporarily forgotten.

Quinton did, leaving out no detail he thought might be pertinent. When he finished, he waited expectantly. She looked over her notes and tapped her finger absent-mindedly against her chin.

When she shook her head, Quinton felt as though the tunnels had collapsed on top of him. "I don't think there's anything I can do. Before, your demon was dying, which was healed by contact with the nexus. But from what you're telling me, there's nothing wrong with you. The demon has recovered, and you've resumed your descent into madness, just like any other host."

"If I touch the nexus again, will it heal me?"

"No," Rachel's answer left no doubt in Quinton's mind. "We've connected plenty of demons who are in the latter stages of madness, and there's no difference between them and a younger demon. Obviously, I'd love to have you on the machine again, but for my own selfish reasons. I might keep your body alive, but I can't heal the madness."

Quinton took a deep breath and stood straighter. If he was doomed, he might as well meet his end in a dignified manner. "Thank you for your honesty." She could have lied to get him back on the machine without a fight.

He bowed. "Good luck with your research."

He turned and left.

It was nothing, he tried to tell himself. He'd always known, from the moment he'd welcomed the demon into his flesh, that his days were numbered. He'd done well with them and served the Creator like few before him had. This desire for more time was foolish.

He would spend what time he had left contemplating the glory and majesty of the Creator he served. And as soon as Father saw him, Quinton would die and enter the next life as a hero.

"You don't have to do this," Tomas told Angela.

The statement would get him in trouble, but it needed to be said again.

She didn't look at him as she answered. "As much as I appreciate your concern, I've already decided." Her reply was firm, but then she sighed and glanced at him. "Why does it bother you so much?"

"As long as I've known you, you've been a peacekeeper," Tomas said.

"And before that, I was in the army. This isn't exactly unfamiliar territory."

"I'd hoped you could keep it in your past."

Angela's attitude softened. "Me, too, but if there's ever been anything worth fighting over, I think it's this. I've seen what you've seen, and I know what's at stake. I *want* to fight."

"Will you be able to fight like this?" he asked.

She understood his vague question, and her answer didn't come as quickly this time. "I can. It's not what I'd like, but the way I see it, the guards' hands aren't clean of what happened. They stood by as Ghosthands herded innocents into a cargo car in chains. They're as guilty as he is."

Tomas swallowed the last of his objections when he heard the determination in her voice. Of course, she was correct. He didn't have the right to question her decision. "Then let's do this."

They found Hardin, Myra, and a young host named Alec waiting for them to the west of the camp. Another squad of hosts from Alliston lay in the grass and stared up at the stars. Gavan and a handful of his commanding officers were also present. They were standing with Hardin in a loose, silent circle. Farther to the west, a smaller group of Gavan's soldiers stood around three carts, loaded heavily with weapons Tomas didn't care to think about.

"Everything good?" Gavan asked.

"Solid," Tomas answered. Gavan waited for Tomas to elaborate, but the veteran host saw no need.

Gavan shrugged. They didn't have the time for long discussions or farewells. It would be an arduous journey already. "I suppose it's pointless to tell you how much is riding on this," he said.

"We'll do everything we can."

"As will we. We'll keep their eyes turned toward us for as long as we can."

Gavan wasn't pleased by his role in all of this, though he well knew there was none other he could fulfill. But the nature of their plan meant he wouldn't be in control of the most crucial parts of the fight. As they'd forged their strategy, there had been times Tomas thought Gavan might resign his command of the 34th just so he could join Tomas, Hardin, and the rest of the impromptu unit.

Tomas believed Gavan took solace in the knowledge that his role wasn't without risk. While Tomas and the others made their big move toward Corrin, Gavan would lead a dangerous assault to the south.

They said their farewells, and the hosts joined Gavan's soldiers by the carts. Gavan and his commanders rode south to meet with the main force of the 34th and begin their brutal march south. Tomas watched them go and wished them well, then turned his attention to the carts and soldiers.

This little expedition was commanded by a fiery woman named Hayla. Tomas knew her from his time with the 34th, mostly by reputation. Legend around the army camp was that she'd never failed to complete a mission given to her, even when a wiser commander would have retreated.

So she was the perfect choice for this wild deed.

Hayla gave the order to move out, and they started west. The carts groaned under their load, but once they picked up speed, they bounced happily down the rough paths leading toward Saxton. Tomas couldn't help but stare. He understood he was openly showing his ignorance of modern developments, but the carts handled the journey better than any he'd seen before. Given the weight they were carrying, Tomas would have expected to fix several broken axles back during the war.

After a few miles, Hayla gestured to Hardin, who nodded and passed on the command to the other hosts.

"You ready?" Tomas asked.

"I am."

Tomas hesitated for a moment longer, then let Elzeth burn.

After so long without Elzeth's aid, the extra strength felt more potent than usual. Tomas's senses sharpened as he kept pace with the other hosts, pulling away from the carts. His hands were steady, and he prayed they remained so.

Hardin led the way, bounding through the tall grass like a deer. Returning to the battlefield had been a beneficial change for him. In Alliston, his guilt had consumed him. But now that he was out, actively attempting to retrieve his friends, a good deal of his former personality had returned. He had a purpose, and Tomas almost felt sorry for anyone who stood in his way.

They would need that anger and skill, not to mention a whole cartload of luck. Tomas almost wished he believed in the Creator, just so he would have someone to pray to. On paper, the plan they'd come up with seemed perfectly reasonable, if one ignored the fact that they were attempting an infiltration into the very heart of church-controlled territory.

By the time Tolkin was high in the sky, Tomas and the others had run most of the way to Saxton and were several miles ahead of the carts. They rested as a group for a moment and caught their breath.

Hardin aimed his first question at Tomas. "How are you feeling?"

"Good enough for this," he answered honestly. He'd felt fine the whole night, to the point where he started to doubt how mad he thought he was.

Hardin sent them off in pairs in different directions. Tomas and Angela took the southernmost approach to Saxton. Their mission, the same as the other hosts', was to find any patrols and kill them without raising an alarm.

Tomas already knew what to expect, thanks to army informants living in the town. Two watchtowers stood on the east side of town, with clear lines of sight to any approach. A handful of patrols with dogs wandered even farther out, armed with rifles. The rifles served both as weapon and as warning. The church soldiers would defend themselves if necessary but were also trained to fire a round into the sky at the slightest sound of trouble. Dogs complicated the challenge. The sound of barking or gunshots would reach the watchtowers and warn the town.

It wasn't as secure as building a wall, but didn't fall much short, and apparently, the town was growing so fast that a wall would have been impractical. If there was any weakness to Saxton's defenses, it was that they didn't have many knights. The church, it seemed, was spread thin.

Gavan and Hayla trusted the hosts to be the spear that found the crack in Saxton's defenses. With their supernatural senses, the army commanders expected the hosts to get in close. Ideally, they would silence the watchtowers, too, but they had plans if that seemed an unreasonable ask.

Tomas and Angela proceeded slowly, using what cover was available as they advanced on the town. Thankfully, it was a cloudy night, which blocked most of Tolkin's light. Tomas kept Elzeth at a simmer, trusting Angela to carry most of the load.

To his surprise, they reached Saxton without crossing a patrol. He'd assumed that with his luck, he'd find the only patrol filled with knights. He and Angela crouched in a wheat field and studied Saxton.

The watchtower was the most prominent feature, standing thirty feet high and well-lit. It marked the southeast corner of Saxton, though Tomas suspected it wouldn't for much longer. Neighborhoods were bulging around it both to the south and the east. So far, they had kept the land around the tower clear, but it wouldn't be long before Saxton tore the tower down and moved it.

Farther to the west, Tomas could see the terminus of the

railroad tracks the church had built. An engine and cars sat there, ready to depart for Corrin first thing in the morning.

"How do you want to attack the tower?" Tomas asked.

Angela grunted. "Can't think of anything brilliant. I only see four guards within, and they aren't disciplined. If you let me use my rifle, I think I could kill them all."

"And alert the rest of the town? Sorry but no."

Tomas burned Elzeth a little brighter, so he could see more clearly. Angela was right about the guards. Four wandered around the watchtower, but they spent as much time looking at something inside the tower as they did watching their surroundings. They laughed at something, and one even leaned with their back to the outside.

Definitely not knights.

He didn't dare risk approaching straight on, though. The wheat fields weren't great cover, and one unlucky moment would be enough to jeopardize the entire mission. He was grateful for his enemies' incompetence, but he didn't count on it.

He pointed toward the south end of Saxton. "We work our way around and enter when they aren't looking. Then we approach the tower from the cover of the town. They won't be expecting an attack from that direction."

Angela agreed with the plan. They retreated until Tomas felt comfortable circling around and approaching the town from a different angle. He asked Angela to keep a sharp eye on their surroundings so he could let Elzeth rest. His sagani complained about being treated like an old man but became still the moment he was no longer needed.

The land within a hundred yards of the town's outskirts had been cleared, and Tomas and Angela paused there. Tomas reignited Elzeth and turned his gaze toward the tower. None of the guards were even visible.

Tomas didn't question his luck. "Let's go. Slow, though."

They broke from the cover of the fields and walked toward the nearest street. The back of Tomas's neck itched as though someone was standing behind him and staring hard. He fought the urge to run. On a cloudy night, sudden movement would alert the guards faster than a casual walk. The distance between them and the cover of the first houses seemed to lengthen, and Tomas was sure someone would spot them.

But the night remained quiet. Tomas released the breath he didn't realize he'd been holding when they took cover behind the first building. They gave themselves a minute to calm their nerves and listen for any sign Saxton had noticed their crossing. When Tomas was certain they were safe, they worked their way toward the tower, pressing themselves tight against the buildings so the guards wouldn't spot them.

A part of Tomas's brain screamed that it was all too easy, but he ignored the warnings. The church wasn't invincible, no matter how many times Ghosthands had gotten the better of him. At the last building before the tower, Tomas poked his head slowly around the corner. Fifty yards of open street separated him from the tower, but no one guarded the foundation. Tomas looked up and, once again, saw nothing.

He pulled his head back and whispered to Angela. "The way looks clear. Let me lead the way."

She looked like she might argue, but when she studied his expression, she relented. "I'll be right behind you."

Tomas expected nothing less. He poked his head around the corner one more time to ensure the way was clear, then ran across the street. Elzeth burned brighter, and they started up the stairs.

The solid construction of the tower made Tomas's

work easier. This was no rickety watchtower hastily constructed. The timbers that served as the tower's support were thick and dug deep into the ground, and the ladder didn't so much as squeak when he started climbing. Soft laughter from above masked what little sound he made.

He climbed fast, aware of how exposed the ascent left him. He reached the top of the watchtower and hauled himself over the lip. The guards were slow to notice him, as most of their attention was centered on a table in the middle of the tower. Some sort of game was being played, though Tomas didn't recognize it.

By the time the first guard saw him, it was already too late. Elzeth burned comfortably in Tomas's core, and Tomas drew his dagger. The first guard to die had his back turned to Tomas, allowing Tomas to plunge the dagger between the ribs and straight into the heart. He drew the blade across the throat of the second guard as he was about to cry out, then pounced on the last two as they retreated from the sudden and unexpected carnage.

The only sound they made was when their bodies slumped to the floor.

As soon as the last body dropped, Tomas let Elzeth rest. He felt unwell, though it had nothing to do with his encroaching madness. The guards had all been young and barely trained. Yes, they'd chosen to serve the church, and as Angela had said, they had likely watched Jonasson's hosts being marched like cattle without lifting a finger.

It still sickened him. He turned to tell Angela not to join him, but it was too late. She'd climbed into the tower a couple of seconds after him, but the battle was already over. He couldn't decide if the horror he saw on her face was something real or a product of his imagination.

He didn't want to stick around and think about it. "Tower's clear. Let's scout out the train."

Angela nodded, letting her stare linger on the corpses before she descended.

As Tomas followed, he understood how the years had altered him. Once, he would have taken pride in such a successful mission. Now he wished they'd been able to find another way. It made him think that maybe walking through the gate wouldn't be so terrible.

They rushed away from the watchtower, looking left and right for threats. The streets of Saxton seemed unusually quiet, though. Tomas was fairly certain it was because it was a church town, so there'd not be any places serving drinks this late, but it still made his skin crawl, like he was walking through a trap.

He took comfort in the dark shadows of the buildings. Once again, he asked Angela to take the lead, and she guided them down a narrow street that ran roughly from east to west. Tomas felt like a ghost haunting an abandoned city, but the illusion was dispelled when they found the train guards.

A glance told Tomas these were a higher quality of warrior than those in the watchtower. There were two pairs walking in steady circles around the train, and at least one wore a knight's uniform. Tomas and Angela watched them make several rounds, then ducked back into hiding.

"What do you think?" Angela asked.

"I'd like to wait for the others, but if they aren't here before long, we should move. The carts will arrive soon."

Tomas took heart because he hadn't heard any rifles yet. The quieter the night remained, the more likely it was that Hardin and the others had also been successful.

"I'll see if I can get higher and watch for them," Angela said.

Once she was gone, Tomas asked Elzeth how he was feeling.

"Not as bad as I'd feared. It's almost like old times."

"Almost."

Tomas appreciated Elzeth's forced good humor. Even if neither of them were sincere, it felt good to pretend.

Angela reappeared sooner than Tomas expected.

"Found Hardin and the others. They're heading this way."

Soon, the hosts reunited and shared their experiences. Hardin and the others had eliminated the remaining patrols and the other watchtower, meaning only the train remained. Now that everyone was here, Tomas let the others take the lead. He watched as the other hosts ambushed the train guards. Hardin himself took the knight, killing the man before he had time to draw his sword.

It was as successful a start as they could have asked for. Less than an hour later, the wagons appeared from the south. Hardin and the others had already opened all the cargo doors on the train and prepared the way. Unloading the weaponry from the carts took longer than Tomas was comfortable with, but soon they had everything aboard, including the wagons and their horses.

Everything was locked up and secure when the first alarms cracked the air. Fresh guards came to relieve the tired guards, only to find their friends fallen. They fired rifles into the air, and the silent town of Saxton stirred. They were too late, though. Hayla's engineer had the train ready. Tomas, Hardin, and others shoveled coal, and Hardin let the steam whistle blow long and loud as the train pulled out of the station. It was a defiant and triumphant shout.

The guards fired their rifles, but the steel of the engine protected them well. Two of the guards tried to jump on the train, but Angela swatted them off like flies with her rifle.

They left Saxton in chaos. Tomas leaned out the window of the engine and hollered, momentarily overcome by their success.

His excitement died quickly enough, though. Stealing a train had been the simple part of their plan. Now they had to reach the other end of the line and mount an assault in the heart of church lands.

26

"Do you have any idea what this is about?" Quinton asked Rachel. They were seated across from one another in a carriage, surrounded by an absurd number of knights.

Quinton didn't think Father traveled with such an escort, and he didn't understand why he wasn't allowed to walk. The tight confines of the carriage made him feel sick, and the knights had ordered him to leave the curtains on the windows closed.

If it was any consolation, Rachel didn't seem any happier. She flipped through pages in her notebook randomly, then closed it. She shifted uncomfortably in her seat, then opened the notebook again. "No, and I'm annoyed. I can't think of anything so important that Father couldn't have sent a messenger. We're too close to the answers."

The ride grew less bumpy as they entered Corrin proper. Quinton risked a quick peek behind the curtains. The knights hadn't thinned at all, meaning their carriage and escort pushed all other traffic off the road as they passed. He caught a few citizens openly staring at the carriage, trying to puzzle out who was within.

"I don't need such an escort," Quinton complained.

"Unless Father thinks you're in the grip of madness," Rachel said. "Although, in which case, I'd want to know why I'm here, too."

Quinton glared at her, but it didn't cause either the harm or distress he'd hoped for. She returned her attention to her notebook, studiously ignoring him. Quinton leaned back and closed his eyes. It was petty, ignoring her because she slighted him, but he couldn't deny he took pleasure from it.

They didn't stop outside Father's home but outside the enormous mission. The door opened, and the commander of the guards bowed deeply. "Hurry inside, please. We'll wait here for your return."

Quinton almost told the knight he would not return, but he held his tongue. He'd been back in Corrin for a week, and Father hadn't seen him nor sent him a message. His resistance to the demon crumbled, but he couldn't take his life until Father granted his permission. The lack of response added to his demon's frustrations over the last week and made him feel close to the three hells.

Father *had* to let him die today.

Quinton obeyed the knight and hurried through the main doors of the mission. Knights waited inside to direct him and Rachel down a long set of stairs to a vast underground maze of rooms. Aides ushered them through a large door.

A heavy oak table, polished until it shone, sat in the center of the table. It was full. Quinton recognized many of the knights around the table. Almost every commander in the region was here. Off to the side, Father sat on a raised chair, watching the proceedings.

Quinton took a knee as soon as he saw Father. Rachel did the same, though not nearly as enthusiastically.

Father gestured for them to rise, but Quinton's heart sank. He'd thought Father had finally summoned him to grant him his last request, but he wouldn't do so with all the commanders present. This was something else, which could only mean that Father had another request for him.

Quinton's knees trembled. He couldn't bear this burden for much longer. Even he had limits, and he feared he'd passed them weeks ago. He refused to give voice to his complaints, though.

Father said, "Quinton, Rachel. Thank you for coming on such short notice. We've been receiving disturbing reports throughout the past couple of days." He gestured for High Knight Davis to continue.

Quinton's position within the church meant he rarely crossed paths with the High Knight, but the man's reputation preceded him. He was a clever strategist but a master planner. It was his leadership that had swelled the ranks of knights over the past decade. He was competent, faithful, and long-sighted. Quinton considered him one of the church's best leaders.

Davis continued Father's explanation. "We've received pigeons from several sources, and we're putting together what happened. Boiled down to its essentials, we believe the 34th penetrated Saxton and stole the train headed for Corrin."

Quinton was dumbfounded, both because such a thing had happened but also because it was a foolish plan. What did they hope to accomplish? "How?"

"Reports indicate the 34th launched a two-pronged attack. Their primary force has been under the watchful eye of scouts ever since they made their way toward the demon settlements. They weren't there long before they started marching west." Here, Davis grimaced. "We underestimated them, though. The 5th was defending our borders and was more than ready for the conflict if the 34th tried to advance. They did, and the 5th sent them packing with heavy losses. But it appears that before the battle, a small contingent of warriors split from the 34th and attacked Saxton."

"But how did they steal the train?"

"They killed the patrols around the town, as well as the guards in the watchtowers, without raising an alarm. By the time the intrusion was noticed and our forces responded it was already too late."

A shiver went down Quinton's spine, and now he understood why he'd been summoned. It was the same reason they always summoned him. "They have demons."

Davis nodded. "That is our assumption, too. The 34th picked up demonic warriors in the settlements and is using them to strike at Corrin."

"Is this part of some larger strategy? What do they hope to accomplish?" Quinton asked.

"I wish we knew. As far as we can tell, there's no other coordinated effort among the army units. The main branch of the 34th has been repelled, so the borders remain steady. It seems a fool's errand, but we won't make the mistake of underestimating our enemies. We've bolstered our defenses around Corrin, and we've summoned both of you."

Father took over from Davis. "Quinton, I'd like you here as part of the defense of Corrin. I can't imagine what they're planning, but you and the host-knights will be the tip of our spear."

The orders felt like a punch to the stomach, and Quinton found himself at a loss for words. Fortunately,

Father's attention had already turned to Rachel. "Is the cannon ready?"

"It is."

Davis said, "Then prepare it for firing. We'll destroy the train before it arrives. There's no point risking ourselves by letting them get too close. For all we know, they've packed the train with dynamite and hope to explode it once it enters the city."

Rachel pleaded with Father. "Holy Father, isn't there any other way? The cannon is ready to fire as often as you wish it, but remember that demons are our ammunition, and I need them for my research. If too many die to power the cannon, I won't be able to continue my research."

The room went silent as Father considered the question. Quinton hadn't expected him to deliberate. High Knight Davis no doubt spoke with Father's voice, and such decisions were usually well-considered.

"How close are you? Honestly," Father asked.

"We're modifying the machine for a large-scale test. We already know the theory is solid, so the problems are more mechanical in nature and easier to solve. I could be ready to try within a day or maybe two."

Quinton couldn't believe what he was hearing. The fort buzzed with rumors of the long hours Rachel and her researchers were working. All the church's top scholars called her subterranean station home, and few ever saw the sun. But to hear they were so close was still a surprise. His thoughts turned suddenly from ending his life to surviving for the next few days. He wanted to see the results of all his sacrifices.

Father's chin fell to his chest as he pondered the question. The nearness of their ultimate victory seemed to catch him by surprise as well.

"I'm sorry, Rachel, but the cannon takes precedence. We will do all we can to limit the number of times we use it, but we can't allow that train to reach Corrin. We can always find more demons, but we've lost too many believers in this conflict already."

Rachel opened her mouth to object, but Father prevented her. "My decision is final, daughter."

She exhaled sharply through her nose but had the wisdom not to argue.

Father's sharp eyes found Quinton. "My son, I also know what you desire, and I know your struggle, but you must hold a while longer."

The statement left no room for debate, but Quinton wasn't sure he even wanted to. If they could destroy the train in one cannon shot, Rachel should still have plenty of demons to complete her experiments. The knowledge of the church's success could sweeten his eternal reward.

Quinton bowed. "Your will be done, Father."

(###)

Quinton stood on top of a high roof near the eastern edge of Corrin. Wind from the fields tugged at his hat, threatening to pull it off and send it sailing away. All around him, the highest-ranking church officials struggled to keep their vestments presentable. Fortunately for the cardinals and knights, no one in the crowd below paid them much mind. Every eye was turned toward the west, where the plume of steam from the incoming train could clearly be seen.

Quinton watched the scene with a growing sense of dread. He understood well enough what Father and the others intended by the demonstration, but it still represented an unnecessary risk. The power of the cannon would no doubt inspire the people, but only if everything went according to the plan. They had placed dynamite by the tracks less than a mile outside of Corrin, but it was reserved only as a fallback plan if Rachel's cannon failed.

Father would tell him to have faith, but Quinton believed there was a time for faith and a time for preparation. This was one of the latter, and they should have blown the tracks the moment they knew danger approached.

At least, he had one of the best views around. All the highest rooftops had been sectioned off for the church officials, and Quinton was allowed into one of the prized viewing areas. Crowds had gathered in the hurriedly constructed stands below, but the air of the gathering was more of a celebration than anything else. Everyone knew a train full of demons barreled toward them, but they gathered with their friends and their picnics to watch. Quinton admired their faith even as he cursed their foolishness.

The train was now clearly in view, and the excited babble of the crowd quieted in expectation. There was no official countdown, but Quinton knew before the others when the cannon was about to fire. Rachel had warned him what he might experience, but it still didn't prepare him.

One moment the world was peaceful and understandable, the next, he felt as though a thousand voices were screeching in his ear. His demon redoubled its efforts at breaking through its cage, and its attacks had a manic quality.

Quinton forced himself to stay standing, and he walked between the gathered onlookers with as much grace as he could summon. When he reached the west end of the roof, where every back was to him, he fell to his knees and clutched at his stomach. He swore he could feel the demon beneath his skin, clawing and biting its way out.

The moment passed, and though Quinton's knees trembled, he pushed himself to stand.

He was just in time to witness the awesome power of Rachel's weapon. She'd told him this one was bigger and more powerful than the design she'd used in Kimson, and it was terrifying.

He saw the wave of energy as a translucent haze arcing from the fort toward the train. Nobody around him reacted, leading him to believe he only saw it thanks to the demon's powers.

Everyone shouted when the power crashed into the train. The locomotive crumpled like a giant fist squeezed it, and after a moment under the cannon's power, it was tossed from the tracks like a hat caught in a tornado.

The cars on the train had lost their engine, but they'd built up so much momentum that it didn't matter. They ran into the wall of power and shattered under its assault. Train wheels, passenger benches, and windows went chasing after the locomotive.

It ended faster than Quinton would have believed possible. With one shot, Rachel's cannon had destroyed a train. Quinton looked down at his sword, feeling rather meaningless. What use was he when the church had weapons like that?

The crowd had gone completely silent as the train was destroyed, but now a cheer began that shook the roof Quinton stood on. Men embraced one another and pointed as children clapped.

Father's faith had been rewarded. The citizens of Corrin had long believed themselves special, but now they felt safe.

And why shouldn't they? With Rachel's cannon active, no one would be foolish enough to approach.

He climbed down a ladder to join some knights. Their duty now was to check the wreck and see if they could learn what the demons had intended.

It was mostly idle speculation, now, though.

Nothing could have survived that blast.

27

For as much pain as he was in, Tomas couldn't help but laugh at the scene. A few moments ago, they'd been sitting in a circle quietly discussing the night's assault, and then a moment later, they were all rolling around, clutching at their stomachs and trying not to moan too loudly. Two of the hosts were passed out, but when Tomas checked on them, their breathing was steady.

Tomas locked eyes with Hardin. "So, they've got a cannon here, too."

Hardin grunted as he forced himself to sit up straight. "Seems that way."

"You think we should change anything about our plan?" Tomas asked.

Hardin deliberated for a few minutes before shrugging. "I assume it's in the fort where they took everyone. I'm not sure I see how it changes our plans, but you're the one who actually had to fight it last time. If you'll remember, I was in a cage the last time it was firing. What do you think?"

Tomas had considered the question and reached the same conclusion. "If it's like Kimson, we might destroy it pretty easily." He tilted his head toward where Hayla and the soldiers of the 34th rested.

"That's pretty damn optimistic. You think it will really be that easy?"

"Not a chance, but a man can dream, right?" Tomas didn't think they'd leave the machinery of the cannon as exposed as before, but perhaps they had no choice. If it was exposed, Hayla and the others would destroy it quickly.

"I suppose you can. Speaking of, I'd like to get a bit of sleep while I can, and you should do the same."

Tomas nodded and took his leave. Hardin tipped his hat over his eyes and leaned back against a tree, and was soon fast asleep. Angela was, too, and Tomas envied them both. Normally he had little trouble sleeping on the eve of battle, but he had butterflies in his stomach like when he'd faced his examinations in the sword schools as a child.

He wandered near the edge of the grove and found a place in the shade. He didn't think sleep would take him, but he could rest. Hayla's soldiers had volunteered for the first few watches, but Tomas didn't want to disturb them. He leaned back against a tree and closed his eyes.

It should have worked. The last couple of days had been quite the adventure. They'd kept a full head of steam on the train the whole way to Corrin. Everyone had pitched in and taken turns shoveling coal. They'd blown through stations, fighting off whatever meager resistance the church assembled in each town. In most, a few squads of rifles rushed out to meet the train, but even bullets were useless against the massive engine.

One town had tried to block the line with crates and carts, but the cowcatcher lifted and split the obstacles and successfully kept the engine on the tracks.

They'd only slowed when they were several miles

outside of Corrin. A direct assault on the city was suicide, and they assumed the church would be well-prepared for their arrival. They disembarked, unloaded the horses, carts, and supplies, then started the train again. It charged toward Corrin, empty as a mission would be in Jonasson. Hayla ran up church flags on the carts and dressed everyone in church uniforms. The ruse wouldn't survive even a meager challenge, but they made a giant circle far away from Corrin that kept them in nearly empty farmland. Now they approached the fort from the south. The last few days were enough to make the most spirited warrior want a nap.

Sleep continued to elude Tomas, though. His stomach refused to settle, and it wasn't because of the cannon firing. When he held up his hands, they trembled. He'd felt fine burning Elzeth back in Saxton, but his worries had come true. The fight had sped his descent into madness. He'd need Elzeth at the fort, and he wasn't entirely sure he'd return from the fight, even if his body survived.

"Where's your head at these days?" he asked Elzeth.

The sagani, who had been resting as he usually did, stirred. "Truthfully?"

"Of course."

"It's hard for me to even think about. I'll confess there was a period where I looked forward to returning to a nexus. Sometimes I still feel a hint of that, but our recent explorations in the nexuses and the heart have made me realize something."

"That I'm the best host you're ever going to be with?" Tomas meant for it as a joke, but some bitterness crept into his voice.

Elzeth ignored the jibe. "That I think humans and sagani are supposed to work together. Even if you let me lead the way in the nexus, I still need you to survive.

Everything we've accomplished has been together, and knowing that I'm going to lose that makes me unbearably sad."

Tomas swallowed the lump that formed in his throat. "I assume you'll find a new host as soon as you can. I want you to."

Elzeth had no problem leaving the sincerity of his previous statement in the dust. "Oh, don't worry. The moment I'm free, I'll start searching for someone taller, smarter, and better looking."

Tomas snorted softly. "You're going to be alone for a long time if you're so picky."

"Are you kidding? I'm expecting a day of searching at the very most."

Tomas smiled, but the smile fell quickly. The shard of the nexus wrapped up in his pocket seemed suddenly very heavy. "I know we've talked this to death, but if you wanted out, I would understand."

Elzeth didn't reject the opportunity right away, and for a moment, Tomas worried the sagani might take him up on his offer.

"No," Elzeth said, "tempting as it is, I don't want to live knowing that I didn't do all I can here. And besides, given the number of researchers the church has in that fort, if we don't do something, it might be the end of me, too. It's worth the risk."

"I'm glad we agree."

Tomas opened his eyes and saw a large bird circling high above them. It was hard to see with the leaves in the way, but he thought he saw a glint of gold reflected in the bird's eyes. "Is that the same sagani from earlier?" he asked.

"I'm not sure. It could be, though it seems like one hell of a coincidence."

"You and I both know there's no such thing."

Tomas watched for a few moments more, then shrugged and closed his eyes again. The bird wasn't coming down, and Tomas wasn't about to break cover and attempt to chase it across the nearby fields.

His conversation with Elzeth had settled the butterflies in his stomach. So much so that he thought he might be able to sleep.

"Until the end, right?" he asked.

"Until the very end," Elzeth confirmed.

Neither of them said it, but both were thinking the same thing. The end they always spoke about was coming closer than ever. One way or another, they'd seen their last sunrise.

28

———

"Why are the gates open?" Quinton asked.

He had just returned to the fort. The guards at the gate had recognized him and let him pass, just as they would any other day.

Except this wasn't any other day.

Quinton had just spent the better part of his afternoon combing through the wreckage of the train, searching for any clue about what the demons had hoped to achieve. They'd found nothing, but that was evidence enough.

"The gates are always open during the day, sir," the soldier replied defensively.

"Close them now, and don't let anyone in until I speak with the fort commander."

Quinton went searching for the commander but stopped two paces after starting. He spun on his heel and stared at the guard. "I don't hear the gate closing."

The guard stared hard at the ground. "I'm sorry, sir, but you aren't my commander. I need someone above me to give the order. Until then, though, I'll make sure the guards are very cautious about who they admit."

Quinton stepped forward, then stopped himself. Shaking the soldier by the neck wouldn't accomplish anything useful. "Where's your commander?"

"I believe he's in the mess, sir."

Quinton made a straight line for the mess hall. Thankfully, the commander was there, eating with his officers. Quinton walked up to them and bowed. "Sir, I recommend we close the gates to the fort immediately."

The commander didn't dismiss Quinton out of hand. "Why?"

"I just returned from the site of the train destruction. There was no evidence that any demons were on board when the cannon hit it."

The commander's eyes narrowed. "And you think the fort is their destination?"

"I'm uncertain, but it seems the best guess. They'll be searching for the demons we took from Jonasson."

The commander decided quickly. "I'll pass down the orders. It would take more than they have to besiege this fort, but there's no reason not to be cautious. We'll be ready for them if they come."

Quinton thanked the commander, then searched for the person he most wanted to speak to. He suspected he would find her deep in the bowels of the fort.

As soon as he opened the door to the subterranean passages, a wave of heat and noise greeted him. Hammers clanged against steel pipe. The air was humid, and men shouted to one another. Sweat broke out across Quinton's forehead as he took his first step into the abyss.

All the defining characteristics of the tunnels had become more extreme since his last visit. More pipes ran along the walls and ceiling, many of them scalding hot to the touch. The growth of pipes made the tight tunnels nearly impassable. Quinton took one cautious step at a time, grimacing every time his bare hands brushed against the hissing pipes.

He passed bare-chested workers hammering, twisting, and bending the pipes according to a plan he couldn't guess. They made room when they could, but the going was slow.

At least the cages were quieter. There were fewer demons than when Quinton had first delivered them, and those that remained were subdued. Their lips were cracked and bleeding, their hair plastered with sweat. None shouted at him as he passed, which was a welcome change.

The demons harvested the fruit of their sins, and their punishment was sweet indeed.

Quinton passed the cages and knocked on the heavy steel doors that separated Rachel's research space from the rest of the tunnels. She, at least, had the good sense to keep herself safe. A bar of metal slid aside, revealing a peephole. The aide on the other side slammed the bar shut, then opened the door.

"Where is she?" Quinton asked.

"In the main chamber."

Quinton went straight there. The air here didn't press upon him as thickly as it had in the tunnels beyond, but it wasn't pleasant to breathe. Every inhale felt more like another's exhale than a proper breath of fresh air. Quinton wasn't claustrophobic, but the tight passages and nearly unbreathable air combined and made him feel as though the walls were closing in on him.

He found Rachel scurrying around the larger chamber, oblivious to the heat, the air, or the weight of the fort above them. It took Quinton two tries to get her attention, and even then, it seemed like she'd rather be doing anything else.

"How soon can you fire the cannon again?" he asked.

She looked puzzled by the question. "Within minutes. All we would need to do is grab some demons from their cages and attach them to the machine."

"Is there any part of the cannon or the machine that could be easily destroyed?"

Rachel shook her head. "We learned from Kimson. Unlike a traditional cannon, we don't need a barrel. Everything is underground, but why?"

"I believe the demons are going to infiltrate the fort and attempt to retrieve the ones we stole."

That finally focused Rachel's attention. "The odds of them reaching down here are slim, but why even take the chance?"

Now it was Quinton's turn not to follow. "What do you mean?"

Rachel's eyes glittered in the unnatural light of the chamber. "We've solved the last set of mechanical hurdles. The last I checked, the builders were telling me they needed another eight hours or so. But once they're done, we should be able to send a spear into the central nexus. It will kill all the nexuses, as well as all the free sagani. Never more shall demon and human flesh be joined."

Quinton took a step back. Her intensity unnerved him, but her declaration made his knees weak. Ever since he'd let the demon into his flesh, he had lived only to see the Creator's will be done. And he would live to see the fruits of his labor. It was more than he could have asked for. More than he deserved. His heart felt as though it might leap out of his chest.

He'd expected more fanfare, though, a ceremony with Father present. He wondered what it would take to have Father here, then dismissed the idea as foolish. They could send word to Corrin, so that Father could prepare for the moment in absolute safety. The Creator would tell Father when it was done. Quinton had no doubt.

Rachel inched closer, and Quinton realized she was waiting for an answer, though he didn't know what the question was. Then he understood. "Do it," he said.

She smiled, and it was one of the most terrifying visions Quinton had ever beheld. He was grateful that she was allied with him instead of against him.

He left her to her work. Until the spear launched, he would stand vigil and protect the fort. Already, a plan formed in his mind. One he expected the commander would welcome. Tonight, they would save the world. No matter what the demons intended.

29

They debated long and hard how to cover the final miles between them and the fort, and they didn't reach a conclusion until the sun had set.

Tomas had been the loudest voice arguing for a quiet approach using the tall wheat in the fields as cover. It would have been a grueling approach, with everyone crawling and carrying as much weight as they could, but he argued it provided the greatest opportunity to surprise the knights in the fort.

Hayla argued they should proceed as they had already, under the guise of a church caravan. The thought made Tomas's stomach churn. The cannon felt stronger than outside of Kimson, and he could imagine a dozen ways their plan could go wrong.

Hardin pointed out, correctly, that Tomas's method was no less fraught with danger and had the added drawback of exhausting and delaying them. Hayla's plan saved time and strength. In the end, her strategy won out over Tomas's objections.

As soon as night fell, they broke from the cover of the

grove, raised their church flags, and climbed into the carts. Hayla's soldiers bustled within the carts, preparing their weapons. Tomas watched for a bit, but his discomfort eventually forced his gaze forward. He rode as a passenger to save his strength.

He watched Angela walking ahead of him. The view slowly melted his worries away. It had been a great run while it lasted. "Elzeth?" he asked.

The sagani didn't stir, but he answered, "Yes?"

"Ghosthands is almost certainly at the fort. We'll need the nexus and unity if we're going to beat him."

"Last time, you couldn't bring yourself to do it," Elzeth said.

"I couldn't," Tomas admitted. How much of this could have been avoided if he'd just had the courage to fight with everything back then?

"I couldn't back then," Tomas repeated, "but I'm ready now. Are you?"

The sagani answered without hesitation. "I am."

"If the fight turns against us, you don't need to ask. Flee into the nexus. Please. There's no reason both of us have to die tonight."

He halfway expected Elzeth to argue, and the sagani was silent for several minutes. Eventually, though, Elzeth said, "Agreed."

"It's been good. Thanks for everything."

Elzeth's annoyance traveled through their connection. "Sentimentality doesn't suit you." Elzeth paused. "But you're right for once. It has been good."

Elzeth went silent again, and Tomas figured they had said all that needed to be said. They'd been too close for too long. Their feelings were obvious to each other.

Eventually, Angela climbed into the cart beside Tomas.

She said nothing. She just leaned against him, and he basked in the feeling of her shoulder against his. If he took any memories through the gate, he hoped this was one.

His peace and contentment faded as the fort finally came into view. Their trip had been quiet and fortunate. Enormous fields surrounded Corrin to support the growing population. Thankfully, they were sparsely populated. A few farmers had seen them and waved as they passed, never suspecting it wasn't a church caravan they greeted.

Despite their luck, Tomas didn't think they'd catch the church entirely by surprise. He didn't know what had happened to the train, but the church officials would certainly know something was wrong. And it didn't take a strategic genius to connect the short line between the theft of the train and the kidnapped hosts.

Their first glimpses of the fort confirmed it. The gates were locked tight and the walls crawled with soldiers.

It was nothing more than they'd expected, though, and they'd come prepared. Hayla's soldiers redoubled their effort at the sight, but the cart drivers kept prodding their carts forward. So far, their deception served them well, as there was no cry of alarm from the walls. Tomas would have given almost anything to know what happened within, though.

His shoulders tightened. Angela sat straight, and Tomas snuck a quick kiss. Then he crawled over her and dropped from the cart. He didn't want to be near the weapons when they went off, and he wanted to stretch his legs before the battle. If nothing else, he hoped it would reduce some of the nervous energy crackling through his body.

He kept glancing back at the carts, wondering when Hayla would call a halt to the advance. The soldiers had gone still, so their work was done. The decision to stop and begin the assault lay completely in Hayla's hands.

The closer they got, the more devastating their weapons would be, but they'd also be more exposed to rifle fire from the walls. Their advance also risked sacrificing their surprise. Tomas reminded himself to breathe. He shook out his arms and shoulders. The walls loomed ahead, and he swore they were in rifle range. Elzeth picked up on his nervousness, circling in Tomas's core like a dog chasing its tail.

Hayla rode on the lead cart, and Tomas wondered if she could feel every eye on her. If she did, she gave no sign. Her posture and bearing indicated nothing more than a bored soldier tasked with carrying goods from one fort to another.

When she raised her hand and gave a little wave, Tomas almost thought he'd imagined it. The motion was too casual, as though she'd just passed a friend on the road. But the cart pulled up to a stop, and Tomas knew the time had come.

No one spoke or shouted. They had drilled the plan relentlessly before they left. Each soldier and host moved quickly but silently. Those close to the weapons already had wax in their ears, and everyone else spread out into the wheat.

The sudden movement caught the attention of some guards on the wall, and a moment later, Tomas heard the peal of an alarm bell.

He swore softly. He'd even started to believe they might launch their attack without warning. Fortunately, it was too late for the warning to do much good.

Loud *thumps* announced the beginning of the assault. Hayla and her soldiers had carried four mortars and more shot than Tomas thought they could use in a week. It was, they hoped, the weapon that reduced this assault from impossible to merely very difficult.

Tomas had never seen the small cannons before, but he didn't like them any more than their larger brethren. Hayla's soldiers had trained extensively with the weapons, and their training showed. No sooner was the first shot in the air than a second was being prepared. Tomas had been told they had no specific targets. They only wanted to crack the walls open and kill as many people inside as possible.

One last time, Tomas was grateful for the information they'd gotten prior to leaving. Their informant had seen the inside of the fort and had seen no cells like the one Tomas had been a guest in outside Chesterton. The only part of the fort the informant hadn't been allowed to visit was the underground research station, so they operated under the assumption that was where the hosts were being kept.

It made sense. That was the same as the station Tomas had discovered outside Razin. The knowledge that the prisoners were safe allowed Hayla's soldiers to fire at will.

The first explosions rocked the walls. Some of the mortar shells fell inside the fort. Others struck the wall directly. One of the initial shells was short, and the crew altered the angle of their mortar in response.

Tomas ducked into the wheat as the church soldiers returned scattered rifle fire. He didn't hear any bullets pass too close, but he didn't fault the soldiers. If he was standing on those walls, he'd be seeking cover instead of returning fire.

Hayla's crew continued their shelling. The mortars weren't nearly as powerful as full-sized cannons, but they were still devastating. In a few minutes, the few rifles firing back stopped. Tomas stood and watched the assault.

Never before had he been more certain that the age that

was coming wasn't for him. Perhaps such weapons would quench humanity's desire for war. A piece of him wished it were true, but he feared they would instead just keep building greater weapons. He didn't want to watch the devastation the mortars caused, but he couldn't turn away.

Hayla ordered two of the mortars to shift their aim to the main gate. The mortars weren't strong enough to crack open the walls, but the gate might fall if given enough encouragement. Now the process changed. Instead of launching as fast as they could, each mortar crew fired, then waited to see where their shell landed. Eventually, they found their range and kept hammering at the door.

It lasted longer than Tomas expected. He supposed if he could say one thing for the church, they knew how to build. But the gate could still only take so much damage, and eventually, they broke open.

Hayla cut the mortars off with a sharp gesture. The last shell exploded near the center of the fort, and then the world went strangely silent. Tomas crouched lower in case one of the rifles on the wall had survived and sought revenge.

When no response came from the fort, Hayla ordered the carts forward. The crews remained ready with their mortars, but as the carts rumbled forward, they slung rifles across their backs and prepared for the next stage of the assault.

They reached the broken gate without a single shot from the walls repelling their advance. Hayla and her soldiers finally abandoned their mortars and dropped from the carts. Two crews remained behind, protecting the mortars and their escape. The rest of the soldiers fanned out, rifles forward and barrels pressed into their shoulders. Hardin drew his sword and walked straight for the gate. They didn't have time to waste. Corrin would already know of their assault and be gathering reinforcements. They needed to be gone by the time those reinforcements arrived.

Tomas entered the fort behind Hardin, then paused to take in the destruction the mortars had unleashed. The air was filled with dust. One long building on the southern side of the fort bowed almost to the ground. Bodies and parts of bodies were scattered everywhere. Tomas found himself grateful that the dust obscured the details.

He heard weak groans and cries coming from different corners of the fort, but the scene was all wrong. For as many of the dead and wounded as there were, Tomas would have expected more. The interior of the fort was nearly empty.

"I don't like the feeling of this," Hardin said.

"Same," Myra agreed, "but we need to explore if we're going to find our people."

They proceeded deeper into the fort. Tomas looked around, trying to imagine what it looked like before Hayla's mortars had fallen from the sky. In many ways, it reminded him of the fort outside of Chesterton. The walls were tall and sturdy, and most of the living quarters, storerooms, and offices were adjacent to or embedded within the walls, leaving a relatively large courtyard open for various purposes.

"Where's all the tubes and wires we saw in Kimson?" Elzeth asked.

The question froze Tomas in place. He hadn't even thought of that, and now he felt a fool for missing something so obvious. "Do you think we're in the wrong spot?" Tomas asked.

His worry grew as the dust settled.

It was too quiet, too easy, and the inside wasn't anything like what he'd expected.

Suddenly, he was certain that their information had been wrong. This fort wasn't where they needed to be.

He was just about to say so when doors opened around the fort and more knights than he'd ever seen in one place poured out.

30

During the peaceful days of his long meditations, Quinton had often speculated on what an eternity in the three hells of the old faiths would be like. He'd imagined all sorts of horrors, from endless battles to torture to gruesome deaths. Creative as his imagination had been, he'd never created a period of time as mind-numbingly terrifying as enduring the cannon fire in the tunnels beneath the fort.

The fort commander had heard Quinton's warnings and responded with a caution that saved not just their lives but very likely the future of the church. He'd kept church guards on the walls, but he'd ordered the dozens of knights into protected locations. Many were in the reinforced barracks near the walls' foundations, but Quinton and at least two dozen knights took shelter in Rachel's tunnels.

The air was thick with dust and exhaled breath, and Quinton's head pounded both from the effort of containing the demon and the constant hammering of metal on metal from deeper in the tunnels. Though the night air was cool up top, they only opened the door to the surface for brief periods. Quinton wiped the sweat from his hand and waited for the attack he was certain was coming.

At first, the initial explosions were almost a relief. The tunnel rumbled as the cannon fire landed. Lights flickered, died, then returned. As he was with knights, no one screamed or cried, but Quinton saw nervous glances and pale faces around him. Like many others, Quinton reached for his sword, though there was no point in drawing it. So long as he hid in the tunnel, he was more likely to hurt someone than he was to be useful.

The shells continued to land. Sometimes they hit a ways away, noticeable only as a slight tremor in the tunnel. Other times, they would land right above them. The wood supporting the tunnel would groan and bend, squeezing the knights and Quinton like they were worms caught in a fist.

Nothing Quinton could do would make any difference. The opening salvos of the battle were fired, and all he could do was pray to the Creator for His blessing. He was weak and helpless against these new weapons. If the tunnels survived the shelling, Quinton swore he'd never go underground again. Far better to die under the open sky with a sword in his hand.

What frightened him most, though, was the doubt that lingered in his thoughts. The bars of the mental cage trapping his demon weakened by the minute, and he swore he felt the tendrils of madness reaching out and wrapping around his mind. In the moments when his doubts were strongest, he took heart in the ceaseless pounding behind him. Rachel was close. They were all so close.

They only needed to survive this desperate attack.

In time, the cannons went silent and the tremors stopped. The knight commander cracked open the door to the inside of the fort. Thankfully, the doorframe hadn't been bent or broken by the shelling. Knights checked on one another, then turned the lights off in the tunnel, casting themselves into darkness. They sat in wait for the inevitable assault.

The traitors didn't make them wait long. The knight commander signaled that over two dozen invaders had entered through the main gate. Quinton wiped the palm of his hand one more time. He didn't plan on unleashing his demon unless absolutely necessary. Even without it, he was as good as almost any knight. Though, if it was demons daring to tread on this holy ground, he might have no choice.

When the invaders had reached the predetermined point, the knight commander gave the signal, and the knights poured out of the tunnel. Across the fort, the same scene was taking place from other fortified positions.

Quinton's spirits lifted as the knights roared. They burst from their hiding places like a massive lake bursting from the hold of a dam. Knights pushed him forward like a piece of driftwood down a raging river, his shout mixing with all the others.

A volley of rifle fire cut down several knights, but the distance between the doors and the invaders wasn't great, and the soldiers had no chance to fire a second volley. They clumped up tight, dropped their rifles, and drew swords.

The knights crashed against the invaders, squeezing them from almost all sides. Quinton crossed swords with one young man whose reactions were too fast to be human. Alone, it might have been an interesting duel, but Quinton didn't fight alone tonight. He deflected the demon's sword, leaving the demon wide open to the knight commander standing beside him. The commander's sword cut deep into the exposed flesh. The demon fell to a knee, but Quinton refused to give it any chance to recover. He brought his sword down, taking off the demon's head.

Unlike the old demon in the cave, this demon had the decency to slump to the ground when it died.

The demon's defeat gave Quinton an opportunity to look over the battlefield. Everywhere he looked, the story was the same. The overwhelming press of knights was too much for the invaders to handle. The point of their formation held strong, anchored by Hardin, who stood a head taller than anyone else. Quinton angled toward the giant demon, eager to end his life.

He stopped when he came across Tomas. Quinton would have guessed the demon was dead by now, but Tomas had never been good at understanding when he was supposed to die. Quinton shouted, but his voice was lost in the battle's din.

Any dream of controlling his sagani vanished the moment he saw Tomas. The reaction was so raw, so primal, Quinton wasn't prepared to deal with it. He burned his demon in the pyre of his anger, cutting at Tomas's neck with savage intensity.

Tomas leaned away. Then his eyes went wide when he saw who'd attacked him. Quinton cut up, then prepared to bring his sword down again. Tomas stumbled half a step back, eyes widening further as Quinton's blade reflected Tolkin's light. Quinton bared his teeth, certain of his victory.

A change swept over Tomas as Quinton struck the killing blow. The demon's eyes narrowed and glowed gold, and he slid aside with unbelievable speed. Quinton's certain victory blew away like a puff of smoke, and when Tomas struck back, Quinton wondered if he'd even survive.

He'd seen this strength and speed from Tomas before when he and the Family assassin had worked together to bring the demon down outside the train station. That spelled trouble enough, but there was a deeper change, too. Tomas fought with a calm detachment Quinton had never witnessed from him. In the past, about the only guarantee with Tomas was the fact he'd become too invested in the battle. He was an emotional child, simple to manipulate.

Not today. Quinton tried to draw him away from the other demons, but Tomas refused to follow, even when Quinton tempted him with openings. Quinton swore to himself.

His own demon reached through the bars of its cage, hoping to ensnare Quinton for good.

Faced with both an unflappable host and his damned demon, Quinton retreated from the front line. Eager knights jumped into his position, and Quinton took satisfaction in the knowledge that the battle was still over. Even Hardin was giving up ground as Bond and Fabian attacked him.

Quinton could wait a minute or two while the knights picked off the protection around Tomas. The invaders had walked straight into a trap, and its jaws had closed with devastating finality. Soon, Tomas would be alone, and Quinton could enlist the aid of his knights to bring the demon down once and for all.

The Creator wasn't just going to give the knights victory over the invaders. He was going to give Quinton the opportunity to rectify the mistake of letting Tomas live.

He was great indeed and worthy of Quinton's worship. Quinton smiled and dedicated this victory to the Creator.

31

———

Tomas should have known better. Their informant had told them the knights had a massive presence in the fort, and it was too much to think their stunt with the train had fooled anyone for long. Tomas had thought the mortars would make enough of a difference, but the flood of knights pouring out of the doors proved that assumption wrong.

The suddenness of the ambush gave them no time to think. Tomas stepped back so he was beside the others, then met the charge. Immediately, two knights teamed up against him. One cut high while the other cut low. Tomas deflected the blades and stabbed out at the closest knight but didn't score a hit.

Steel clashed up and down the lines. Tomas and the others had the advantage of being hosts, but they were severely outnumbered, and the knights were strong. Tomas cut down one knight, which gave him enough space to risk a look around.

He knew the signs of a losing battle when he saw one, and this was as losing a battle as he had ever seen. Knights pressed everywhere. Hayla's soldiers were already collapsing under the assault, and near the point of the formation, Hardin and Myra were hard-pressed.

Then Ghosthands was in front of him, cutting down with his sword. Tomas cursed his distraction and dodged away from the first attack.

For once, there was no need to discuss their decision with Elzeth. They had spoken before and fought with one heart. Tomas gripped the shard of the nexus between his hand and the hilt of his sword. He connected to it while dropping all the flimsy barriers that remained between him and Elzeth.

The transition only took a moment. Thought dropped from his mind as he dove deep into the present. He expected anger to accompany the transition. It usually flared when he saw Ghosthands. But instead of anger, he felt an unusual sense of calm. He met Ghosthands's next attack and pushed him back.

Surprised, Ghosthands took a step back, but Tomas did not pursue. Here, among the others, he might survive. But if he broke from the pack and pursued, enemies would close in on him from all sides.

Ghosthands tried to tempt him, but Tomas had no interest in pursuing. His pack was here, and they needed his help. He fought among the others, keeping the bloodthirsty knights at bay. With the help from the nexus, any church warrior who came too close to him met a quick end.

He felt pressure from the side, and when he glanced over, he saw that Hardin and Myra were being pushed back. Only host-knights possessed such a skill. Tomas searched for a way to help, but the press of bodies was too tight. Hardin and Myra were less than a dozen paces away, but they might as well have been on the other side of the continent.

Tomas redoubled his efforts, but Ghosthands interfered, protecting the knights near Tomas just as Tomas protected the hosts that surrounded him. The two warriors were islands of protection in the violently shifting sea of the battle, and the space between them churned with sharpened steel.

Instinctively, Tomas knew it wasn't enough. The knights fought relentlessly. One host fell behind Tomas, and he suddenly had to worry about the swords behind him as well as the swords before him. For every knight he killed, two appeared, eager to avenge their fallen friends.

He glanced back when he bumped into someone else. It was Angela, who had slung her rifle over her shoulder and turned to her sword. She fought a pair of knights, but Tomas trusted she had them well in hand. He turned to his own fight.

No knight could stand against him, and if he had more time, he might have cleared a path through the church's best, but their formation collapsed too fast. Tomas fought on, determined to find a way forward, even as every possibility closed.

In the middle of a cut, his stomach began to feel sick. He shoved the knight back and tried not to clutch his gut. Beside him, the other hosts suffered similar ailments. Tomas looked up, expecting to see the warping of the air that accompanied a blast from Rachel's cannon.

But the air was clear.

This feeling was familiar, but it wasn't the cannon. Where had he felt this before?

The answer bubbled up from a memory that wasn't his own. In the mountains to the west, it was a call from a sagani, ordering others to do its bidding.

But why here, and why now?

The hosts' distraction nearly spelled the very end of the desperate attack on the fort. Knights noted the weakness of their enemies and surged forward. Hayla was the last remaining soldier of those that had followed Hardin into the fort, and she fought with a careless disregard for her own life. Two more hosts fell.

Tomas wished he had the time to apologize to Angela for dragging her into all of this. If not for him, she'd be in Razin, a well-respected marshal. But the knights didn't even give him enough time for that.

He felt them before he heard or saw them. The rumble of their approach tickled the bottom of his feet, and when he looked, he saw something he had hoped never to see again.

It looked like the fields beyond the fort were alive. Hundreds of sagani, eyes glowing gold, charged the fort. The battle within the walls came to a standstill as knight and host alike stared in confused awe.

The knight commander didn't hesitate. He ordered the knights attacking Hayla to the gate. To their credit, they obeyed, though Tomas wasn't sure what they hoped to accomplish. Sagani didn't often attack humans, but when they did, the attacks were vicious.

A few knights made halfhearted attempts to resume the battle against the hosts, but every eye was inevitably drawn to the flood coming closer.

Overhead, a familiar sagani cried out. Tomas looked up and frowned. He couldn't be sure, but it looked so much like the bird from before, the one he'd seen since being outside of Razin.

There was no more time for wonder. The sagani charged into the knights guarding the gates, and the knights fell in a moment under the sheer mass of the sagani. Tomas turned away as the sagani tore into the knights with tooth and claw.

He felt no love for the knights, but he wasn't sure he'd wish such an end on anyone.

The fallen knights didn't distract the sagani for long. They pushed and shoved through the gate, flooding the area.

Tomas drew his sword and prepared to meet the new threat, though he doubted he would last much longer than the knights.

32

Quinton's mouth hung open. Demons flooded the fort, dropping knights left and right. The knight commander was one of the first to fall, throwing the rest of the knights into chaos.

He saw the demons avoid the invaders, and he snarled. Tomas still stood, surrounded by a meager number of his friends. He was responsible for this. There could be no doubt.

As much as Quinton wanted to punish Tomas, he couldn't. His demon had cracked the bars of its cage and fought for control. Quinton wanted to jump on the nearest knight and bite into his throat. The instinct was so strong that he was crouched and ready to pounce before he realized what was happening.

He couldn't be here, not if he wanted to help Rachel.

One glance around the fort told him all he needed to know. The battle, which had easily been theirs, had turned against them. Countless sagani burst through the gates, and it was only a matter of time before the knights were all killed.

"Retreat!" he shouted.

The order was superfluous. The knights who still survived were already running for shelter, and Quinton was no different. He cut down two sagani foolish enough to approach, then sprinted toward the door leading underground. He glanced back before shutting the door behind him.

The sight horrified him. Bond and Fabian were on all fours, killing one of their fellow knights. Hardin stood over them, sword raised high for the killing blow.

Quinton swore. He understood the temptation to recruit the host-knights, but the church still didn't understand the demons well enough. Bond and Fabian had been stellar knights. It was a shame to see them come to such an ignominious end.

There was no point worrying about it, though. He had his own life to save and a mission to complete, if that was even possible anymore.

A handful of knights had reached the tunnels before him, and he waited as long as possible to give others a chance. No one followed him, though. The demons bunched together to attack, so Quinton slammed the steel door shut. He turned to the knights.

"Guard this door with your lives. The scientists might still save us, but they're going to need all the time we can give them. Understand?" Quinton said.

The knights didn't look pleased with the order, but it wasn't like there was another exit out of the tunnels. They bowed. "Yes, sir."

Quinton raced deeper into the tunnels. They were as hot and dusty as ever, but the pounding of the hammers had stopped, and there was no flood of demonic creatures here, so he considered the tunnels quite the improvement over the surface. Behind him, the steel door shook as an enormous force barreled into it.

He closed each door behind him, ignoring the questioning looks of the workers. Most were sitting with their backs to the wall, sweat dripping down the sides of their dirt-stained faces. Quinton stepped over extended legs and ducked under newly constructed pipes. Eventually, he reached Rachel's research station.

She and the other scholars were clustered around each other, speaking so fast Quinton could hardly keep up. Rachel noted his arrival and glared at him. "What's happening up top?"

"Our position is overrun," Quinton said.

"How?"

"Sagani have flooded into the fort from the wilderness. I've never seen so many in one place, and they seem to be under the command of a more powerful force."

"Who?"

"Tomas, I think."

She scowled. "I should have knifed him when I had the chance. It's no matter, though, I think the machine is ready to kill the central nexus. Once it does, all the sagani in the fort should die."

That was exactly what Quinton was hoping to hear. "What do you need from me?"

"We have separated all the hosts from the humans in the cages. Ten remained at last count. Help bring the six strongest to the main chamber. Once we get them chained to the machine, we should be ready to fire."

Quinton nodded and gestured for some knights to join him.

He returned to the cages. The demons within stood now, listening to the steel door above bending against the relentless assault. Hope sparkled in their eyes, even if their bodies sagged when they stood.

Quinton opened up one cage that held two young men. They were emaciated, but they growled at him as he came close. Good. They had the fighting spirit Rachel desired.

As soon as the door was open, the young men attacked. Which was foolish. A moment later, they were both rolling on the ground, groaning. Quinton shook his head as the knights came in and shackled the prisoners. What good was being infected by a demon if you didn't even learn to make use of your new strength? He found these youths even lower than Tomas, in his estimation. At least Tomas knew how to fight for what he believed in.

The third and fourth hosts surrendered without a struggle.

Their next problem developed when Quinton pulled a young woman from her cage. Across the hall, where the humans from Jonasson were being kept, a girl cried out, "Mother!"

The young woman, who'd been cooperative, bolted. She picked up one of the knights and tossed him like he was a small bag of flour. He cracked against the steel of another cage, where the hopeful demons reached out and grabbed him. They tore at his uniform and held him firmly in place.

Quinton struck the young woman before she could harm the other knight. He slammed the side of his blade against her head, and she folded to the ground. Then he stabbed through the bars at the hosts that held the knight until they backed off. The girl in the cage cried, but Quinton ignored her. He urged the knights to get the mother chained and into the main chamber.

The last host he gathered by himself. She tried to struggle, but there was little fight left in her. He hoped she was strong enough for whatever Rachel needed her to endure.

He lingered for a moment longer. Up the hallways, the workers were waiting. There was nothing for them to do and nowhere for them to go. They were innocent, though, and thoughts of their predicament made Quinton want to swear. Beyond the workers, metal screeched as it bent under the force of the assault.

There wasn't much for him to do, either. He retreated deeper into the tunnels, locking the two steel doors behind him. Neither was as thick as the first, but they'd slow the demons down a little. When he closed the last door, he stood behind it, ready to defend the main chamber with his life.

He turned to watch Rachel and her fellow scholars chaining the hosts to the pillars. The knights helped, overpowering the weak hosts when they fought. Those Quinton had knocked unconscious were already in position.

The six hosts were arranged around the circular room. Pipes ran in every direction, a mess Quinton didn't think he'd ever understand.

When the hosts were all in position, Rachel and the others retreated. She went over to a large switch, then paused for a moment.

Quinton still wished there could be more fanfare. But at that moment, he heard the first door finally falling. They were out of time. He caught Rachel's gaze and nodded.

She smiled and nodded in return, then flipped the switch and turned the machine on.

Immediately, the air in the center of the machine distorted. Every host, whether or not they'd been unconscious, screamed.

Quinton struggled to describe what he saw. A darkness

spread in the center of the room, almost as if light was attempting to flee the space. He stepped toward the door, only to run into something that made his shoulder ache. He turned and saw a barrier protecting the room and the machine within.

He pressed against the barrier and was rewarded only with pain. He grinned. Even if the doors fell, Tomas wouldn't reach them.

He relaxed and let his eyes settle on the growing darkness.

"What is it?" he shouted.

He couldn't hear Rachel's answer over the screams of the hosts, but he could read her lips.

"The spear."

The darkness grew and solidified, and Quinton was enraptured.

All his dreams were finally coming true.

33

———————

Tomas had expected a fight, so he almost cut at the sagani before realizing they weren't attacking him or his allies. He stood in an eddy of a river of chaos. Knights screamed as the sagani tore them limb from limb. They fought with all the skill their training had granted them, but it was for naught.

The tip of Tomas's sword fell until it almost touched the ground. Grateful as he was to draw breath, he feared the horror of the moments would linger in his memories until the end of his days.

On the other side of the massacre, Tomas caught sight of Ghosthands running through a doorway and closing the door behind him. Tomas gripped his sword more tightly. That was where the prisoners would be, where Rachel and the others were.

He stepped forward, ignoring Angela's cries to remain. The sagani parted around him, feeding on the fallen knights. A pair of giant sagani, bigger than bears but maintaining a similar shape, slammed into the door Ghosthands had fled through. It shook but didn't break.

Tomas approached, leaving Hardin, Angela, and the others behind.

A shriek from above drew his eyes upward. The familiar sagani dropped toward him, this time in complete control of its descent. It spread its wings and landed two paces away. They stared at one another, then the bird spread out its wing and reached for Tomas. Its feathers brushed against his arm.

It wanted to step into the nexus together.

Tomas watched the enormous sagani pound at the door. It would be a minute or two yet, so he let the nexus pull his spirit in. He passed through the river of power without a ripple, the smoothest transition he'd ever made. On the other side, mountains stretched as far as the eye could see. He didn't recognize the area.

The bird appeared before him, human-sized. "Tomas and Elzeth. It's a pleasure to finally speak with you."

Tomas grunted. He'd heard snippets of the conversations between Angela and her sagani, but he'd never heard another sagani as clearly as he'd heard Elzeth in his head. The voice was familiar, though, another memory that wasn't his. A name rose, unbidden. "Telarion."

The bird bowed, eerily imitating human behavior. "Elzeth's memories have returned, then."

"Some." Tomas didn't have patience for the conversation. "Why are you here?"

"The same reason you are. To stop the children of the spires from destroying the world. We've been gathering for weeks to prepare for our own assault. When their weapon fired, we knew we could wait no longer."

Tomas frowned. "That was what happened in the woods, wasn't it? You were summoning sagani."

Telarion tilted his head to the side, then said, "Ahh, yes.

You witnessed that, didn't you? Yes. Safer to have my brothers and sisters rejoin the nexus and then be reborn out west."

"You organized all this?"

"Along with some of my brothers and sisters, sagani like Elzeth."

Tomas had dozens of questions, but they didn't have time. "They intend to kill the heart, if they can."

"We're aware. We'll break down the doors, but I fear we'll be too late. The children of the spires are clever. Already the machine draws upon the strength of the hosts."

"What can we do?" Tomas asked.

"I'm not sure. We'll see what's possible when the doors fall. Follow Elzeth's lead."

"Why?"

"He's unique, even among us. He's carried us through periods of darkness before. Now he might need to again."

Telarion threw Tomas out of the nexus, and he found himself once again in the fort. The sagani had finished their destruction of the knights, and with one loud roar, the oversized bears crashed through the steel door. As soon as the doors fell, the bears charged, only to be stopped by the narrowness of the tunnel.

The delay only lasted a few moments. The bears shifted before Tomas's eyes, becoming lean mountain cats with razor-sharp claws. The sagani rushed through the door before Tomas could get close, and screams echoed from up the tunnel.

Tomas followed, trusting the others to remain behind him. He hurried down the tight hallways. The floor was slick with blood and bodies, and he had to step carefully. A few sagani chewed on severed limbs, not even looking up as Tomas and the others passed.

"What in the hells is going on?" Angela asked as she caught up to him.

"The sagani are finally getting their revenge," Tomas said.

Behind Angela, Hardin swore.

The scent of blood and bile seared Tomas's nostrils, but he kept walking. He heard the second doors crash, and he wondered what form the sagani had used to accomplish their goals. No screams accompanied the destruction. Tomas heard the meaty sound of swords carving into flesh, but the forward press of the sagani never faltered.

When Tomas passed the site of the battle, he barely recognized the knights' uniforms. Again, the sagani munched happily away. Myra finally could take no more and threw up. They went deeper and found cages filled with familiar faces.

"Find the keys and free them," Tomas called to Hardin and Myra, "then return to the carts and retreat."

"We're not leaving you here," Hardin growled.

"Church reinforcements will be here soon. Only Ghosthands remains, and Angela and I can handle him."

Hardin was about to argue some more, but Tomas cut him off. "This is why you came. Don't throw away your chance to save your people."

Hardin swallowed his objections and nodded.

Tomas and Angela left the cages to the other hosts and proceeded deeper into the dimly lit station. The sagani hammered on another steel door up ahead. Tomas figured this was the last. Even he could feel the power gathering directly ahead.

Tomas turned a corner and found the sagani finishing their task. The hallway opened up before the last door, and the sagani had assumed the shape of bears once again. The bears knocked down the last door without a problem, but when they tried to enter, something threw them back. The force of the recoil launched them at Tomas, but the hallway narrowed, and they struck the walls and stopped.

They lay on the ground and shrank to the size and rough shape of dogs. Tomas knelt next to them. Their chests still rose and fell. He patted them. "Rest now. You've done enough."

He stood and strolled toward the doorway. The air just on the other side shimmered like the surface of a bubble. Ghosthands strutted on the other side of the disturbance like a fighter who'd just won the duel of a lifetime. Behind Ghosthands, a void grew and spread in the air. It reminded Tomas a little of the vision he'd seen in the heart. The weapon was pure black, with hundreds of cut edges that gave it the shape of an enormous carved diamond. Its strength was already unbelievable, and it was growing by the minute. That was the spear Rachel intended to send into the heart.

Tomas extended his hand until he touched the shimmering surface. It vibrated like a bell. After a moment in contact, his arm bones felt like they were about to vibrate out of their joints. He removed his hand and shook it out, waiting for feeling to return.

Sound traveled through the barrier without a problem. Tomas endured the screams of people he'd met in Jonasson as the machine drained them of their lives. Rachel laughed at Tomas and said something to one of the other scholars about learning from her past mistakes.

A smarter man might have come up with a different plan, but Tomas had always believed the most straightforward approach was the best. He pointed the tip of his sword at the barrier and pushed. When the tip struck, light flared so brightly he had no choice but to close his eyes.

Both sword and arm vibrated, but he just shoved harder. He planted his feet and dug in with his toes. No machine was going to stop him.

Angela stepped up beside him, took her blade, and mirrored him. He felt the barrier bend as she added her strength to his. He nodded and pushed harder. Teeth gritted, he channeled more strength through the nexus.

The barrier warped. Rachel swore.

Then the barrier shattered, and Tomas and Angela were through, standing next to Ghosthands. Tomas struck at the surprised host, driving him back. Their swords crossed as sagani poured in behind Tomas. Tomas didn't know if it was surprise, if he was fighting better than he ever had before, or if it was something else, but for once, he was faster than Ghosthands.

He knocked Ghosthands's sword away, and the host dropped to all fours and snarled. Tomas was about to finish him when a motion out of the corner of his eye drew his attention.

As he'd fought Ghosthands, Angela had advanced on Rachel, who looked at Angela as though she stared at a ghost.

"I killed you!" she screamed.

"Almost," Angela said and raised her sword.

Rachel lunged for a switch on the wall. Angela cut, severing the lower part of Rachel's spine, but Rachel still reached the switch. She wrapped her hand around the handle and pulled down.

Tomas swore.

Angela stepped forward and cut again, killing the church scholar for good.

But it was too late.

The black diamond in the middle of the room shot straight toward the heart at the center of the planet. It passed through the stone without disturbing it, but Tomas felt it traveling toward the core.

The sagani in the room savaged the last of the church scholars while others ripped apart the machine with claws that tore through steel like it was warm butter. The machine would never fire again, but it had already done its duty.

The weight of their failure threatened to crush Tomas. They'd given everything. He met Angela's gaze and saw his own shame reflected there.

Something in his core pulled toward the nexus in the room, the heart of the machine.

Tomas didn't question the desire. He stepped toward the nexus and raised his hand, then saw Angela following.

His throat tightened. This journey wasn't one he was coming back from. He turned to Angela and kissed her, lingering longer than he should have. Then he stepped back. "I love you. But please, don't follow me. I'll wait for you on the other side of the gate."

She nodded, tears in her eyes.

He turned back to the nexus and extended his hand. The last thing he heard was Angela saying, "I love you, too."

34

When Quinton's senses returned, he was on hands and knees, the bloody corpse of a church scholar beneath him. He scrambled back until he was pressed against a wall. The sagani destroyed the room, wrecking years of work. Even worse, they were slaughtering the last of the scholars, a loss that might set the church back even further.

Where was the weapon? It had been here a moment before, but now it was gone. Had Tomas and his allies destroyed that as well?

Then he felt the answer. It was below him, dropping fast. He'd recognize that feeling anywhere.

He slumped back against the wall, already feeling the impulse to get back on hands and knees and resume feeding. His demon had broken free of its cage, and he'd lost the will to fight back.

Until he saw Tomas step toward the nexus and *disappear*.

Even now, that sinful bastard sought to destroy everything Quinton stood for.

And once more, Quinton would stop him.

He grabbed his demon by the throat and squeezed every drop of strength from the creature. He found the strength to stand, then the strength to run. Angela had thought him out of the fight and was still stunned by Tomas's disappearance. He sprinted by her before she could react and jumped, hand outstretched, toward the nexus.

The power was unlike anything he'd ever known. It filled his muscles and veins, stretching his skin until he thought he would burst.

But he wasn't here for power. He was here to kill Tomas. As soon as he focused on the thought, it became real, and he was standing before his hated enemy, who'd been sprinting across an open prairie.

Quinton appeared in front of Tomas, and the demon came to a stop, confusion written on his face. "Ghosthands?"

"It's too late! You can't stop Rachel's spear."

Tomas cocked his head to one side, staring at Quinton like a curious owl. "I think I can. Time runs differently here. I can be at the heart in a moment, then search for a way to stop the spear."

Quinton drew his sword. "You'll have to get past me first."

Tomas vanished. Quinton cut at where he'd been, but there was nothing, not even bent grass on the ground where he'd stood.

Quinton sensed a presence behind him and turned. Tomas stood there, as calm as Father when he meditated. Quinton choked the last strength out of his demon and attacked, but Tomas batted away the sword with the side of his hand. He moved so fast that Quinton barely caught the motion.

"You can't beat us here," Tomas said. "Not the way you fight your sagani."

Quinton roared and cut at Tomas's neck. Tomas took the blow without moving, and the sword barely scratched the host's skin.

Something inside Quinton started to realize Tomas might not be lying. His determination cracked but still held. He pushed harder on the sword, but it didn't budge. "Why?"

Tomas shook his head. "For the longest time, I tried to figure out why you were so much stronger than me. I thought maybe you'd found a way forward, like Ulva. But it was always much simpler than that, wasn't it? I can see your sagani here, beaten and bruised almost beyond recognition. You squeezed it for everything it was worth, which made you one of the best swords in the world. Maybe even the best. But it makes you weak here. Here, the closer you are with your sagani, the stronger you are."

Quinton swore and attacked. Tomas sighed and kicked him in the chest. Again, Quinton barely saw the move. One moment he was swinging his sword at Tomas, the next, he was on his back, staring up into a partly cloudy sky, and his ribs felt like they'd cracked.

He sat up just in time to see the grass off in the distance bend. The disturbance rushed toward them both, and when it passed over them, Quinton's eyes went wide. When the wind blew past his ears, he was again in that place he'd found when he'd first joined with his sagani, and the wind was the voice of the Creator. It was the same force, the same order, that had called him to his second life.

Tomas looked back in the direction the wind had come from, but Quinton repositioned himself on his knees. He clasped his hands together. "Holy Creator, your will be done!"

He'd never felt it so clearly.

Tomas turned back to Quinton, his eyes narrowed. "You believe that is your Creator?"

"How can you not? Can you not feel its goodness? It is the order in a fallen world."

Tomas continued to stare at him strangely. Abruptly, their surroundings disappeared. They floated in a void, but it wasn't the emptiness of Rachel's weapon. Quinton felt the presence of the Creator surrounding him, embracing him.

Tomas spoke softly. "The prairie was my creation. The expression of my will upon the nexus. Without it, what do you see? Look deeply."

Quinton searched, hoping to find the answer to Tomas's power in this place. He fell into a meditative state and allowed his awareness to expand.

He'd done the same hundreds of times in the home Father had given him as a gift for his service. Alone on the frontier, he'd always been aware of the weighty silence of open places. It had covered him like a warm blanket, reminding him he was just a small piece of a much larger plan.

Though his eyes told him he stared upon an endless darkness, his other senses told him the space was alive with the Creator's presence. As he sat with the presence, it took form, becoming the most intricate and expansive spider web he'd ever seen. It became visible, faint at first, but growing more clear as his awareness expanded further.

"What is this?" he asked.

"You already know," Tomas said.

Quinton didn't, but the sight stole away any of the anger he should have felt. He continued exploring, and more detail resolved itself. And then he realized Tomas was right. He did know. He felt the nexuses, the demons—no, the sagani, and humans, all connected.

The Creator pulsed through them all.

The Creator pulsed through them all.

Quinton shook his head, recoiling from the very image he'd created. "No." He shook his head harder. "No. It can't be."

Tomas said nothing, and it was the most compelling argument the host could have made.

Quinton took a step back, then another, but the image followed him. He pointed his sword at Tomas. "You're doing this! You've never done anything but lie, and this is another deception."

"Trust your senses," Tomas said. "Is that what they're telling you?"

"You're deceiving my senses!"

"You know that's not true. Be brave, Ghosthands. Find the truth for yourself. It's right in front of you, maybe for the first time in your life."

Quinton calmed his pounding heart. If this was a trap, an intricate lie Tomas had created, Quinton would find the way out. Tomas was nothing compared to him. If he had mastered this space, Quinton would still surpass him, and the process started with becoming more aware.

He let his awareness expand, probing his surroundings with his complete focus. He turned first to Tomas, seeking the evidence of his wrongdoing.

All he found was more surprises. Tomas had claimed he could feel Quinton's sagani, a claim Quinton had dismissed as a lie. Except now that when he focused, he could feel the same. Tomas and Elzeth were unified, two that had become one. If he pushed his senses hard enough, he could feel the thousands of connections between human and sagani forged through a lifetime of cooperation.

That wasn't all he felt. One connection was brighter than

the others, and when Quinton followed it, he shook his head again. It couldn't be.

But then the connection pulsed again. The feeling was as clear as a cloudless sky. Elzeth and the Creator were connected with a glow that was far brighter than Quinton's own.

Quinton followed the thread from the demon, and it ended at the central nexus, which pulsed with the love of the Creator.

Tears fell down Quinton's face, and he threw his awareness at the central nexus, searching for the lie that had to be there.

Except there was nothing. His senses weren't being deceived. Tomas and Elzeth did nothing.

The Creator was within the central nexus, and he sent a spear at the Creator's heart.

Everything was wrong. The church was wrong about the sagani, wrong about the primacy of humanity. His world was made of crumbling bricks, and he couldn't hope to hold them together.

The enormity of the error froze him in place.

Then the moment passed. He felt empty inside, as though his demon had carved out his insides and served them for supper. When he'd been younger, he'd believed the world was meaningless, and he'd almost lost his soul to that realization. Then he'd found the Creator, and that brief encounter had made meaning out of the chaos.

What did he do when he learned the Creator wasn't what he expected?

"What does any of it matter?" he asked Tomas bitterly.

The host swept his arm back so that he encompassed the whole image Quinton had created. "How can it not? We're all connected."

Quinton closed his eyes, shutting out everything. It couldn't be. He couldn't have been so wrong.

Quinton chuckled. The chuckle grew louder until he was laughing so hard he was holding his gut. In time, he regained control of himself, and he felt better than he had in ages. He pushed himself to his feet and grasped his sword in both hands.

"If I'm going to be the one that helped kill the Creator, I might as well kill you, too."

His heart felt light. If nothing mattered, he could do as he wanted, and he wanted to kill Tomas more than anything in the world. He hated the sight of the host and hated him more now that he'd stripped away Quinton's illusions.

Tomas didn't draw his sword.

Quinton shrugged. He burned his demon hotter than ever before, demanding everything. He leaped forward with a yell.

Tomas blinked out of existence, then reappeared in front of Quinton. He punched before Quinton could cut down, but when the punch landed, Quinton didn't feel the impact. It was as if Tomas's hand had passed through him.

Quinton landed and spun around, ready to pass again, but he stumbled. He clutched at his chest, not understanding.

Tomas had his back to Quinton, and he was kneeling. Beyond Tomas, a snake was slowly gliding away, returning to the central nexus.

Quinton raised his sword and stepped forward, but a sudden pull arrested his movement. He glanced back and saw a gate, glowing the same pale blue of the nexuses. His eyes went wide, and he swore. He scrambled forward, but the gate grew larger.

"No!" he shouted. He stabbed his sword down, searching

for purchase, but the blade struck nothing. The pull of the gate was irresistible.

"I'm going to kill you!" Quinton shouted.

And then the gate took him, and the last of his worries disappeared.

35

Tomas watched the gate fade. He'd always thought there would be some greater feeling of triumph. When he'd imagined defeating Ghosthands, he'd imagined rejoicing above a corpse and buying drinks for anyone nearby. Today, the victory left him somber. He would make the same journey through the gate soon enough, and Ghosthands had died as broken as he'd lived. There seemed little reason to rejoice.

There was also little time.

He'd probably taken too long fighting Ghosthands. Time passed much slower here, but it still passed. The spear rushed toward the heart, and Tomas didn't have the slightest clue how to stop it.

He blinked and appeared at the entrance to the heart. The darkness of the spear grew closer, blotting out the sky.

Tomas stared at it. Here, in the nexus, the weapon was no longer the enormous dark diamond. His imagination and will had shaped it into an actual spear. Both shaft and point were a lightless black, and it was hundreds of feet long.

It fell slowly, Tomas's perception far faster than the progress of the weapon. But as it fell it cut through the heart's connections. Here, it meant the sky darkened, but Tomas understood he was watching dozens of nexuses and sagani die.

With an effort, Tomas started rebuilding the wall that separated him and Elzeth. The sagani helped. The process wasn't easy, but it was less difficult than it had been on their last few attempts. Once Tomas felt himself again, he turned to his sagani for advice. "Telarion said I should follow you. So what do we do?"

He felt Elzeth questing toward the spear with his senses. Finally, he said, "The heart needs a shield."

Tomas nodded. It had been one of his ideas, too, but he didn't know if it was a good one or not. He trusted Elzeth's instincts, though. In unity, perhaps they'd have enough strength. Elzeth could pull from the heart.

"Together until the end?" he asked.

Elzeth didn't answer.

"Elzeth?"

"I think this is where we part ways, old friend," the sagani said.

Tomas stepped back as though it was possible to run away. "What do you mean? Didn't you say we needed to be together to have any effect on the heart?"

"I did, and I'll hold on to a single thread to satisfy the heart, but I'm not sure I'm strong enough. I'll try first, and if I fail, well, then it'll be up to you. Best to have two attempts instead of one."

"We're stronger together, Elzeth. We always have been."

"We can't risk it. Two shields against the spear are better. And I think I can draw more from the heart if I don't have to worry about your well-being."

Elzeth started to pull away. A glowing head grew out of Tomas's stomach, and it felt like his insides were being ripped away. Tomas clutched at his gut as though he could hold Elzeth in with his hands.

They did not deter Elzeth.

"Stop," Tomas groaned.

"I'm sorry, friend, it's the best way."

Tomas clutched onto Elzeth with his mind, locking the sagani in place. "I can't do it without you."

The fragments of Elzeth that had escaped lost their form. They floated until they surrounded Tomas, then gently squeezed him. The glowing embers warmed him.

"It's time, Tomas. You need to let me go."

Tomas squeezed his eyes shut and shook his head, but he released his mental grip. It reminded him too much of Ghosthands, choking the life out of his poor sagani. If this was the end, he could at least meet it with more dignity.

Elzeth resumed pulling away, and the pain surpassed anything Tomas had experienced before. Even the inquisitors of the church had never hurt him like this. He was being torn apart.

The feeling wasn't just in his head, either. He watched some of Elzeth's fragments pull away from his body, and it was as though a thousand tiny hairs had intertwined with his bones, muscles, and sinews. The sight reminded Tomas of their experience in the heart, where Elzeth had made countless tiny connections.

The sagani had done the same in Tomas's body, a process that had probably been going on for years. Now he broke those connections, not with a clean cut, but with a brutal pull.

Tomas's legs gave out, but there was nothing for him to

fall onto. He floated by the heart as his companion finally left him.

They'd agreed to let Elzeth return to the nexus, but it took all of his will not to force Elzeth to stay.

Finally, it was done. Elzeth had returned to his feline form and stood apart from Tomas. One thin connection between them remained, allowing Elzeth more control over the heart.

The spear grew ever closer. It ripped through connections to more nexuses as it approached, killing them with a touch. Even with time passing differently here, Tomas guessed they didn't have more than a minute or two before the tip of the spear struck the heart. Elzeth looked up. Then he stared at Tomas. "It's been an adventure, old friend."

Tomas twisted until he felt like he was standing. With Elzeth mostly gone, he felt the pull of the gate. He didn't have long. "Let me. That way, at least one of us survives."

"You don't have the strength, Tomas. Humans are still too far removed from the heart."

"Then why split up? We're both going to die, anyway."

The mountain cat shrugged his shoulders, an absurdly human-looking gesture. "Even if I fail, perhaps I'll weaken it enough for your strength to be enough. This is the way."

Tomas's throat tightened. He trusted Elzeth more than he'd trusted anyone in the world. "I know. I just—"

His voice cracked, and he couldn't continue.

"I know. Me neither." Elzeth paused. "Thanks."

Tomas nodded. "They've been the best years of my life."

Elzeth nuzzled up next to Tomas, and Tomas wanted to embrace him and pull the sagani back into his core. He held the mountain cat tight, soaking in his friend's power. His own body felt weak and shredded, emptied of its animating force. Finally, he let go.

Elzeth took a step back, then leaped toward the spear.

The sagani trailed countless threads behind him, and as Tomas followed them, he saw they connected to the heart. Elzeth glowed brighter and brighter, the contrast more pronounced as he neared the falling spear. Rachel's weapon overshadowed Elzeth, and it seemed impossible the tiny sagani would have any chance. But soon, he was glowing brighter than the sun, and Tomas had no choice but to look away.

The pull of the gate grew stronger. When Tomas glanced back, he saw the pale arch welcoming him after their long time apart. He could still resist the pull, but not for much longer.

The light surrounding Elzeth focused into a small round shield, floating just above the sagani's head. Elzeth dipped his head down a moment before impact, so the shield caught the spear dead center.

The collision shook the void. Light and darkness fought for dominance. The reality of the nexus warped, making Tomas feel like a piece of paper being folded, twisted, and torn.

The light of Elzeth's shield faded. Darkness pressed against it, seeking to devour the sagani on its way to the heart. Strong as Elzeth was, the spear hadn't been stopped. It kept falling toward the heart, as though pushed by an army of angry warriors. The nexus grew darker and colder as the spear fell closer. Tomas tried to position himself between the spear and the heart, hoping to honor Elzeth's wishes by acting as a second shield.

His body refused his commands. Even in this space, he

no longer possessed the strength to fight. And the gate pulled him farther away from the battle.

He watched the spear descend, and he bowed his head. Elzeth's shield had almost faded completely, and the sagani was moments away from failing.

An unexpected warmth made him look around. Floating threads, like spiderwebs blowing in a gentle breeze, surrounded him. They were glowing with a faint light, the same golden color as a sagani's eyes.

The light grew brighter and warmer until Tomas was surrounded by blazing tendrils of light. The tendrils shot upward, wrapping themselves around Elzeth's shield until it glowed brighter than the sun.

Once again, hope and despair warred, the duel balanced on the edge of a razor-sharp blade. Tomas had no idea how Elzeth channeled the power he did. The sagani had somehow known. Attempting this would have killed him.

Then Elzeth's shield exploded, and a wave of light and dark consumed Tomas.

36

When Tomas opened his eyes, he lay directly before the gate. The heart was behind him, beating as strong as it ever had. Tomas closed his eyes and allowed himself to feel the power of the heart, calm as a frozen lake.

Elzeth had won, then.

Tomas looked up, but there was no sign of the sagani.

His chest tightened. It wasn't fair. It should have been him. Elzeth could have lived on, could have helped another host.

He understood it couldn't be any other way. His own strength was nothing compared to the weapon Rachel had created. Elzeth, as usual, had been right.

He stood, brushed himself off, and took a step toward the gate. His body was in shreds, and Elzeth was too dead to heal him. The fact he'd lived this long without Elzeth was remarkable, but he could feel his body failing. Every organ, muscle, and bone had been connected with the sagani, and now they were all breaking together.

His eyes narrowed.

It *was* remarkable that he'd lasted this long without a

sagani. As far as he knew, the moment a sagani left the host, the host died. As much as he wanted to believe that he was special enough to break that rule, he wasn't convinced. Sure, he was at the very gate of death, but he wasn't on the other side.

Why not?

He sought for Elzeth, hope bursting in his chest. Try as he might, though, he could see no sign of the sagani. The pull of the gate grew stronger, and he took a step forward before realizing how close he was.

He searched one last time. Elzeth had kept a thread between them, so where was it now? Tomas turned his attention inward and found it, one weak thread connected to his core. He followed it, then stopped.

It led straight to the other side of the gate, which was why he hadn't noticed it earlier. It pulled him just as the gate did.

But it wasn't broken.

Tomas wanted to see Elzeth one last time. He grabbed at the thread and pulled.

At first, nothing happened. His fingers slipped on the thin thread. He wrapped the thread around his hands and pulled again, planting his feet. His muscles groaned with the effort, and he leaned back to counteract the pull of the gate.

The thread began to move. Tomas wrapped another length around his hand and pulled again, then again. He picked up speed, and soon he was pulling as fast as his arms could haul the thread in. He no longer had to fight the thread, but he had to resist the pull of the gate.

Elzeth emerged headfirst, as though the gate was a deep lake and he was surfacing from swimming underwater. The gate rippled, then was still. Elzeth floated beside Tomas but didn't move for several long moments.

Then he looked up, lethargic. He blinked, then stared at Tomas as though he were a stranger.

"Tomas?" Elzeth asked.

"Good to see you, old friend."

Elzeth looked back at the gate, still coming to his senses. "I died."

Tomas grunted. "Happens to the best of us."

"You saved me."

"Don't worry, I won't be around long enough to rub it in your face."

With that, he surrendered to the pull of the gate. It drew him toward its welcoming embrace, but Elzeth stood between him and the gate and stopped his progress. A thin hope bloomed in Tomas's heart. "Now that you're alive again, I don't suppose you want to hop back into this body, do you?"

Elzeth shook his head. "I don't think I can. Whatever I am, I don't think I'm a sagani anymore."

Tomas's hope died, but he put a smile on his face anyway. It didn't matter what Elzeth was. He was alive, and that was good enough. "Well, you said it true earlier. It's been an adventure. I'm glad I got to take it with you."

Elzeth grunted. "No need to be so morose. I might not be a sagani anymore, but I'm certainly familiar with healing your broken body. You've given me more than enough practice over the years."

The sagani reached up and put his front paws on Tomas's chest. Warmth spread from his chest through his body, though it quickly burned. Hundreds, maybe thousands, of connections had been destroyed by Elzeth's departure, and now Elzeth healed them all, restoring Tomas's wrecked body.

As Elzeth worked, the gate faded from Tomas's sight.

Elzeth stepped away. "Only one last thing to do," he said.

"What's that?"

"Cut the last thread between us. I suspect the nexus will kick you out as soon as I do."

"Will I see you again?"

"Don't know. But we're both alive, which is more than either of us expected when we woke up this morning. I think we can call that a win, don't you?"

"I'll miss you," Tomas said.

"And I'll miss you. But even I have to admit, Angela is far more attractive than I am. I think you'll be fine."

"You're probably right," Tomas grumbled. Then he bowed. "Farewell, Elzeth. I hope we meet again someday, but if not, I wish you all the best."

"Same to you, Tomas."

Elzeth sliced through the thread with his claws and proved once again that he was right. Tomas blinked. He was on the floor of Rachel's research station, the space illuminated by the pale blue glow of the nexus.

"Tomas?" Angela asked.

Tomas sat up. He felt strange, as though he were only half a person. But he raised his arm and squeezed his fist, and there were no tremors. "Yeah?"

"What happened?"

Tomas pushed himself to his feet. He wasn't as fast as he had been, but he rose without pain. "It's a bit of a long story, but we stopped it. Now we need to get out of here before the church reinforcements arrive."

He looked around and decided he hadn't been gone long. Hardin and Myra were unchaining the last prisoners from the machine. Soon, they'd all be free.

A glowing shard at his feet caught his attention. He reached down and picked it up. It was the piece of the nexus he'd carried for months. It did nothing for him. He felt no pull at all.

He pocketed it. Regardless of its power, it was a beautiful stone.

He looked around the room.

"And we're going to need dynamite."

(###)

They were riding away on the carts when the dynamite exploded behind them. Tomas glanced back to see the fort crumble in on itself. A few oaths accompanied the collapse, but the survivors of the battle were too hollow-eyed and exhausted to cheer.

Tomas experienced the same satisfaction he usually did when he completed a job well.

He'd volunteered to drive one of the two carts. It wasn't much, but it was probably the most useful thing he could do to help. Most of Hayla's mortar crews were dead, and the former prisoners were in no shape to help with the fight to come. He wasn't sure how much use he'd be, either. He had said nothing about his experience in the nexus, but that was only because he hadn't had any time.

Angela sat beside him and rested her head on his shoulder. "When are you going to tell me what happened?"

"When I'm sure distracting you won't be dangerous. As soon as I can."

She sat up straight and put her hand on his leg. "Are you hurt? You seem different."

It was a well-intentioned question, but it was one that stabbed deep into his heart because it was the one question he didn't know the answer to, the same question that had stopped him and Elzeth from joining in permanent unity.

Who was he without Elzeth?

The sagani had nearly been part of his entire adult life.

He supposed he had no choice but to find out, and it started now. "Well, I suppose I should start off by saying I'm not a host anymore, so if you were only sticking around for Elzeth, I think you're going to be disappointed."

"*What*?"

"I'll tell you everything later, but Elzeth and I went our separate ways. He's still alive, too."

"How? Isn't that supposed to kill you?"

"It certainly is, but he saved my life. Saved all our lives, really."

Angela leaned back against his shoulder, and Tomas let some of his worry about the future dissipate. "You always did make him do most of the work."

Tomas snorted and put his arm around Angela.

She jerked away as if something had stung her.

Tomas was hurt until she pointed at the horizon. "We've got company," she said.

Tomas swore. It was the last thing they needed, but something they had all expected. The only question had been when Corrin would catch up with them. "Prepare the mortar crews. Hopefully, we can scare them off," he ordered.

Although every part of their plan had been risky, it was the return trip that Tomas had always felt was weakest. They couldn't hope to steal another train, so their plan was to ride east until they reached the safety of the Green River, where an informant was waiting with a boat that would carry them quickly toward army-controlled territory. They hoped the mortars would dissuade any church forces from coming too close until then.

It looked like they were going to put that idea to the test sooner than expected.

Angela passed along the orders, and the mortars were prepared. The surviving crew gave instructions to the survivors, then waited for the church forces to come into range.

Then, for the second time that night, the sagani saved them.

They'd trailed the carts as they left the fort, and Tomas had expected them to disperse, but they never did. Now, though, they broke away from the carts and attacked the church forces with the same brutal efficiency that had marked their efforts all night long.

In the last dark hours of the night, Tomas couldn't see what had happened, but Angela soon confirmed they were no longer being pursued. The sagani returned to trailing the carts, and Tomas breathed his first sigh of relief since discovering Jonasson and Alliston had been attacked.

Between the sagani and the mortars, the church would be foolish to attack. If they wasted too many of their forces, they wouldn't even be able to defend their borders. They weren't to safety yet, but Tomas didn't think they'd have any problems for the rest of the trip.

Telarion flew above them, screeching out a cry of victory. Tomas tipped his hat toward the sagani, and the sagani replied by dipping its wing.

They rode into the breaking light of dawn together.

EPILOGUE

Angela held onto Tomas's elbow as they returned home after supper. The evening was a quiet one, although it wouldn't be long before the last of the snow melted, and it would be time to plant once again. Tomas could imagine the fields now, though he knew an enormous amount of work stood between the present moment and his dreams.

"I know I say this all the time, but I still can't believe Nester and Bertha let you settle next to them, especially after their hospitality almost got them killed last time," Angela said.

Tomas smiled. She did say that often, and his answer was always the same. "I can't help being this charming. It just comes naturally."

And as always, she scoffed, and they fell once again into the natural silence of their new life.

"Radd is growing up so fast. I swear he's shot up a foot in the last few months," Angela said.

"You're not wrong. I think he's going to be looking down at me before long."

"Considering how tall his parents are, that's not that surprising."

Angela's free hand went down to her belly, hovering over it protectively.

"Worried?" Tomas asked.

"A little, if I'm being honest."

"We'll figure it out. Most other parents seem to do well enough. I suppose if it ever becomes an emergency, we can visit Ben and Olena for a few years."

As they followed the path to their home, their front porch slowly came into view. A man sat on one of the chairs, his hat pulled down low. Tomas's hand instinctively went to his sword, but it wasn't there. He rarely carried it these days. His callouses remained, but they were due more to the digging fork and shovel than the sword.

Angela's pace didn't falter. "There's something strange about him, but I can't say what, exactly. I'm sure I've never seen him, but he seems familiar."

The two of them stopped just before the porch. Tomas wished he still had Elzeth. Angela could defend him from almost anyone, host or human, but he didn't want to hide behind his unborn child.

The stranger wore a long black coat. He was lanky, but Tomas noticed he didn't carry a sword. The stranger spoke first. "Do you have any idea how long it took me to find you?"

Tomas shared Angela's thought. There was something about this man that was familiar, but Tomas couldn't place it.

"Here I am, so say your piece and be on your way," Tomas said.

The stranger laughed, and the sound made Tomas

frown. He'd heard that laugh before, often. But it couldn't be.

The stranger lifted his hat. The face was unfamiliar, but the eyes glowed with a golden light. "That doesn't seem like a way you should greet an old friend."

"Elzeth?"

"In the flesh."

Tomas's jaw hung open. "How?"

Elzeth shrugged. "Mimicking a human isn't that hard anymore. Don't do it too often, though. Walking on two legs is dreadfully foolish. I'm still not sure why you do it."

Tomas was onto the porch and picking Elzeth up before he even thought about it. He wrapped the former sagani up in an embrace, ignoring the warmth radiating off him. "Come in, come in, we have so much to talk about!"

He led Elzeth in and got water boiling for tea. Once it was prepared, they spent the rest of the daylight catching up on recent events. Tomas and Angela recounted the journey that brought them to Nester and Bertha, and Elzeth told them about his wanderings.

Tomas's old friend had been all around the world since they'd parted ways outside of Corrin. Since then, he'd traveled extensively in the east, learning more about his new abilities. In an interesting twist of fate, Elzeth's explorations made him the most informed of the trio.

"Did you hear the church finally signed a treaty with the army?" Elzeth asked.

Tomas shook his head. "When did that happen?"

"A few months ago. It's not in any of the papers, but I think the collapse of the fort was the deciding factor. It set the church's weapon development back years they didn't have, and I think they feared the return of the sagani." Elzeth twirled his teacup, just the same way Tomas always did. He laughed. "People out east don't know what to make of it. Most out there haven't seen a sagani in their lives. They're mythical creatures, but everyone claims they're part of the reason the conflict ended."

"What were the terms?" Angela asked.

"The church settled for less territory than they'd hoped for, but it's theirs to keep. Believers are welcome enough out east, but they're barred from holding office or advancing beyond squad commander in the army. A lot of believers are heading west, but a fair number have parted from the church now that it doesn't carry the same possibility of advancement. There's also been a resurgence of interest in the old faiths, but who knows how long that will last?"

Elzeth gestured to Angela's stomach. "Congratulations, by the way. Is it his?"

Tomas grunted and considered throwing his tea, but it had been a gift from Gavan after they returned from Corrin.

Angela took the joke as it was intended, smiling widely. "I sure hope not, but we'll have to wait until it comes out. And thank you."

"So, you decided to become parents?"

"We did." Tomas could have said much more. The decision hadn't come easy, as there were still a lot of unanswered questions about their future. In the end, though, there were always questions about the future. It didn't change what they wanted.

"I'm glad. I'll have to stop by more often to watch this disaster unfold."

"What about you?" Tomas asked. "We've talked your ear off, but you haven't said much except about what's happening in the world."

Elzeth looked down at his hands. "I'm still figuring out what I am. I mean, I feel the same as I did for years, but now

I'm not stuck in your body, which means I end up in far fewer deadly situations. But I'm alive, and I spend a fair amount of time studying the nexuses and the heart. There are still mysteries out there, and I intend to learn as much as I can."

"There's a part of me that's jealous," Tomas admitted.

"Only a part?"

Tomas reached out and held Angela's hand. "I'm happy here. Truly happy."

Elzeth looked between the two of them and smiled. He stood and put on his hat, tipping it toward the two of them. "As am I. It's been good to see you both."

"You're leaving so soon?" Tomas had hoped he would stay for at least a few days.

"I worry if I stay too long, Angela might realize she was really settling when she found you," Elzeth said.

"Sure," Tomas said, "but why are you really leaving?"

"I learned a trick from the sagani, and now I can travel from nexus to nexus. Now that I know where you are, I can be here whenever. There's no need for me to stay. You've got your life, and I've got mine, but I promise I'll visit often. Someone needs to liven this place up."

"I'm glad you found us. I've thought often of you since that day."

Elzeth grinned. "I am hard to forget."

They embraced again, and Elzeth went into their bedroom.

Tomas needed a minute to understand. "Wait, you came in through *my* nexus?"

"It was the closest. Trust me, no one was as surprised as me to end up in a closet."

They said their final farewells, and Tomas held the nexus out in his hand. Elzeth placed his hand over it, bowed deeply, and was gone in a blink. Tomas stared at the open space with a rueful grin. He turned to Angela, acting serious. "I think we're going to have to put the nexus in a different room."

"Why?" she asked.

He took her hand and led her to the bed, a mischievous grin growing on his face. "Because I really don't want Elzeth showing up in our bedroom at times like these."

THE ADVENTURES CONTINUE!

Top of the morning!

I hope that wherever you are in the world, this finds you doing well. Thanks for reading, and I hope you enjoyed the story. In an age of endless entertainment options, the choice to spend your time in these pages means the world to me.

Last Sword in the West has been a pleasure to write, and someday, I may return to the world and meet some new characters, but Tomas's and Elzeth's journey together has come to a close. Thank you for joining me on this ride, and I hope to see you again soon!

Ryan

August 2023

ALSO BY RYAN KIRK
FIND THEM ALL AT RYANKIRKAUTHOR.COM

Saga of the Broken Gods

Band of Broken Gods

Fall of Forgotten Gods

Rise of the Resurrected God

Last Sword in the West

Last Sword in the West

Eyes of the Hidden World

A Sword Named Vengeance

Wraith's Revenge

Frontier's End

Song of the Sagani

Oblivion's Gate

The Gate Beyond Oblivion

The Gates of Memory

The Gate to Redemption

Relentless

Relentless Souls

Heart of Defiance

Their Spirit Unbroken

The Nightblade Series

Nightblade

ABOUT THE AUTHOR

Ryan Kirk is the bestselling author of the *Nightblade* series of books. When he isn't writing, you can probably find him playing disc golf or hiking through the woods.

RyanKirkAuthor.com
contact@waterstonemedia.net

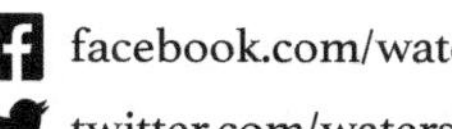 facebook.com/waterstonemedia

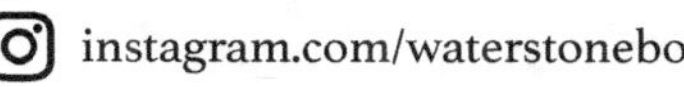 twitter.com/waterstonebooks

instagram.com/waterstonebooks

www.ingramcontent.com/pod-product-compliance
Lightning Source LLC
Chambersburg PA
CBHW060906210726
48293CB00006B/1977